THE PHARAOH'S DAUGHTER

ISABELLE WEBB

OTHER BOOKS AND AUDIO BOOKS BY
N. C. ALLEN

Faith of Our Fathers Vol. 1: A House Divided
Faith of Our Fathers Vol. 2: To Make Men Free
Faith of Our Fathers Vol. 3: Through the Perilous Fight
Faith of Our Fathers Vol. 4: One Nation Under God

Isabelle Webb novels*:*
Legend of the Jewel

THE PHARAOH'S DAUGHTER

ISABELLE WEBB

a novel

N.C. ALLEN

Covenant Communications, Inc.

Cover image Pyramids © Sculpies

Cover design copyright © 2011 by Covenant Communications, Inc.

Published by Covenant Communications, Inc.
American Fork, Utah

Copyright © 2011 by Nancy Allen

All rights reserved. No part of this book may be reproduced in any format or in any medium without the written permission of the publisher, Covenant Communications, Inc., P.O. Box 416, American Fork, UT 84003. This work is not an official publication of The Church of Jesus Christ of Latter-day Saints. The views expressed within this work are the sole responsibility of the author and do not necessarily reflect the position of The Church of Jesus Christ of Latter-day Saints, Covenant Communications, Inc., or any other entity.

This is a work of fiction. The characters, names, incidents, places, and dialogue are either products of the author's imagination, and are not to be construed as real, or are used fictitiously.

Printed in the United States of America
First Printing: January 2011

16 15 14 13 12 11   10 9 8 7 6 5 4 3 2 1

ISBN 978-1-60861-116-4

For Nina, Anna, and Gunder: owners of my heart.

Acknowledgments

I would never have finished this book without the encouragement of family and friends—especially those who fly in V-formation with me, and the special ladies of the Goldenpens who allowed me into their circle and made me feel at home. Extra thanks go to Josi Kilpack for providing space for our late-night writing sessions, and to our husbands and children who held down the fort while we made up stories.

Prologue

November 19, 1865
Suez, Egypt

THE BRIGHT EGYPTIAN SUN SHONE down on the arid landscape. A lone man stood in the shade of a palm tree, awaiting a messenger. It was warm, but the locals insisted that within weeks, if not sooner, the air would cool and nights would actually be quite chilly. He looked forward to that. The sweat that gathered under the brim of his hat was uncomfortable, as was the heavy fabric of his suit. Had he the money, he would have bought something much lighter in feel as well as color.

His mind raced, as it was known to do, with thoughts of wealth untold, *power* untold, contained in the form of a stone, a jewel. He had possessed the ticket to obtaining it, only to lose it and very nearly his freedom as well. The fever, however, refused to subside. He would spend his life, if necessary, seeking to obtain it.

The man checked his pocket watch for the third time in five minutes. The note had said he was to wait here, that at one o'clock he would be approached with a business opportunity that could prove lucrative. As he was absolutely penniless, he figured he had nothing to lose. The note had been a surprise, though; he knew nobody in Egypt save the two young girls he had sailed with from Calcutta and then befriended in hopes of gaining information to use when the opportunity presented itself. He was beginning to wonder if the young girls were going to be "rescued" after all. If his hunch proved incorrect, then his serendipitous passage on their same ship was all for naught.

The thoroughfare on which he stood was fairly crowded, but his position off to one side afforded him an unobstructed view of the street vendors and the local populace, interspersed with European travelers who had come to take a gander at Egypt's ancient secrets. Several times he thought someone was coming toward him, but then they would veer away at the last moment or pass on by.

Just when he was ready to dismiss the whole message as utter foolishness, a tall European in a light linen suit approached him and said in an Italian accent, "Mr. Jones? Or is it, perhaps, Mr. Sparks?"

Sparks looked up in surprise. His silence must have equaled assent, for the European jerked his head slightly and said, "This way."

Sparks, his curiosity gaining the upper hand, followed the man down the street and into the dining room of a lavish hotel. The Italian led him to a quiet corner where several men sat around a table, finishing lunch.

"Ah, you must be Mr. Sparks," said one man. He looked Egyptian and spoke in heavily accented English.

"How do you know who I am?" he asked the man and refused the chair offered him by the tall European.

"Please, sit," the Egyptian said to him. When Sparks acquiesced, the Egyptian smiled. "One does not go about India openly searching for the Jewel of Zeus without attracting some notice."

Sparks looked at the men seated around the table, trying to gauge his personal safety. In addition to the men at the table, there were several others placed at intervals around the room. One, in particular, stood close to the Egyptian who had spoken to him, probably security for the man. He couldn't ignore the sense of unease that crept up his spine.

"One certainly does not go about searching for the Jewel of Zeus with a companion bearing the mark without attracting significant notice."

"Who are you?" Sparks finally managed.

"We represent a group of people who are interested in certain antiquities. You, my friend, have . . . what is the phrase? Stirred up a hornet's nest."

"What do you know of my activities?" Sparks asked, finally feeling a bit of outrage on his own behalf. "Am I being watched? Followed? For how long?"

The Egyptian laughed. "My friend, you made quite a scene in your homeland, searching for sponsors for your quest. You were followed before you ever left American soil."

Sparks looked at the man and felt his heart increase its rhythm. His uncertainty must have shown on his face.

The Egyptian lowered his voice a bit, and his face lost some of its mocking humor. "What, exactly, do you know of the legend and from whom did you hear it?"

"That's no business of yours! Your note to me mentioned a service for payment. Unless you care to explain the details to me, I'll be leaving."

The Egyptian studied him for a moment from under intense black brows that were at odds with his graying hair. His face relaxed into a smile as he sat back in his chair. "Of course. You know nothing of our organization and here am I, expecting you to willingly share private information with strangers.

"We are followers of the legend ourselves. We are diverse and multinational. Naturally, when people speak of the legend, we take notice because the legend itself is not commonly discussed. Very few know of it."

Sparks nodded impatiently. "I am aware of this."

"We find ourselves wondering if you will be an asset to our quest, or a hindrance." The Egyptian let his pronouncement hang in the air and regarded him with eyes that never blinked or broke contact.

Sparks considered the men seated at the table. They watched him with unnerving directness, every last one. He was unable to ascertain all nationalities represented but knew enough to recognize they were varied.

"Of course I would be an asset," he finally answered the Egyptian. "What is it that you need? My companion who bears the mark?"

The Egyptian raised a brow. "You are perceptive. I believe you may indeed become an asset."

"It happens that I am in pursuit of him myself," Sparks said, feeling the upper hand for the first time since entering the room. "I expect that he will soon be in the country."

The Egyptian nodded. "And when he does arrive? You will demand he return with you to India to resume your journey?"

Sparks frowned. "It will not be as simple as all that. I will convince him, however."

"Perhaps your time might be better spent in Egypt."

Sparks shook his head. "The jewel was last known to be in India."

"I believe you may not be in possession of the entire legend."

One of the other men seated at the table cleared his throat and leaned forward a bit as though to interrupt, but the Egyptian held up a hand to silence him.

Although Sparks's interest was piqued, he was unwilling to give the man the satisfaction of begging for details. He waited patiently for him to continue.

"It is thought that the jewel was taken from India by traders and brought to Egypt approximately 1800 BC. Certain hieroglyphs suggest it."

Sparks digested the information. His pulse quickened, and he felt a familiar sense of excitement surging through his veins. If he could find the jewel in Egypt, he wouldn't need to return to India. He made every attempt to maintain an outward calm. "If you know so much about the jewel, why have you not yet found it? Why do you need me?"

"We have searched, but to no avail. We are beginning to believe that it can be found only by one who bears the mark. I believe this was your original belief as well."

Sparks reluctantly nodded. It had indeed been his original belief. His mistake had been forcing the issue, though. He should have let their journey be guided by Phillip Ashby. Instead, Sparks had assumed the British had been in possession of the jewel during the Sepoy Mutiny of 1857, and that therefore, the jewel would lie somewhere in one of the major playing cities. The legend held that the jewel would find those worthy of it, those who bore the mark. Sparks wouldn't make the same mistake twice.

"What do you want of me?" Sparks asked the Egyptian.

"We will cover your expenses, and you will trail Phillip Ashby. Should the opportunity present itself for reconciliation, you will do that. You will need to watch his every move. If he is led to the jewel, you will tell us."

Sparks felt another moment of outrage. He wanted, and always had wanted, the jewel for himself. It would do no good to admit it to the men seated around the table. He had no doubt that to them he was expendable. Should he ruffle too many feathers, he likely wouldn't make it to sundown alive. He decided his best course of action would be to play their game. "So I am to trail Phillip Ashby, secure his trust, and if he obtains the jewel, tell you."

The Egyptian nodded. "We do not have any in our inner circle who have an established relationship with Mr. Ashby, so we are dependent upon you, even though your relationship with him is, at present, not on the best of terms."

Sparks swallowed. He was amazed at the information they had gathered about him. He had kept the young man with him using coercion and threats against the man's mother. Phillip wasn't likely to embrace Sparks with open arms. He could hardly admit this to the Egyptian. It was the only card he had to play.

"And what will I receive for this service?"

"A substantial payment."

"I am in need of money now."

The Egyptian nodded. "And I repeat, we will fund your venture." He motioned with his hand, and the man standing near him withdrew a piece of folded paper from his inner pocket. "This is a list of contacts both up the Nile and along the Red Sea coast. Europeans rarely venture farther west than this. Should the young man arrive, as you say he will, and then stay, you will need to follow him. If the legend holds, he will find the jewel."

"You're assuming he will want to stay," Sparks cautioned. "Perhaps he and his brother will simply collect the girls and return to India. Or home, even."

"I suppose that is a risk we all take, you included, no? If he is not vulnerable to the legend, then perhaps he will leave. But the jewel is here—I believe he will stay."

The jewel had supposedly been in India as well. Phillip Ashby had been of absolutely no use to Sparks there. Again, he chose to keep that to himself. After all, perhaps the reason for their failure had been because the jewel truly was no longer in India. "Very well," he said. "I will do my part." He accepted the paper and pocketed it. He also accepted an envelope the man extended to him, glancing inside. He made an effort to control his features—it was full of money.

"This should set you off well enough," the Egyptian said. "We will be in contact with you, and should you need to reach us sooner, see the list of names. I will be leaving shortly for Cairo; my guess is that you will be soon to follow."

Sparks nodded and pocketed the money with the list. He stood then hesitated. "I know nothing of you. How am I to know you are trustworthy?"

The Egyptian smiled. "You don't know. It will be a leap of faith, yes?"

Sparks gave the man a nod and slowly left the room. As he saw it, he did have a few things working in his favor. He felt reasonably sure he could work his way into Phillip's life once again. Also, he did know of Phillip's traits, his habits. He knew enough about the young man to know how he was best manipulated.

He put his hand in his pocket and felt the thick, reassuring mass of money he'd received. Within the space of twenty minutes, he'd gone from destitute to well-enough off. If he were careful, the money would last.

And in the end, he'd claim a much bigger reward.

1

THE SHIP TOSSED AND TURNED, the sea hurling it about like a toy. The sky was dark, and Isabelle fought to remain at the railing. It wasn't long before rain began to fall from the skies and she knew she'd have to go back to her cabin. When she was below deck, she was disoriented and felt uncomfortably out of control. At least, here at the rail, she could see where she was headed.

"Isabelle, for the love of heaven!" James Ashby approached her in long strides, the wind whipping at his hair and long black coat. "I've been looking for you for nigh unto an hour," he shouted over the wind.

She turned, strands of her hair blowing across her face and around her neck. "It makes me sick to go below!" she yelled back.

"You'll get sick if you stay up here." James took her elbow and pulled her from the railing.

"I'll be fine!" Isabelle stumbled to keep up with him.

"Has it escaped your notice that you're the only one topside?"

"I don't much care."

James turned her toward the staircase and led her down, breathing an audible sigh of relief at being away from the elements. "When the entire deck is deserted, that might be a good sign that it's not the best place to be."

Isabelle sniffed as she reached the last of the steps and swayed into the wall as the ship heaved again. "Not the best place to be if one is faint of heart, perhaps."

James steadied her and ushered her down the passageway. "You are exhausting," he said. "Belle, really. You're soaked through and shivering. Why would you stay up there?"

Isabelle scowled. "I can't see outside in my cabin. I want to know where we are."

"I'll tell you where we are. We're in the middle of the ocean, traveling through some sort of freakish squall. That you feel perfectly comfortable standing out in it is something I find fairly alarming."

"I warned you," she said. "I am not a conventional woman. You'd be better served to turn your attention elsewhere."

James growled in the back of his throat and shoved her into a dark corner. "Why do you think I've been looking for you for more than an hour?" His mouth came down on hers swiftly, and he smothered her exclamation of surprise. He was warm, and as he pulled her shivering frame tightly against his, she felt the heat from his body seep into hers. His arms tightened across her back and she felt entirely enveloped, warmed, and protected.

"I'll not be turning my attention elsewhere, so you might as well stop suggesting it," he said when he finally broke the kiss.

"Mr. Ashby," Isabelle said when she found her voice, "what will the other passengers say if they find us here?"

"They will envy me," he said, and in the darkness she saw his mouth curve into a smile. "They will wonder how I've managed to capture the affections of the most beautiful woman in the world."

"Such flattery," she said, meaning to sound coy but realizing it came out rather breathless. "What's a girl to do?"

"Succumb."

Isabelle actually sighed as he kissed her again. Had someone told her that she would one day be so smitten, she'd have laughed.

James had kissed her for the first time two days before as they'd sat on the shore in Calcutta, India. Now they were on a ship bound for Egypt in an effort to finally catch up with Isabelle's young ward, Sally Rhodes, and Alice Bilbey, the young daughter of a recently murdered British officer. The girls had mistakenly boarded a ship headed for Egypt in their attempt to escape a kidnapper.

James lifted his head and looked closely at Isabelle. "Better?" he asked.

She nodded. "How did you know I wasn't . . . that I needed . . ."

"I can read you like a book." James rubbed her nose with his.

Isabelle laughed. "No, you can't. Nobody can."

"Hmm. Nobody but me. You think I don't know you by now? Every expression, every comment?"

She smiled and reached up, kissing the tip of his nose. "You've not known me that long."

"Long enough." He moved his face downward, trailing his lips along the sensitive skin at the side of her neck. "Besides, one needn't have known you for long to realize there's something amiss for you to be standing in the middle of a hurricane."

She sighed. "I suppose that's true enough. I'm worried."

"I thought so." He lifted his head and moved his hands to the sides of her face. "We'll find her soon, Belle. She's perfectly safe now."

Isabelle nodded and folded her arms across her midsection, snuggling into his chest for warmth. "I'm cold."

"I know. Silly woman," he said, and Isabelle felt him shaking his head. He wrapped his arms around her again and held her close for a moment before finally rubbing her back. "Let's get you to your cabin. You can change your clothes and then meet me in the dining room. It's time for supper."

Isabelle bit her tongue to keep herself from asking him to wait for her outside her cabin. She didn't need a guardian; she never had. Why she would want one now was beyond her comprehension. Her relationship with James was unlike anything she'd experienced; not only was he attractive and set her pulse to racing, he was solid and reliable. It was tempting to lean on him and let him take charge of all her problems. She knew he would if she asked. It was in his nature to control and lead.

She shook her head to herself as he led her out from the darkened stairwell, her brow creased in a frown. Her instinct was to pull away, to distance herself from any sort of vulnerability. She was fortunate, however, that she recognized it in herself, and she knew that any chance at a good future with James meant that she stay open and honest with him.

And brave.

She was discovering that there were different kinds of bravery. There was the kind that allowed one to go incognito into an enemy's circle and infiltrate their defenses, learn all their secrets. Isabelle possessed that kind of bravery in spades. It meant becoming someone else for a while, living another life, almost. That was easy enough for her. It was being just Isabelle that was proving to be the challenge.

"How's our cargo?" she asked James, trying to distract herself. She spoke of an iridescent purple jewel roughly the size of her palm.

He smiled as he guided her down the hallway, pulling her hand through his offered arm. "Safe and sound," he said.

"Alice may be relieved to know her batty mother was right all along." Isabelle blew a strand of hair away from her eyes, finally tucking it behind her ear when it didn't seem to want to behave. She fell silent, pursing her lips. As much as she was looking forward to seeing Sally and Alice again, she still hadn't settled on a good way to tell young Alice that she was now an orphan. It had been confirmed that Alice's mother had been murdered weeks before on a steamship from London to Bombay; the same murderer had then shot her father in a hovel in Delhi.

Ari Kilronomos was the name of the gunman, and when Isabelle had last seen him, he lay unconscious on the jungle floor, holding the attentions of a very large snake. His body was never recovered, but Isabelle found it hard to believe that he might have survived. That, at least, gave her some measure of peace. The fact that he had abducted Sally and Alice and had made arrangements to sell them into slavery in Egypt still made her seethe. It was for that very reason that she found herself, along with James and Phillip, bound for Egypt's east coast in pursuit of the two girls, sixteen and seventeen.

They came to a stop before Isabelle's cabin door, and she withdrew a key from her pocket. The ship lurched again and she missed the lock, scraping against the door with the metal before regaining her balance. "I don't know how they're going to manage dinner tonight," she muttered. "How will we keep the food from sliding off the plates?"

"I'm going to make an effort," James said with undisguised glee. The ship was run entirely by British staff, and the food was like a long-lost friend for James. He hadn't much found Indian food to his liking.

"Where is Phillip?" Isabelle asked James as she finally got her door open.

"A little under the weather," James said, motioning across the hall.

"Making friends with the chamber pot, is he?" Isabelle asked.

"Intimate friends."

Isabelle grinned. "Gauche of me to mention it, of course."

"I would expect nothing less."

"Undoubtedly, few women of your acquaintance would ever mention a chamber pot," she said.

"I don't recall my *mother* ever mentioning a chamber pot."

Isabelle laughed and reached a hand up to his neck. He followed without a fight as she pulled him down for a quick kiss.

"Now go," he said, nudging her into her room, "before you're ruined entirely."

"There's nobody about," she said. "I'm sure they're all in their cabins, becoming intimate friends with their chamber pots."

He shook his head at her, his mouth partially drawn into a rueful smile, and she closed her door with a chuckle. She was fortunate to have found one of the few men in the world who would abide her bluntness and rather jaded sense of humor.

* * *

Dinner had been a laughable affair, James admitted as he loosened his tie and took a seat on the small bed across from his brother's.

"How was it?" Phillip groaned, his face looking decidedly green.

"Interesting. Amusing, really. People trying to use their best manners, and more often than not, missing their mouths entirely. How are you feeling?"

"Just the thing," Phillip said. "Ready to take on the world."

James shrugged out of his coat and hung it on the back of a chair. He looked at his brother, grateful he was there, sick or not. It was a quest to find Phillip that had led James to India in the first place, and while James wished that Phillip had never fallen for the stories of Thaddeus Sparks and his pursuit of a legendary jewel that would grant the possessor untold powers, he was glad it had led him to Isabelle. If not for Sparks, James would never have met her.

He looked in his trunk for a fresh nightshirt, and his hand brushed against a box that lay nestled among his clothes and other personal items. He paused for a moment, tipping his head to one side at the slight vibration he felt against his fingers. He grasped the box more fully, holding it in his hand. Odd. He'd not noticed that before. He raised his eyebrows and lifted a shoulder in an unconscious shrug. Must have been the vibration from the ship's massive engine.

"I'm anxious to get to Egypt," James said to his brother as he closed the trunk and finished readying himself for bed.

"As am I," Phillip muttered from the doorway. "If I ever set foot on another ship again, it will be far too soon."

"How do you propose to get home, then?"

"Fly. It works for the birds."

"Well," James said as he settled into bed with a book, "if you can manage that, I would love to see it."

"Don't tempt me. I'm desperate enough to try anything. Maybe I'll just find myself a nice pyramid and stay in it."

"Where are you going?"

"None of your business." Phillip swayed a bit with the motion of the ship and closed his eyes, wincing. "Definitely going to find myself a nice pyramid and never leave it," he muttered as he stumbled out into the hallway.

"I wouldn't get too comfortable," James said as he donned his reading glasses. "I don't expect we'll be staying very long."

2

The ship settled into place alongside the dock at Suez, and Isabelle stood on deck with James and Phillip. She knew the girls had no idea she was coming for them, but she scanned the crowd anyway, hoping for a silly chance that they might actually be there, watching for her.

People milled alongside the ships, hawking wares and accepting the shipments now being walked down the gangplank. The air was rife with the sound of seagulls, and palm trees lined the streets. The sky was a brilliant blue, the temperature pleasant. Isabelle had heard that Egypt was uncomfortably warm in the summer—she supposed she should be grateful the girls had gone on their accidental voyage in the later autumn months.

As she continued to scan the crowd, Isabelle caught sight of a woman whose stately form was forever etched into her memory. Her jaw dropped and she squinted, wondering if her eyes deceived her. Feeling slightly weak in the knees, she tightened her hold on James's arm and swayed into him.

"What is it?" he asked her. "Do you see the girls?"

"The Ben . . . the Ben . . ." she stammered

"Who is Ben?" James asked, looking out over the crowd.

"The Benefactress," she managed. "The woman who took in my sister and me and sent us to school."

"She's *here?*"

Isabelle nodded. "I can't believe it. There she is, watching for me like she knew I'd be coming!"

"It must be a coincidence," James said as he looked in the direction of Isabelle's gaze.

"I've been dreaming of her," Isabelle said. "Do you remember me telling you? She came to me in my dreams and told me all would be well when Sally and Alice were kidnapped." Isabelle suddenly felt detached from herself, as though she looked down on the scene from far away. Why would Genevieve Montgomery be in Egypt?

"She might have asked friends of your whereabouts."

"They thought I was going to India. Only just before we left did I send a letter to my friends in Boston that we were headed here. They probably have just now received it."

James frowned and looked out at the crowded dock again before turning his eyes back to Isabelle. "Belle, are you certain?"

She nodded. "That is most definitely her."

"Are you . . . upset?"

Isabelle considered his question. Genevieve had been a mother figure to Isabelle when she desperately needed one, yet she had always held a part of herself back from the older woman. She couldn't deny now, though, the sense of longing that surged through her at the sight of the woman whose kind ministrations she'd never understood.

"No, I'm not upset," she said. "I'm confused." She found herself wanting to call out to Genevieve to be sure the woman wouldn't leave before she had a chance to talk to her. It was unnecessary, though; Genevieve caught Isabelle's gaze and held it fast. A smile began at the corners of Genevieve's mouth, the same smile she had bestowed upon Isabelle each time a term had finished and Isabelle presented her with top marks in all of her classes.

Isabelle unconsciously reached up and smoothed a hand over her hair, suddenly wanting to appear spotless. "You look fine," James said to her.

She nodded and dropped her hand to her side, steeling her spine. "James," she said, "you're about to meet the closest thing to a mother that I have."

Isabelle moved toward Genevieve Montgomery and had just opened her mouth to speak when the older woman closed the distance between them and surprised Isabelle by enfolding her in an embrace. "Genevieve," Isabelle finally managed to say, "what on earth . . ."

"You're much remiss in your duties, you know, to make me travel to Egypt to find you." Genevieve pulled back and grasped Isabelle's upper arms in her firm grip. "I heard about your accident in Washington, and by the time I was able to track you down, you had left the country." Genevieve's sharp blue eyes examined Isabelle's face, and she found herself wanting to fidget.

"But I hadn't planned on coming here. How did you know I would be arriving today?"

Genevieve smiled and gave her arms a quick squeeze. "Plenty of time to explain everything over a good meal." She indicated behind her. "You'll find this place to be a treat for a good appetite."

Isabelle's head swam. James cleared his throat and she looked back at him. "Oh, James. This is my, my . . ."

Genevieve extended a gloved hand to James. "Genevieve Montgomery. Isabelle's good friend."

"James Ashby. I, also, am Isabelle's good friend."

"And this strapping young man must certainly be a relation," Genevieve said as Phillip approached with two Egyptian dock workers and the travel trunks.

James made the introductions, and the small group fell silent for a moment. It was then that Isabelle finally registered a shorter, pleasant-looking woman standing to Genevieve's side. "Oh!" Genevieve said as she followed Isabelle's gaze. "This is my dearest friend, Maude Davis. She is an expert on Egyptian history and antiquities, and I could never have managed this expedition without her."

Isabelle felt as though she'd been transported to the moon. "Expedition?"

Genevieve waved a hand in dismissal. "Too much to discuss while standing out here. And if I'm not mistaken, you're looking for two young girls?"

Isabelle tilted her head to one side and stared at the woman.

"I've met them. I assured Miss Rhodes that you were to arrive shortly, but I'm afraid she must think me batty. At any rate, the girls have gone on a local excursion with their ship's captain and will return this afternoon. Plenty of time for you to eat and for me to explain myself."

Isabelle was rooted to the spot. It was James who finally took her arm and extended his hand toward the hotel. "Lead the way, my lady," he said to Genevieve. "We are at your disposal."

* * *

James watched Isabelle throughout the meal. She ate mechanically but seemed to have recovered enough of her spirits to again show color in her face. He had been fairly alarmed at her pallor dockside and had wondered if she were going to faint.

He also watched Genevieve carefully, looking for signs of deceit or dubiousness of character but found he was enchanted in spite of himself. The woman seemed genuine in her affections for Isabelle and possessed a certain no-nonsense quality he appreciated. Perhaps it was this quality that lent her story credence.

"The past two years, I have dreamed of you being here. At least once weekly, and the dream was always the same," Genevieve was saying to Isabelle, her gaze unwavering and unapologetic. "You, here, with an entourage and something . . . dangerous . . . in your possession." She paused for a moment. "Perhaps *dangerous* is the wrong word. *Unpredictable* or *unstable* might better suit the situation.

"Well," she continued, spearing a piece of lamb with her fork. "Maude and I have talked of funding and hosting an Egyptological expedition for, oh, what has it been, five years or so?" At her companion's nod, she said, "We were trying to divert our thoughts from something other than the war, I suppose, but suddenly it became something I rather knew I needed to do."

"Why?" Isabelle asked.

"Absolution."

Isabelle frowned. "What do you mean?"

"Nothing. The reasons are, well, they are complex. At any rate, I began corresponding with associates in Britain in January who put me in contact with the Stafford brothers. They, in turn, brought on the Frenchman, and with my two sons rounding out the group, we have ourselves an actual expedition. When I discovered you had left for India, I knew the time had come. I have met each ship that docks here. By the time the girls arrived I knew you could not be far behind."

Isabelle dabbed at her mouth with her napkin and took a drink. "How are the girls?" she asked, emotion thick in her voice.

Genevieve smiled. "They are well. They are amusing."

Isabelle's shoulders relaxed a bit. "That they certainly are," she agreed. "I'm sure they've entertained you with all manner of tales."

"Yes, and mostly about you," Genevieve said. "You have quite a champion in young Sally."

Isabelle shook her head. "Misplaced affection."

"I think not."

When Isabelle refrained from reply, James leaned forward. "Mrs. Montgomery," he said, "I cannot speak for Isabelle now, but it was initially our intention to collect the girls and return home. I gather you had hoped for an extended visit?"

Genevieve turned a thoughtful expression on him. "Of course, you must do what you must do. But wouldn't it be a shame to be in Egypt and not enjoy it, just for a little while? In fact, as a group we are sufficiently varied in talent; however, we do lack a certain element of physical . . . prowess, I suppose I should say. I've been looking to hire on some men to serve as security for us. You and your brother would fit the bill nicely."

"A moment," Isabelle said, holding her hand up. "The brothers and I will need to discuss this." She might have said more, but a shriek from the door had her whipping around in her chair.

Isabelle stood as Sally Rhodes crossed the floor and launched herself at her. James smiled, and he and Phillip stood. Sally laughed as tears filled her eyes, clearly heedless of the spectacle she was making in the hotel dining room. She was followed closely by another young woman who appeared much improved by her recent adventures. Her trials seemed to agree with her; there was a flush to her cheeks and a genuine happiness in her countenance that had been missing before.

"You came!" Sally said. "Oh, Belle, I can hardly believe you're here, and yet Miss Genevieve said you would be! We were to be aboard a ship in two days with our captain for a return voyage to Calcutta—only think if we'd missed you!"

Isabelle pulled back and smiled at Sally. Her face relaxed in a way it hadn't for weeks. "But we didn't miss each other. I'm here and you are never again leaving my sight," Isabelle said. Then she pulled the other young woman close, wrapping her in a gentle embrace. "Alice, I'm so glad you're well."

"As am I, Miss Webb. Sally has been an excellent caretaker."

"Girls, you must sit," Genevieve said and motioned for a waiter to bring extra chairs to the table. "Have you eaten?"

Sally shook her head. "Not yet. Oh, Belle, we have so much to talk about!"

James watched the young Alice Bilbey with a pang of sadness. Isabelle had the unpleasant task of telling the girl she had been orphaned. Isabelle caught his gaze and her expression tightened fractionally. He didn't envy her.

They all resumed their seats as the girls sat down and Genevieve placed an order for more food. Sally's eyes strayed more than once to James's brother, and when it seemed she was about to bounce out of her seat with excitement, he took pity on her.

"Miss Rhodes, Miss Bilbey, allow me to introduce my brother, Phillip Ashby."

"Mr. Ashby, I simply cannot tell you how glad I am that you were found, well and whole!" Sally said, her eyes bright.

"Thank you, Miss Rhodes," Phillip said with an incline of his head. "It's a pleasure to finally make your acquaintance. I have heard many good things about you."

Sally blushed very prettily. "Oh," she said with a glance at Alice. She looked a bit chagrined. "And as your brother said, this is my friend Alice. We met her and her father while looking for you."

James raised a brow at Sally, impressed. The last time he'd seen the two girls, they'd been grudging friends at best, and Sally had been explicit in her instructions that she be given preferential treatment when introductions to Phillip became a reality. Seeing the young woman make a point to include Alice in the conversation spoke much of the friendship's progress.

Conversation continued, significantly lower in volume when the girls were chewing, and James was gratified to see Isabelle looking at peace. The only time her smile faltered was when she looked at Alice.

3

Isabelle sat in the girls' hotel room, cross-legged at the foot of Sally's bed. She gave them their clothing she had brought with her from India, which the girls received with much delight. After they took turns telling her what had happened since their abduction in India, Sally then demanded that Isabelle tell them what had happened on her end, how they had found Phillip, and what had ever happened to Ari Kilronomos.

"You must tell me how my father is doing," Alice finally said. "All this time, you've not mentioned him even once."

Isabelle took a deep breath. "Alice, I'm afraid I have some distressing news about your father." She rose and sat on Alice's bed, reaching for the girl's hand.

Alice pulled back, and Isabelle gave her some space. "Is he ill? Has he died?" the girl asked, her eyes widening.

Isabelle winced and nodded. "Sweet girl, I am so sorry to tell you this. Your father has passed on."

"No, he has not," Alice flatly stated. "My father is a strong man. You must be mistaken."

"Oh, Alice, I wish I were. I was with him when he died." Isabelle paused. "I am so very sorry."

"What happened?" Alice looked at her through wide, dry eyes.

Isabelle hesitated.

"What happened?" Alice repeated.

"He was shot," Isabelle said.

"In a battle? The country has been relatively stable of late."

"Not in a battle." Isabelle wished desperately that she could somehow soften the blow. "It was Ari."

A spark flashed in Alice's eyes. "Ari Kilronomos killed my father?"

Isabelle nodded. "I wish I could have prevented it . . . it happened so fast."

"I don't blame you, Miss Webb," Alice said. She rose from the bed and paced, her nightgown flowing behind her as she moved. "I will, however, take my revenge on Ari with my bare hands."

"I've already done it for you," Isabelle said. "At least, I think I have."

Alice came to a halt. "What do you mean?" Her face was set in angry lines, but the tremor in her voice belied her true emotion.

Isabelle explained what had happened that fateful night in Delhi, sparing no detail. About how she'd left Ari to die in the jungle. She also told her that the military received news that Ari had also killed Alice's mother at sea. She had underestimated Alice's strength; it was only a matter of time, though, until the dam would break.

Alice contemplated Isabelle in silence for a moment. Her eyes were still wide open, luminous, but there was an uncomprehending quality to her expression that led Isabelle to believe that the news had yet to really penetrate Alice's consciousness.

Alice frowned, her brow creased. She made her way to the bed and slowly sank down next to Isabelle. Her shoulders sagged a bit, and her hands lay limp in her lap. "What am I to do, then?" she asked.

"The military is in the process of contacting your brothers and your parents' relatives in England," Isabelle told her gently. "You'll be well cared for by people who know you."

Alice glanced askance at Isabelle with a light sound of derision. "They don't know me. Nobody there knows me, and I haven't seen my brothers in years. A fortnight at Christmas hardly signifies." She shook her head. "I don't want to go home to live with people who know me only as Hortence's spoiled daughter."

"You could stay with us," Sally interjected. "Can't she, Belle?"

Isabelle cast a sympathetic glance at Sally. "I wish it were so simple," she said. "Alice's relatives are hardly likely to turn her welfare over to the hands of a stranger."

Alice shook her head. "They're more strangers to me than you are,

Miss Webb. But that's hardly the point. I don't expect you to take on another orphan. Please take no offense, Sally."

Sally answered with a sad smile. "It's true."

"We all are," Isabelle said. "I lost my parents at fifteen, Alice. A year younger than you are now. It does hurt, but I promise you, it does get easier."

Alice stared into the corner of the room, her gaze unblinking, unfocused. Isabelle watched her, knowing that nothing she could say would help at that moment. Finally, unable to help herself, she murmured, "Alice, I am so sorry."

Alice shrugged a shoulder, and finally a tear formed in her eye and escaped, trailing slowly down her cheek. She drew in a shuddering breath and softly blew it out. "I am afraid," she whispered. "And I wish I could tell my father I love him." She paused and wiped the tear with her finger.

"I'm sure he knew," Isabelle said, although she hardly believed it herself. When they had first met Alice, she had been a petulant child who could barely see past the edges of her frock.

"No, he didn't," Alice said. "He didn't know because I never told him." Tears flowed in earnest then, and Isabelle handed her a handkerchief. The girl's grief was all the more heartbreaking because it was so quiet. Isabelle had expected an intensely outward display of emotion.

Sally moved to sit on Alice's other side and grasped the girl's fingers within her own. Alice's grip was such that her knuckles whitened. "I don't want to live with strangers," she said as she attempted to wipe her eyes. "I only wanted to go home to England with my mother to have a Season—she would have been with me then, and my maid. We were to have gone next year . . ."

Isabelle tried to harden her heart against the sound of the young grief, but her eyes burned in spite of her best efforts.

"I don't know what to do!" Alice gasped out, looking at Isabelle with huge eyes. "I . . . I . . ."

"Alice," Isabelle said, "you need do nothing for now. We will sort everything out. I told the colonel in Calcutta that we would be returning you to him. People are concerned—you have more friends than you probably know. Captain Weber wanted to come with us to find you, but other duties called him away. In the meantime, the colonel is contacting your brothers and relatives. I didn't say exactly when we would return, however."

Alice sniffed and wiped at her nose. "What do you mean?"

"I mean, there really isn't a rush to return."

Sally looked around Alice and caught Isabelle's eye. "We can stay here? In Egypt?"

"Well," Isabelle said, wondering if she would come to count herself ten times a fool later on. "Genevieve seems to think we would enjoy spending some time with her expedition. How do you feel about it, Alice?"

Alice nodded without a trace of hesitation. "Yes, please. I don't want to go back. I don't want to go home—I don't know what I want, other than to stay with you for as long as possible."

"I'll send word with the captain of your steamer that we've decided to extend our stay for a bit."

"I would like that very much," Alice said, and her grip on Sally's fingers visibly relaxed.

"Alice, it does get easier," Isabelle repeated. "And if at all possible, you're welcome to make your home with Sally and me. I cannot guarantee anything, but do know that the offer is extended."

"You're kind," Alice said, and the tears flowed afresh. "I hardly deserve it. I'm not a very nice person."

"Yes, well, neither was I at your age." Isabelle gave the girl a small smile and a wink. "Neither was Sally, for that matter. She's only now becoming nice."

Sally snorted at Isabelle and tossed her own wadded-up handkerchief at her. "Well, then, here's to all of us. The nasty orphans," Sally said and placed an arm around Alice's shoulders. Alice rested her head against Sally's, and it was with no small amount of relief that Isabelle realized Alice was in good hands.

"Get some sleep, girls," Isabelle told them. With a gentle ruffle of Alice's hair and a kiss on Sally's cheek, she left the room and quietly closed the door.

* * *

Isabelle found James seated in the hotel's large parlor. He occupied a chair next to the hearth, his long legs extended and crossed at the ankle. He stared into the fire, seemingly lost in his thoughts.

She fought down a surge of panic that had been building as she spent time with Genevieve. Old feelings assaulted her, worries, defenses she hadn't felt for ages. She couldn't allow herself to rely on anyone, to become too close to anyone. She had never allowed a man to capture her heart. Sabotaging relationships before they even began was her familiar modus operandi.

Isabelle shook her head and willed herself to approach James. Her feet, however, remained firmly rooted to the spot. *This is utterly ridiculous,* she silently fumed. *You know this man, you trust this man. He is here with you still because he cares for you . . .*

Her heart increased its tempo in spite of her best efforts to stay calm. Too fast, perhaps. They barely knew each other, after all. She'd allowed herself to fall too hard, too fast. Time and distance would surely help. She needed some space to breathe.

Isabelle forced herself to cross the floor to James. "Hello, handsome," she said as she took a seat opposite his, determined to return their relationship to a lighter footing.

"Hello to you," he said and straightened in his seat, leaning forward and grasping her hands in his. He placed a kiss on her knuckles, his eyes locked with hers. She quite forgot what she was going to say.

"How is Alice?" he asked her.

Isabelle sighed, and when he released her hands, she sat back in her seat. She was morbidly grateful to have something else to think about. "She is sad. She also doesn't want to go home. She wants to stay with me and Sally." She looked back at James to judge his reaction.

He raised a brow. "What do you want?"

"I wouldn't mind. I doubt it will be possible, though. Her family will likely want her." She paused. "I also told them we would travel with Genevieve for a bit. James, I understand if you and Phillip need to go home." She swallowed, almost wishing he would agree to leave but feeling sick to her stomach at the thought.

He looked at her with a bland expression. "You don't honestly believe I'm leaving you here."

"James, you have a life." She lifted a hand in frustration, and it fell back limply to her lap. "I don't know what this is . . . I don't know what to expect of this . . ."

"Belle, I'm not letting you go. I'll tell you what you can expect of this. I'm staying by your side. I should like to see you try to be rid of me."

She took a deep breath and cursed her racing heart. "I . . . this is sudden. I'm feeling . . ."

"Afraid?"

Isabelle looked at him, unwilling to admit the truth.

"Belle, you've been acting distant ever since we sat down to lunch. You've had a great shock, seeing your benefactress again after so many years. Perhaps you just need some time to accustom yourself."

She nodded. "I'm sure that's it," she said. "I just need to . . . slow down. But," she paused, intensely uncomfortable, "what of money? I hate to ask it, James, but I worry . . ."

He laughed. "You worry that the blacksmith is low on funds?"

Her nostrils flared. "Don't mock me."

"I'm not mocking you, my dear. I have enough money to last Phillip and me for a bit yet. And besides, the Benefactress offered me employment, if you'll remember."

"I'm so sorry, James. She's impulsive."

He smiled. "Think nothing of it. I took no insult; I may, in fact, accept the offer. I am a practical sort, after all."

"So you and Phillip want to stay and travel with them?"

James nodded. "We discussed it earlier, and Mrs. Montgomery is indeed in the right of it. It would be silly to be here and not enjoy it for a while."

Isabelle nodded once and looked back into the fire. For a woman who was usually adept at spontaneity, she found herself strangely conflicted between wanting to know exactly what her future held and the fear of committing to something that could see her abandoned yet again. "What will become of us, James?"

He chuckled and she looked at him. He had resumed his relaxed stance and now looked at her through heavily lidded eyes. "Are you fishing about for a proposal, Miss Webb?"

"Of course not," she shot back. "What would I want with a proposal?"

"What, indeed?"

Isabelle narrowed her eyes a fraction. "Are you toying with me, Mr. Ashby?"

"Certainly not, Miss Webb. I must admit, however, that I rather like having the upper hand."

"You don't have the upper hand."

"Of course not." He smiled.

"You don't!"

"Exactly."

What was it about this one man? In all her adult years, nobody had ever managed to fluster her so. She needed to regain her perspective, find her footing. He was imposing in physical stature and in spirit. If she surrendered to that, and if he were to leave—to decide he didn't want a spy for a wife—she didn't care to consider the devastation. "I do not waste my time with games," she said in a huff.

His expression sobered and his eyes lost all hint of teasing. "Neither do I."

* * *

James readied for bed, lost in contemplation. Phillip already slept soundly, and James supposed he was grateful for it. His thoughts needed some quiet in which to roam.

Were it left to him, Isabelle would already wear his ring. As it stood, he knew she wasn't ready. He wasn't altogether certain what had happened in her life to make her shy away from trusting relationships, but he knew for a fact that she trusted Sally and quite possibly only one or two other friends back in the States. She was beginning to trust him, but something in her eyes gave him pause; it was as though she expected him to bolt at any moment or break her heart and offer it back to her.

Rather than rush into marriage, knowing she felt intense fear and reservation, he wanted her to come to it with confidence and a sense of security. He knew exactly what he wanted. She, however, would require time. He had no doubt she was coming to love him, but he wanted her comfortable and at peace with her heart. It could prove quite a feat for someone whose heart had rarely found peace.

As had become his habit before retiring for bed each night, James crossed to the trunk that held the jewel. He uncovered it and stared for a moment, finally reaching down to touch it. He was forced to redefine what he had dismissed as vibration from the ship's engines when they were at sea. The stone seemed, at times, to quiver on its own. It had happened earlier in the day, when he had taken a moment to unpack a few things, and again before he left to sit in the parlor and wait for Isabelle to finish with the girls.

It now lay still and cold, innocent in its silence. Determined to prove to himself it was nothing more than a lifeless piece of rock, he picked it up and weighed it in his palm. He casually turned it over, tossing it lightly into the air and allowing it to again nestle in his hand. "Just a silly rock," he murmured.

"Wha . . ." Phillip said from his mosquito-netted bed, turning in his sleep.

"Nothing," James answered him.

Phillip groaned a bit and sat up, and James could see through the white netting that Phillip was rubbing his back at the base of his spine. "Ouch."

"What is it?" James asked, pausing as he felt a slight tremor from the stone. He looked at it for a moment and then replaced it in the trunk, covering it with a cloth.

"My back has been bothering me these last few days," Phillip said and rubbed his eyes.

James wouldn't have thought much of it, except that Phillip rarely complained from physical pain. "When did it start?" he asked.

"On the ship, really, but I was so miserably sick that it seemed a minor thing. I suppose it still is a minor thing, but it irritates."

"Hmm. Odd." James washed his face and hands with a cloth from the bedside basin and changed into night clothes. "You're certain you want to stay?" he asked Phillip as he climbed into his own bed and pulled the mosquito netting around it.

"Of course. Home can wait. It isn't going anywhere."

James smiled. "True enough. Sleep well."

"Likewise."

The last sound James heard as he drifted off to sleep was a quiet, steady hum.

4

Isabelle sat alone in the dining room the next morning, enjoying a few moments of peace before breakfast. It wasn't long before she spied a familiar figure. Genevieve was aging beautifully, and Isabelle expected nothing less. Everything about the woman had always exuded class and sophistication with a heady dose of intellect to top it off.

Genevieve spied Isabelle and smiled. She made her way across the dining room with a grace that Isabelle envied. Isabelle stood and accepted Genevieve's offered hands. The older woman placed a kiss on Isabelle's cheek and sat down with her.

"You slept well, I hope?" Genevieve asked her.

"I did. Better than I'd hoped to. I'm afraid I had to give Alice some distressing news last night."

Genevieve lifted a brow.

"Her father died just before I left India. We also received word that her mother had met with foul play as well."

"Oh, dear. How is the girl?" Genevieve asked.

Isabelle shrugged. "Probably much as I was." She studied Genevieve for a moment. "Do you remember? Although it was a few years after the fact that we met."

"I do remember. So young and fiercely independent. Determined to provide for yourself and Claire on your own. You didn't trust me much."

"I could not fathom that a stranger wanted to send Claire and me to exclusive schools and pay for our every need." She paused. "I still cannot fathom why."

Genevieve plucked a piece of lint from her skirt. "I told you why then, and yet you still don't understand me?"

Isabelle let the silence fall between them in an attempt to force the woman to break the awkward pause. Genevieve looked at her with a smile, as though she knew full well Isabelle's ploy. "I knew your parents," she finally said. "Their parents were dear friends of mine, and I wanted to see to their granddaughters."

"And these friends of yours died before we were born."

"Yes."

Isabelle opened her mouth, closed it again, and finally decided to be brave. "What do you know of my parents? What do you remember of them?"

Genevieve sat back and was thoughtful for a moment, looking at Isabelle as though considering something. "Your father was gentle, strong, quite brilliant. He was . . . he was an amazing child who grew into an amazing man. Your mother was equally his match."

"But she was his social inferior." Isabelle still felt the bite: the defensiveness for her mother, the anger at her father's family. "It's hard to believe you would step in where his own family wouldn't."

"Is it so hard to believe someone wanted to care for you?" Genevieve asked her.

Isabelle met the frank, blue gaze and read compassion there. Compassion and something else that had always flickered in and out of the woman's eyes, something Isabelle remembered trying to define even as a young girl. A sort of sadness, as though she were fighting emotion.

"I don't believe in fairy tales," Isabelle said, "and you were a fairy tale. Orphans are never swooped off the streets and into the arms of a privileged godmother. My own grandparents were nowhere to be found. That strangers would care for us was beyond my comprehension."

This time, Genevieve let the silence grow. "Why did you join with Pinkerton?" she finally asked. "I was prepared to launch you into Boston society, yet as soon as school was finished, you left everyone to become a spy."

Isabelle shook her head. "I never intended to be 'launched.' I wasn't ready; I had little liking for the young men in town at the time." She lifted her shoulder in a small shrug. "I wanted to take care of myself."

"Were you angry with me?"

Isabelle looked at her in surprise. "Of course not. I was grateful to you; I made a point to thank you repeatedly."

"Yes. I still have all the letters. And yet I often felt you resented me."

Isabelle looked at the woman's face and a surge of affection overcame her. "I never resented you, Genevieve," she said quietly. "I was embarrassed, horribly embarrassed, and angry that my parents were gone, had left us to the charity of others."

"You loved them very much."

Isabelle nodded once, stiffly. "Very much. I didn't want anyone but them."

"I knew that then. And I want you to know something now. My only regret was not being able to find you sooner." Genevieve leaned forward and clasped Isabelle's hand. "Now, for heaven's sake, let me love you and dote on you, and do not make me travel the world to find you again."

Isabelle smiled past the uncomfortable lump in her throat. "Fair enough." She paused, then couldn't keep herself from asking, "How is Claire? Have you seen her?"

Genevieve nodded and settled back into her chair. "She is doing well. Are you never going to contact her again?"

"She doesn't want me to."

"Pooh. Silly girl. Of course she does."

Isabelle shook her head. "No. The times I've tried, she's made herself very clear. She hates me quite thoroughly."

"No. She didn't understand why you left; she took it very personally."

"And she then proceeded to tell me that she never wanted to hear from me again, that all I'd ever done was meddle in her life, that she was glad I was gone because she was finally free."

Genevieve smiled a bit. "She lashed out in an effort to stem the hurt. Surely now you see that for what it was."

"I don't know. She only insisted more of the same as time went by. I eventually stopped trying to talk to her altogether."

"Well, I should think enough time has passed. It's time to try again."

"Perhaps."

"Now," Genevieve said, "let me tell you about our entourage. You've met Maude. My sons should be arriving for breakfast shortly, and the Stafford brothers usually make an appearance as well. Monsieur Deveraux may show his face, but sometimes he prefers a cup of tea in his room."

Isabelle shook her head. "Why, exactly, are you doing this?"

"Why not? And besides, I told you. I have dreamed of your being here and felt something . . . momentous should happen." Genevieve smiled and looked extremely satisfied with herself.

"Hmm. And here I'd always known you to be the solid, practical sort."

"Yes. And I am solidly, practically here in Egypt, ready to examine tombs and traipse around the desert."

"Are you looking for something specific?"

"We have permission from the Egyptian Antiquities Department to begin digging at a site up the Nile that was the scene of a prior excavation but was abandoned due to lack of funding. I have yet to receive any real information about it or the timeline behind it, but Maude has been piecing details together based on the location and prior findings in the area." Genevieve smiled. "Maude and the rest of them just want to get their hands dirty."

"Not you?"

"And ruin this ensemble?" Genevieve asked, gesturing to her fine clothing.

Isabelle smiled. "'Twould be an outrage."

"Of the worst kind! Oh, look! It's my Eli." Genevieve waved at a man who looked to be in his mid-thirties. He lifted a hand in response and made his way across the floor. He was soon followed by a second man, obviously a brother, who seemed a few years older.

"Miss Isabelle Webb, may I present my two sons, Eli and William."

"A pleasure to meet you," Isabelle said as both men murmured their hellos. Isabelle's attention caught on Eli, the younger brother. There was something oddly familiar about him—his looks, his mannerisms—something she couldn't quite place. "Are you certain we've not met before?" she asked him as he settled into his seat.

Eli looked at her, brows drawn but expression pleasant. "It's possible, but not that I can recall. Mother has certainly told us about you and your sister through the years. It's a pleasure to finally meet you in person."

The room suddenly seemed a bustle of activity as food was laid out on a buffet table and more hotel patrons entered. By the time the food was settled on the table and everyone was seated, the four final members of the expedition had joined the group, in addition to James and Phillip.

James took a seat at Isabelle's side and asked her where the girls were.

"They'll be down eventually," she said. "Those two are night owls, if you'll recall. That, and I don't imagine sleep came easily for either of them once I left them last night."

"I do hope Miss Bilbey is faring well," Phillip said. He flicked his napkin open and placed it in his lap.

"I believe she will be well enough before long," Isabelle said and smiled her thanks to a servant who filled her glass with juice.

Genevieve interrupted the small conversations at the table long enough to make introductions all the way around and ended with, "And these are the Ashby brothers, who have graciously consented to serve as our personal heads of security on our excursion."

Isabelle fought to keep from rolling her eyes at Genevieve's theatrics but couldn't suppress a smile. Genevieve had likely assumed that Isabelle may not have wanted to stay in Egypt had the Ashbys gone home, but Isabelle had to applaud the woman for her ability to orchestrate things to her advantage. Getting James and Phillip to stay with her group was a very strategic move.

Isabelle slowly ate her breakfast and studied the group seated at the large table. Several distinct personalities began to emerge, and her brain began categorizing each person's individual traits. The British brothers, Harry and Henry Stafford, were nearly as identical in personality as they were in appearance. They appeared to be in their late thirties but had an innocence to them that was refreshing. Their excitement for the coming expedition showed clearly in their faces, and they occasionally tripped over their words in their excitement.

They were conservators, experts in their field at preserving and caring for antiquities.

The Frenchman, Jean-Louis Deveraux, was quiet and had a studious air about him. He was pleasant when addressed but kept largely to himself. The reserved nature of his personality was at odds with his young age; Isabelle guessed him to be close to Phillip's age, twenty-two or so.

William Montgomery, Genevieve's oldest son and in his early forties, engendered in Isabelle an immediate dislike. He was fairly obsequious to his mother, but when she wasn't watching, he cast a shrewd eye around the proceedings as if analyzing them to fit his own needs. The comments he made in conversation smacked of condescension and arrogance.

Eli Montgomery, who looked to be a few years younger than his brother, seemed very genuine. He lacked the brash outer edge his brother possessed and was all that was pleasant. He sat to Isabelle's left, and she took an immediate and instinctive liking to him.

Maude Davis sat between Harry Stafford and Jean-Louis Deveraux. She was charming and an affable conversationalist. She switched easily from the animated chatter of the Brit on her left to the more reserved approach of the Frenchman on her right. Isabelle had to admit a certain curiosity about the woman's knowledge of ancient Egypt and looked forward to seeing her at work.

Isabelle was nearly finished with her meal when the girls appeared in the dining room doorway. She waved to them and they crossed the floor, looking lovely and young. Alice looked remarkably in possession of herself and bore only a slight trace of darkness beneath her eyes as a sign of lost sleep.

Isabelle made the formal introductions and saw the girls comfortably seated. She realized how much she'd missed them, especially Sally, in the time since their abduction over a month before. She'd grown accustomed to caring for someone other than herself and found that she enjoyed it.

Phillip began a conversation with Sally, and much to Isabelle's surprise, the girl seemed almost shy. In all their time together, she'd never yet seen this side. Of course, she'd also never seen Sally confronted with a man with whom she was genuinely enamored. Sally drew Alice into the conversation as well, and Isabelle gave a slight nod of satisfaction. The girl was growing up.

* * *

Thaddeus Sparks watched the group finish breakfast and leave the dining room. He sat in a corner, well apart from them, and had been able to observe the key players in action. A surge of anger swept through him as he watched James Ashby lean over to his brother, Phillip, with a smile, and whisper something in his ear. Phillip reacted with a laugh and a shake of his head. The two men waited for the Webb woman and the younger girls and followed them from the room, looking physically large and self-assured.

Sparks's nostrils flared. He would exact his revenge on the Ashby brothers. When he had what he wanted, he would finish James before Phillip's very eyes. Disgust had Sparks shaking his head as he remembered the first time he'd met Phillip. Phillip had been young and idealistic, and he possessed the one thing Sparks needed in order to obtain the Jewel of Zeus: a birthmark on the lower left of his spine in the shape of a star.

Phillip had become uncooperative and suspicious as their journey had progressed, and by the time they had reached India, he had been ready to beat Sparks senseless and return home. It was only by threatening future harm to Phillip's mother that he'd been able to maintain control of the younger man.

Phillip was still the key—of that Sparks was convinced. Even the Federation knew of the legend regarding the birthmark, and so few would ever possess it that Sparks could not afford to let Phillip escape him a second time. He would follow them as they made their voyage up the Nile and played in the sand. When the time was right, he would know, and he would again secure Phillip's cooperation. Phillip was nothing if not chivalrous, and one of the young girls could prove useful.

Sparks looked up at the approach of a European-looking man in a nondescript suit. He looked like any one of a dozen European tourists and possessed a face that could easily be forgotten in a crowd. He doubted he would ever forget that face, however. Periodically, Sparks could swear the man was watching him as he went about town. He sat at Sparks's table and withdrew a packet from within his coat pocket.

"Mr. Ashby did indeed come to Egypt," the Italian said.

Sparks couldn't keep the irritation from his voice. "I told you he would."

"So you did." The man nudged the packet toward the middle of the table. "Your next payment."

Sparks looked into the envelope to see that the money was substantially less than the first payment had been. "You tell your employers that they are tying my hands by portioning the money this way," he said.

The man leaned forward and dropped his voice. "What I might tell them is that I do not understand why you have not already spoken with Mr. Ashby. You insist you are well-acquainted and that he trusts you, yet you hang back."

"I have already explained this!" The Italian glared at him, and Sparks cast a furtive glance about before dropping his voice. "Mr. Ashby's brother harbors misconceptions about my activities in pursuing the . . . prize . . . and he has warned his brother about me, telling him lies. It will take some time and distance before I am able to gain Phillip Ashby's trust again."

"And if you are unable to gain that trust?"

"I have other plans should that happen. You needn't concern yourself with the details."

"The very reason for my employ is to concern myself with details." The Italian sat back in his chair and regarded Sparks with a cool, assessing eye.

"And again, *sir*, allow me to remind you that your employers contacted me. So I repeat, do not concern yourself with my affairs!"

The man watched him for a few unnerving moments. "It appears from your last communication with my employers that Mr. Ashby and the rest plan to travel to Cairo and then proceed up the Nile."

Sparks nodded stiffly.

"Should that be the case, you'll find a *dahabeeyah* arranged for your travel." He slid a piece of paper across the table. "Contact this man at the docks. He will handle the matter for you."

"Very well."

The Italian nodded once and then stood. "I'll be seeing you again," he said, and left the room.

***

The Italian walked a short distance to his employers' hotel and made his way through the rooms to a private suite befitting a pharaoh. When he was admitted, he bowed to the group of men seated together in comfortable chairs around a low table filled with fruit and frosted tea cakes.

"The money and instructions have been delivered," he told the group, specifically addressing the Egyptian.

"Excellent. And how did you find our man?" the Egyptian asked.

"Nervous."

The Egyptian eyed him in quiet speculation. "You wish to say more."

The European paused. "I believe him to be skittish. I wonder at his ability to comport himself and actually be able to again ingratiate himself with Mr. Ashby. He seems rather a security risk, sir." He bowed his head slightly in a show of respect.

The Egyptian nodded. "What you say is true. However, he is, at the moment, the best option. If we were to merely abduct Mr. Ashby, he couldn't very well lead us to our goal. Mr. Sparks, however, has at least a chance of again capturing his friendship."

The Italian could feel the dubious expression on his face, and he tried to soften it so as not to appear critical. "I'm not certain he will be able to do so. He is very uneasy. I believe the relationship might be beyond repair."

"Rest at ease. I know you have the best of intentions with your concerns. There is, however, another matter to consider. Mr. Sparks is entirely too inquisitive about the jewel. He is a threat to the Federation, inept or no. We cannot have bungling amateurs thrusting their noses into this business. So we shall simply keep him close, use him for our own ends, and dispose of him when the time presents itself."

"Yes, sir."

5

Isabelle moved with the swaying motion of the train as she walked into the lounge car. The group had packed up their belongings and boarded the train earlier in the afternoon for a three-day journey inland to Cairo and the mighty Nile River. Her excitement matched that of the girls, although she was a bit more discreet. The diversion was proving a welcome one for Alice, whose only indication of her inner sorrow was an occasional bout of silence where she stared into the distance at nothing in particular. She was quick to recover, however, sometimes with a slight shake of the head as though making a physical effort to break free of her grief.

The group had settled into a comfortable rhythm, each personality fitting itself into the dynamics of the others. The Brits were always to be counted on for laughs, the Frenchman for thoughtful insight, the elder Montgomery brother for a snide remark, and the younger for something considerate. Genevieve was often to be seen sitting back and watching the proceedings with an astute eye, and Maude Davis regaled the group with tales of ancient Egypt and what she hoped to see along the Nile. James provided Isabelle with a dual sense of both unnerving scrutiny and heart-thumping breathlessness. Phillip was endearing, charming, and made her laugh.

Isabelle surveyed the group in the lounge car for a moment before taking a vacant seat next to Maude. She supposed the weather would soon change; she felt rain in the air long before it ever made itself manifest. She absently rubbed her suddenly achy leg, thinking that later she would apply a warm cloth to it for some relief.

"How are you feeling, dear?" Maude asked her.

"I am well, thank you," Isabelle said and folded her hands together. Darn that Sally; she had regaled both Maude and Genevieve with tales of Isabelle's wartime exploits before Isabelle had reached Egypt. Now both older women looked at her in concern if she so much as sneezed.

"Are you hurting?" Maude probed.

"No, no. Well," Isabelle amended at Maude's arched brow, "not much, anyway. I suspect it will always be a nuisance."

"Perhaps not. Your injury is less than a year old, isn't that right? It will heal."

Isabelle nodded, uncomfortable talking about herself.

"Take a look at those two," Maude said, swiftly changing the conversation to address the laughter of the Stafford brothers. "Have you ever seen such infectious joy?"

Isabelle smiled. "Truthfully, no. They are refreshing."

Maude nodded and shifted some papers she held on her lap. "I think they'll be just the right balance for what we'll need on this trip."

"What do you have there?" Isabelle asked her.

"Some notes on our proposed excavation site. I've been searching my books for months now to learn as much as I can about the tomb that we'll be looking for, but I can find precious little." Maude frowned and perched her spectacles on her nose. "All we know is that the group before us unearthed some tombs along a rock face but was unable to find anything of significance.

"No guesses as to the dynasty, possible royalty?"

"Nothing, really."

Isabelle gestured toward the papers. "May I see them?"

"Certainly."

Maude handed her the sheets, and Isabelle studied the careful, neat script. "What do you know of the region itself?" she asked, turning a page.

"The area has seen much archaeological activity of late, and with incredible success. Our site, however, is more remote, and many in the field have thought it beneath notice. I suppose that would explain the relative ease with which we secured permission to continue the excavation. Nobody expects much to come of it. The Antiquities Department is willing to let the bored Westerners play in the sand for a fee."

"The Antiquities Department itself is staffed with Westerners, is it not?"

Maude nodded. "We can't keep our hands to ourselves, now, can we? If there ever is anything of interest somewhere, expect to find an American or European making it his business." She softened her remarks with a smile. "And it works to my benefit, of course. Here I am, pursuing a passion I've harbored for years. When I was very young, I read of Napoleon's exploits in Egypt. Ever since, I've been dying to see these things myself."

Isabelle returned Maude's papers to her and looked around the car as the older woman began making more notes after consulting a book she held open in her lap. Sally and Alice were stifling yawns, no doubt unwilling to go to bed and miss something interesting, and even some of the older members of the group were showing signs of fatigue.

James and Phillip had been playing a hand of whist with Sally and Alice. James now tossed his cards on the table and leaned back in his seat. "I do believe it's time for me to retire," he said. He must have felt Isabelle's eyes on him; he looked up and held her gaze. Finally, he winked at her and stood. Phillip yawned and followed suit, prompting the girls to rise as well.

"I think I'll make sure those girls actually get into bed," Isabelle said to Maude.

Maude glanced up and studied them for a moment. Alice was laughing at something James had said, and Sally blushed as Phillip sent a smile her way. "They are having the time of their lives," Maude said. "How many young girls can claim such adventures?"

Isabelle cast a dubious glance in their direction. "Not many, most likely, and I'm sure their parents would feel that to be a good thing."

Maude looked at Isabelle with a smirk. "Abduction aside, I mean."

Isabelle laughed. "Yes, abduction aside, they are having a wonderful time. And you know, even the abduction served its purpose. It solidified their friendship when little else might have."

"There is always a silver lining, then."

Isabelle bid the woman good night and moved across the room to kiss Genevieve's cheek. Genevieve showed obvious surprise at the demonstration of affection and looked as though she were trying to accept it with nonchalance.

Isabelle felt herself blush, which was certainly an oddity. "I've missed you," she said in a huff and turned to follow the girls.

Genevieve's soft laughter followed her out into the hallway where James stood waiting for her. He motioned for her to precede him down the narrow corridor and she marveled, as she often did, at the odd sensation of walking in a direction opposite of that which the train traveled. The clack of the wheels along the tracks was familiar, and she found that she'd rather missed it since leaving India, where they'd traveled across the country in a relatively compressed amount of time.

Ahead of them, Isabelle saw Phillip bid the girls good night and then move down the hall to his berth. The girls entered the cabin they shared with Isabelle, and she caught a snippet of their conversation as she neared.

". . . know I saw him at the train station," Sally was saying to Alice.

"Mr. Jones? Are you sure? I thought he said he was returning to Bombay. In fact, I know he said that, because we told him we were headed for Calcutta and would have to travel so many more days than he."

"I know, but there he was! Truly, could I have mistaken those eyes?"

Isabelle smiled. The girls were growing into womanhood, and she was glad she and Sally had fortuitously come across Alice Bilbey. It gave Sally the companionship of a girl her own age. They entered the cabin and closed the door just before Isabelle reached it. She wasn't certain if she was relieved or alarmed. She'd been casually avoiding spending time with James alone.

James smiled at her when she stopped at her door and turned to him. He took both of her hands in his, leaned forward, and instead of kissing her, nuzzled the spot just below her left ear. She drew a shuddering breath, and he finally laid the softest of kisses there before releasing her hands and moving on to his cabin with his hands in his pockets and a whistle on his lips.

She looked after him with narrowed eyes. She gritted her teeth and yanked her door open, inwardly cursing him as he entered his own cabin without even a backward glance. Just that blasted whistle!

"Says he doesn't play games," she muttered. "What was that all about, I'd like to know?"

"What was what all about?" Sally asked her as Alice untied the back of her dress. Sally released a breath as the material loosened. "Oh, that's better," she said and turned Alice's shoulders to do the same for her.

"Nothing," Isabelle said and rubbed her forehead. What was he trying to do? Prove he could make her want him? Try to make her think she couldn't live without his affection? She frowned a bit. It wasn't until some time later that she realized being frustrated with him kept her from being panicked about him.

Perhaps he knew it as well. He was too perceptive by half.

* * *

Isabelle wasn't certain what had pulled her from sleep, but as she lay in her bunk, she knew something specific had awoken her. The train made its usual soothing sounds. Night outside the small window was black and fathomless, only just beginning to show the slightest glow from the moon as it made its journey across the sky. Isabelle sat up and quietly rose, pulling on her robe. She glanced at the bunk above hers; Sally lay sleeping peacefully, as did Alice, in her bunk across the small space.

Frowning, she tied her robe securely and quietly opened the door. Looking first to the left, then the right, she saw that the corridor was empty. She pulled back into the room and then decided against it, quietly exiting and closing the door behind her. She debated whether or not to awaken James; he had made her promise on more than one occasion not to "walk around alone at night," as though it were a common occurrence.

She was forced to admit, however, that it had happened more than once in India, and several times she had met with danger. She turned to walk away when she heard James and Phillip's door opening. "I just need some air," Phillip said to James and closed the door behind him. The younger brother was nearly upon her when he noticed her standing in the corridor.

"Belle! I'm . . . sorry, I . . ." He looked disheveled and harried. He wore trousers and his shirtsleeves were open at the throat and haphazardly buttoned the rest of the way down. The shirttails were tucked in the front and mostly around the back, with a portion hanging out at the side.

"Not at all, Phillip, I'm fine. What are you doing?"

"I . . ." He paused. "What are you doing?"

"I heard a noise."

Phillip smiled slightly, in spite of his obvious state of stress. "So you went to investigate. James would have your head if he knew."

"He needn't know. Do you mind the company? I'm wide awake now and couldn't sleep if I tried." It was a lie, of course. Isabelle was so tired she could hardly see straight, but her curiosity over Phillip's agitation overcame her desire for rest.

Phillip ran a hand through his hair and looked down the empty corridor. Finally, he offered her his arm with a sigh, and they made their way to the lounge car, which was dark except for a lone lantern. After seeing Isabelle seated, Phillip sat down and leaned forward, placing his elbows on his knees, his head dropping forward slightly.

"What is it, Phillip?" she asked him.

He let out a soft sigh and shook his head a bit before raising his eyes to hers. The lantern created shadows that played on his face, creating worry lines where there weren't any in the light of day. "You'll not believe me," he said.

"You should let me be the judge of that."

He was silent for another moment, avoiding conversation by examining his finger in a gesture endearingly like his older brother's. Finally, rubbing a hand across his knuckles, he looked back up at her again. "I do believe this fanciful part of the world is playing games with my mind."

"How so?"

He shook his head again, and she waited for several moments before he spoke. "I think Sparks's crazy stories have taken their toll on my sanity. I see multiple jewels in my sleep, and I'm constantly trying to find them, but they are always just out of reach. And people are chasing me and I can't run. Sparks is after me again, hoping to find me alone. The worst of it, though . . ."

Isabelle waited again, watching him with sympathy.

"The worst of it is my back." He looked embarrassed to be speaking of it.

"Your back?"

"Yes. My birthmark. Sometimes it itches and burns. It's making me rather mad."

Isabelle studied him, turning the information over in her mind. She wasn't a believer in magic or the occult; she barely believed in God as it was. She did find it interesting, however, that he was experiencing physical symptoms of distress concerning the jewel.

She and James had decided to tell nobody about the fact that they traveled with the real Jewel of Zeus. What exactly she planned to do with it she wasn't sure. Legally it belonged to the Bilbey family. Hortence Bilbey, Lady Banbury, had brought it with her from her husband's ancestral estate in England to India with the intention of selling it to Thaddeus Sparks.

Legend stated that the jewel had been taken from Greece to India; at some point, however, it had fallen into the hands of Colonel Bilbey's ancestors and was removed from India to England. Bilbey and his wife, apparently, were the only ones who had known of its whereabouts. The older generations had since died off, and Colonel Bilbey had regarded the object with a certain amount of disdain. He certainly never made public the fact that it was in his possession, and his wife delighted in sharing the mystery of the legend with any who would listen, all the while knowing the jewel resided on her husband's property.

Lady Banbury had been murdered en route to India from England, her husband killed mere weeks later. Lady Banbury had been, apparently, the only one who knew she'd taken it from its hiding place in England and brought it back across the ocean. Even Alice didn't know about it, and now, Isabelle supposed, the jewel was Alice's by right. Or, at least, it belonged to Alice's eldest brother.

Isabelle turned her attention fully to Phillip and chewed her lip. "Do you suppose you're feeling the burning sensation and are having these strange dreams because of the time you spent with Sparks?"

Phillip nodded, still rubbing his knuckles with the fingers of his other hand. "I thought so at first, but now I'm beginning to wonder if I'm not a candidate for Bedlam."

Isabelle laughed softly. "You're far from that, Phillip. You seem very lucid to me."

"Then what is wrong with me? That sound you heard was most likely me, shouting in my sleep. James had to awaken me again—this happens at least once, sometimes twice a night."

"I wish I had answers for you, Phillip. All I can offer is that I know you've been through quite an ordeal. You were held against your will by a madman, in a strange land, with no money or resources. I should be surprised if you weren't a bit . . . uncomfortable."

He shook his head and in the low light she saw his jaw clench. "It's different . . . the dreams are always the same, down to the finest detail. Sparks is determined to find me, is bent on harming people I care about, and there are others . . . so many people insisting that I find the jewel, threatening me, my family . . ."

Isabelle didn't want to make him feel foolish, so she refrained from repeating herself. It was likely he had been so traumatized by his time spent with Sparks that his overtired brain was spinning fantastic tales while he tried to rest. She had to admit, however, to a certain amount of unease as he spoke. A chill chased its way down her spine as she considered the things he'd said.

"Phillip," she said suddenly, "do you know of anyone else who has a birthmark similar to yours?"

He shook his head. "It's an odd thing, to be sure. It is the exact replica of a five-pointed star. Not just a blotch that might resemble a star."

"And you've said that this is the reason Sparks recruited you in the first place?"

He nodded. "Why do you ask?"

"I don't know." She frowned. "Birthmarks are common enough and yet are different . . . I just wonder if Sparks told you of the mark merely to gain your cooperation."

"But why me?"

"Well, perhaps because you're strong—he may have wanted you along for physical protection . . ."

Phillip again shook his head. "I wish you could see how fanatical he would become. And his eyes, they are an intense shade of green unlike anything I've ever seen."

Something echoed in Isabelle's head, but before she could pin it down, it was gone.

"Besides," Phillip continued, "Sparks wasn't the only one who knew of the mark. The man at the Indian temple mentioned it to James. He told me about it later."

"You're right, I'd forgotten. I suppose I was hoping it was just one man's delusion."

"Why? Because then it would lessen the importance of my own physical reaction?"

"Something like that." Isabelle smiled at him. "Truthfully, I think I'd be more comfortable with the notion that your burning birthmark is nothing more than your own overwrought imagination at work."

He grinned back at her. "So you'd rather that I were crazy than that there might be something mystical afoot?"

"Yes. Entirely. Then I could just say, 'Oh, Phillip. You merely need more sleep.' Then all would be well and solved."

"And you like for things to be well and solved, I presume."

She nodded. "Very much so."

He spread his hands wide and sat back in his chair. "Well, I did say at the outset that I believe I'm losing my mind. Perhaps there really is nothing more to it."

"I don't believe so, Phillip. There may be more here than meets the eye."

They sat in quiet contemplation for a few moments. At length, Phillip stretched and began to yawn. "Do you suppose you're ready to retire yet?" he asked.

"I am." Truthfully, she was now far from it. All vestiges of sleep had fled and left her mind churning and spinning.

Phillip walked back with her to her cabin and saw her safely inside after quietly bidding her a good night. She closed the door and fastened the lock, standing for a while inside and thinking as the train continued on its way to Cairo.

A scant amount of light now shone through the window from the moon outside, and Isabelle crossed the room and opened her trunk. She withdrew her leather-bound journal and a pencil and, sitting near the window, wrote down every detail of her conversation with Phillip that she could remember. She jotted notes that seemed relevant—things she knew about Sparks, things Lady Banbury had said about the legend, anything and everything that popped into her mind when she reviewed the events of the past hour.

When she finished, she felt she was no nearer to an answer than when she'd begun, but of one thing she was certain: she and James needed to tell Phillip about the jewel that James had wrapped in his trunk.

6

Cairo was everything Isabelle might have imagined and more. The streets were congested with market stalls, donkeys bearing tourists, tourists on foot, and locals making a living catering to the tourists. European women wearing lovely day dresses and carrying parasols rode on donkeys, which were proving to be the country's most popular form of transportation. The architecture of the city was a splendid mix of cultures, with domed rooftops, latticed windows and balconies that overlooked the streets, and hotels and restaurants with open-air courtyards.

The entourage made its way from the train station to Shepheard's Hotel, which was, according to Genevieve, the only place for a tourist to stay while in Cairo. Indeed, in terms of its patrons, Shepheard's looked as though it might have been plucked from the civilized streets of a major European city and deposited in the middle of Cairo.

Isabelle herself now rode on a donkey and looked back at Sally and Alice, both of whom seemed torn between fascination and utter bewilderment. "It has been some time since I rode like this," Alice was saying to Sally. "Mostly my father just took me around in his carriages in India."

Isabelle turned to Maude Davis, who rode alongside her. "How long will it take to gather provisions and secure transportation, do you suppose?" she asked the older woman.

Maude smiled. "I hear it can take quite some time. However, if we are firm enough, we might be underway in a week, roughly."

"We are fortunate that Mr. Deveraux speaks the language," Isabelle said with a glance at the Frenchman.

Maude nodded. "That young man is truly remarkable," she said. "Twenty-four years old and he speaks five languages."

The group slowly wound its way through the crowded streets and finally neared Shepheard's Hotel. Isabelle was looking up at the building and missed seeing a small, wizened woman as she darted through their entourage and stopped at Alice's donkey.

"Old woman!" Alice said in some shock. "You might have been trampled underfoot!"

"Don't call her old," Sally muttered at Alice. "That's hardly polite!"

Alice looked at Sally. "She *is* old! And my donkey very nearly ran her down!"

The old woman in question grabbed the reins of Alice's beast of burden and began speaking to her in rapid Arabic. Alice looked at the woman, mouth agape, and blinked once or twice.

Isabelle sat, bemused and wondering at the best course of action when Jean-Louis made his way to the old woman and gathered her attention by speaking softly to her in her native tongue.

"It's as I said," Maude remarked to Isabelle in an undertone. "He'll definitely be useful."

The old woman conversed with the Frenchman, gesturing wildly with arthritic hands that had likely seen years of hard labor. Jean-Louis answered her in placating tones, finally capturing one of her hands in his own and clasping it there. Whatever he said to her appeared to help calm her nerves, for she took a deep, shuddering breath. She spoke one more time, and again, Jean-Louis shook his head and patted her hand, answering her in the same quiet voice.

He gently began to lead the woman from the middle of the group to the side of the street and pulled a coin from his pocket. He handed it to her and, producing another coin, bought a piece of fruit from a vendor. Handing the woman the fruit, Jean-Louis sketched a slight bow and left her watching after him with some bewilderment.

The Frenchman jerked his head in the direction of the hotel, and Isabelle raised an impressed brow at his effectiveness. The entire group lurched forward in response to his unspoken command, and they continued on their way to the front doors of Shepheard's. Isabelle glanced back at Alice, who was staring at the Frenchman with confusion. Sally looked back repeatedly at the old woman, who had turned her hunched shoulders and melted into the crowd.

* * *

Isabelle sat with Maude in the hotel parlor. It had been several hours since their arrival, and Maude, Genevieve, Jean-Louis, and William had wasted no time in securing the services of a riverboat captain and crew for the journey up the Nile. Using Jean-Louis's linguistic services, they not only found a captain and crew but also secured a *dahabeeyah* that had recently been rented to an Englishman who had fallen ill and wouldn't be using it. It was an incredible stroke of good luck. Travelers were often forced to wait weeks before putting together a boat and crew.

While the two older women, the Frenchman, and William were attending to the necessities of the trip, many of the men in the group had taken to the streets of Cairo after seeing their belongings stashed in their respective hotel rooms. Presently, Genevieve and the others had returned with the good news, and the girls and Genevieve were now washing up for dinner.

Isabelle leaned forward a bit and questioned Maude, uncertain she'd heard her correctly. "The old woman said what to Alice, exactly?"

"She told the girl that the mark she bears would bring her strife in the days to come. She also said that what lies buried is better left alone." Maude shrugged. "That's how Jean-Louis translated it."

"Wonderful," Isabelle muttered and sat back in her chair. "That's all the poor girl needs now. Crazed superstition to keep her up nights, alongside her grief."

"Oh, I don't suppose that crazed superstition will bother her overmuch. For all her innocence and occasional flightiness, that girl does seem to have a fairly good head on her shoulders. She might lack some of Sally's common sense, but I believe her to be a quick study." Maude nodded to herself as though confirming her own statement. "She pays close attention when I speak of ancient Egypt and seems interested despite her own best efforts not to be. It's hardly ladylike, you know."

Isabelle snorted. "The poor girl threw her lot in with the wrong group if she is overly concerned about maintaining a properly vapid presence. I don't suppose there's much that is conventional about any of us." She frowned, thinking. "What mark, I wonder, would the old woman have been talking about?"

Maude shook her head. "I haven't the least idea. Nor did Mr. Deveraux. He said he told the woman that the girl bears no mark worthy of such excitement and that she shouldn't concern herself with it further."

"Poor woman. It would be hard to live in a world fraught with delusions."

"I found it odd the way she targeted Alice so specifically."

Isabelle suppressed an involuntary shiver. "Well, it's as you said. Alice is made of sterner stuff than we probably know. I suspect she'll be none the worse for the wear." Isabelle smiled. "Now, had the old woman pounced on one of the men, we'd have had a variety of reactions, depending on the victim."

Maude laughed. "True enough. Can you imagine one of the Stafford brothers? 'My dear woman, I can't begin to imagine what you're saying, but as we're here and having a delightful time, why don't you join us for a spot of tea and we'll tell you all about our coming adventures!'"

Isabelle laughed with her, as much at the feigned accent Maude used as the content of her words. "Those men would try to charm anyone."

"Now, had the old woman approached William . . ."

Maude trailed off and Isabelle waited expectantly. "Yes?" she finally said.

"Nothing." Maude looked slightly embarrassed. "My dearest friend's son. I should hardly be disparaging his character."

"Think nothing of it," Isabelle said, slightly disappointed. Gossip or no, she would have loved the woman's insight into the smug man. "You know, however, I am curious," she ventured. "What, exactly, does William do for the expedition?"

"He has a brain for business matters that is unparalleled. He cares for the financial details of our excursion and is along to look after his mother's best interests."

"Hmm. And Eli? He's an artist, I believe?"

"Yes, and an incredibly gifted one. He'll provide the sketches for our excavations."

"He really is most kind," Isabelle said. "I've chatted with him on a few occasions; he is everything that is polite and considerate. He reminds me of someone I just can't place."

Maude nodded. "You won't find a better gentleman than that one." She glanced at Isabelle, a question in her expression. "Funny that you never met the boys—Genevieve told me you often visited her between terms and such."

"They were never home. They were involved in their own lives by then and had moved out of the family house."

"Even at the holidays?"

Isabelle felt herself flush. "We usually stayed at the school during the holidays."

Maude nodded slightly but was too polite to pry further. Isabelle had no desire to tell the woman that her pride had kept her from accepting any more charity from the Benefactress than was strictly necessary. There were often a few girls who spent the holidays at school, and they had formed a little family of their own.

Pride goeth before the fall . . .

The phrase inserted itself, unwelcome, into Isabelle's thoughts. She finally told herself, *Pride kept me standing upright.* She had figured that to rely on anyone else but herself would be the ultimate folly, and pride had given her a stiff spine when all else deserted her.

She thought of her damaged relationship with her sister and the closeness with Genevieve she'd denied herself and her sister through their school years. She mused that, perhaps, it didn't hurt to bend the spine a little.

All through dinner, Isabelle's thoughts wandered to the odd woman in the marketplace. When Jean-Louis repeated, after much prompting, what the woman had said to Alice, she caught a swift exchange of glances between James and Phillip. Alice herself seemed to pale a bit but recovered well enough and brushed it aside as so much nonsense.

"Well, I've certainly never heard of anything so strange in all my life," Harry Stafford remarked between bites of his kidney pie. "What a perfectly batty old woman! And what a delight to be in a country that produced such a creature!"

Henry Stafford beamed at his brother and joined him in a good chuckle. Isabelle's lips twitched as she watched the pair.

William Montgomery, seated to her immediate right, snorted a bit in a show of disdain. "Dratted nuisance, really," he said. "I'm certain there are laws against accosting the tourists."

"She was harmless," Isabelle said. "Just a bit confused."

Alice nodded in agreement, and whether she did so as an attempt to defend the woman or assuage her own fears, Isabelle wasn't sure. She leaned toward the latter, however; the nod was a bit too quick, the eyes a tad too bright.

"She was absolutely harmless," Alice said. "She startled me, that was all."

"You have every right to be upset," Jean-Louis said to Alice. "That's very gracious of you, miss."

Isabelle silently agreed—abduction and danger seemed to agree with the girl. Had that strange event happened several weeks before, Alice would have been in fits, demanding the woman's head.

Alice blushed slightly at the Frenchman's comment and smiled. "I do care for the downtrodden."

Isabelle bit the insides of her cheeks as she looked at Sally, who had compressed her lips together in a thin line to keep from laughing out loud. Sally finally lost some of the battle and a snort escaped her nose, which she then tried to hide by reaching for her drink and taking a sip.

Alice glanced at her in annoyance and then dismissed her. "Father used to show me the beggars in Bombay and tell me I should be grateful not to occupy their stations. Of course, Mother would then chastise him soundly for showing me such unseemly things."

Genevieve smiled at the girl. "It is important to recognize our blessings," she said. "I do believe your father had the right of it."

Alice nodded, her brows drawn slightly together. "It was ever so sad, really," she admitted in a softer tone. "And it frightened me." She shook her head and tried to laugh, but it sounded forced. "Silly, isn't it?"

"Not at all," Jean-Louis said, regarding her through his round spectacles. "The sight of poverty is upsetting. It can cause one to wonder what keeps one from falling into the same circumstances."

"Caste, for one," William said with a sharp laugh. "Not much chance of Miss Bilbey ever becoming an Unmentionable."

Alice looked askance at William with a light scowl. "One never quite knows when one's circumstances will change in the blink of an eye."

He had the grace to look chagrined and said nothing further.

Maude cleared her throat and steered the discussion to friendlier topics. The boat and crew would be ready to sail in three days' time. They would sail up the Nile for the better part of two weeks until they reached Thebes and an area just south of the Valley of the Kings. The site for their excavation attempts was small, but Maude held high hopes of finding something wonderful, as the whole country was exploding with new and exciting finds each year.

"Isn't it true that the tombs were robbed in antiquity?" Phillip asked.

Maude nodded. "Yes. And numerous times down through the centuries."

"It's a wonder people weren't afraid of incurring the wrath of the gods," James remarked as he finished his meal.

"Greed is a powerful motivator," Genevieve said. "People will do amazing things for wealth. Even risk damnation, I suppose."

Sally's eyes widened a bit at the woman's language, and she exchanged glances with Isabelle, who winked at her. "True enough," Isabelle said. "It's the one thing that doesn't change, no matter the time. Greed is constant."

"As is love," James said in a dry tone and looked at Isabelle with half of a grin. "One might think you are jaded, Miss Webb."

"Merely a realist, Mr. Ashby. One might think you are a romantic."

"And why should he not be, I say!" Henry Stafford exclaimed and lifted his glass high. "To the world's romantics! Were it not for us, the world would be a dull, drab place."

"Hear, hear!" his brother said and raised his own glass.

Isabelle shrugged and raised hers as well, and the table followed suit with much laughter. They drank to romanticism and its benefit on mankind.

* * *

A few hours later, Isabelle sat with the girls in the large hotel room that housed the three of them together. Alice was behind the changing screen and was doing her best to change her clothing unassisted.

"Do you need help?" Sally asked her for the third time.

"No! You can do this by yourself, so I certainly shall learn."

There was the slight sound of rending fabric, followed by a muffled curse. "Oh, for heaven's sake," Sally muttered and joined Alice behind the screen.

"I said no," Alice huffed, and Isabelle heard her smacking at Sally's hands.

"Don't be difficult," Sally said. "Belle helps me more often than not. As we're all here without maids, we must make do. Of course, the last time I had a maid was roughly three years ago, but I suppose that doesn't signify."

"Truly? Who helped you?"

"My mother."

"Your mother? Not your nanny or governess?"

Sally laughed, but it sounded weary. "It was war. We went from a fully staffed household to half of us dead."

Isabelle winced. There was a bit of a pause before Alice said, "I am sorry. I didn't mean . . ."

"I know, silly," Sally said. "There. Now you're untied, corset and all." She came out from behind the screen and flounced on her bed, shoving the mosquito netting aside. She looked around the room at the tall palm fronds in the corners and the warm earth tones that covered the walls. Lights in strategically placed sconces gave the place an exotic glow.

"Belle," she murmured, "we're in Egypt!"

Isabelle smiled. "That we are."

"This is so much more than I ever dreamed of."

"Truthfully, for me also." Isabelle reached over and gave her hand a squeeze. "Thank you for getting abducted so we could come here."

Sally laughed out loud, and Isabelle was glad to hear it. The occasional pain in the young girl's voice made Isabelle's heart hurt.

"How are you faring?" Isabelle asked Alice.

"Well enough," the girl answered, and Isabelle saw her hand reach above the screen to pull her nightgown onto her arm.

"Alice," Isabelle asked suddenly and entirely on a whim, "do you have a birthmark?"

"I *beg* your pardon?" The girl sounded scandalized.

"A mark, a discoloration somewhere on your skin?"

"I *know* what a birthmark is!" Alice muttered to herself for a moment behind the screen as the other hand came up and a sleeve slipped over it. "Actually, yes, I do," she said as she appeared from behind the screen. She presented her back to Sally and motioned for her to tie the ribbons behind her neck.

Isabelle suddenly recalled Alice occasionally rubbing uncomfortably at the small of her back. "You do? May I see it?"

"Miss Webb!"

"Really, Belle!"

Isabelle shook her head. "Girls, you needn't be so offended. We are all women."

"Yes, but really!" Alice said.

"Very well. Will you describe it to me?"

Alice rolled her eyes, her face slightly flushed. "It is a star," she finally said.

Isabelle looked at her for a long moment before speaking. "Is it on your back? And does it ever bother you?"

Alice looked surprised. "Yes, it is, and actually, it has bothered me quite often lately. Burning and stinging."

"Is it to the left of your lower spine?"

Alice's mouth dropped open and she closed it with a nod.

"Let me see!" Sally demanded.

"No!"

Sally pressed the fabric of her friend's white nightgown flush against her back. Alice moved away from her with a screech.

"It is a horrible monstrosity, and I'll thank you not to ever do that again," she said to Sally.

"There's nothing monstrous about a birthmark," Isabelle said, knowing full well that the girl's mother had probably made her feel deformed because of it. "I think they're charming. Look." Isabelle lifted the hem of her skirt three inches to show the girls a light brown spot she had on her lower leg, just on top of the bone.

The girls looked at her, stunned. Isabelle had to laugh at the expressions on their faces; even Sally had never seen much of Isabelle's leg before. She dropped the skirt and stood, motioning for the girls to come close. She gathered one in each arm and gave a good squeeze. "Girls, the body is a beautiful example of both form and function. While I don't expect you to go about flashing your legs in public, you'll certainly be none the worse for the wear should you happen to glimpse another woman's ankle. Now, I'm off to chat for a bit with someone."

"That would be James, I presume?" Sally said and smiled as Isabelle released them.

"Perhaps."

Alice smiled at her. "He fancies you mightily," she said. "I don't suppose you'll be showing him your birthmark?"

"Why, Alice, how scandalous of you!" Isabelle said and laughed as Sally gasped and then also laughed. "Get some sleep, girls. We're off to explore the markets tomorrow, and then I hope to see a pyramid or two."

"Excellent," Sally said and clapped her hands together.

"You don't really want to go into one, do you?" Alice was asking Sally as Isabelle left the room and closed the door behind her. Her smile faded a bit as she considered what she'd just learned. Alice Bilbey had the same birthmark that had created so much trouble for Phillip. Were she a woman of superstition, she'd have crossed herself.

7

JAMES WONDERED IF HE WOULD embarrass himself by losing consciousness. He was bent over, nearly double, and walking behind Isabelle into the depths of one of the seven wonders of the ancient world. Just when he thought he might start screaming and pounding against the unyielding interior walls of the pyramid, the ascending passage opened up to reveal what the Egyptian guide referred to as the "Grand Gallery."

James stood upright and took a deep, shuddering breath. He should have followed his first instinct and stayed outside with Alice and Sally. The thought of tons and tons of rock overhead and surrounding him made him feel as though he were suffocating. Isabelle placed a hand on the back of his arm and gave him a gentle squeeze.

"Are you ill?" she asked him in a whisper.

He glanced at her, expecting to see a teasing smile. Instead, her eyes looked troubled. "I react similarly to high places," she said. "We can leave if you'd like. I wish you'd have said something."

He shook his head. "I've already come this far. No sense in running out now."

"Very well. Perhaps remind yourself that these pyramids have stood for thousands of years. They're perfectly safe."

"Tell that to the pharaoh," he muttered.

They made their way behind their guide and the other members of the expedition through the Grand Gallery and into the King's Chamber.

Phillip was conversing with Genevieve and Maude, both of whom appeared to find him delightful. James was glad. Phillip seemed to have lost little of himself during the ordeal with Thaddeus Sparks in India, but there was an air of caution about him that hadn't been there before. As much as James had been waiting the entirety of his adult life for Phillip to show signs of responsibility, he had no desire to see him jaded along with it.

The Stafford brothers were oohing and ahhing at the hieroglyphs visible in the King's Chamber, and Jean-Louis looked at the walls with intense concentration. James supposed that the Frenchman was translating on the spot. He was a smart one, to be certain.

Genevieve's younger son, Eli, had taken a small sketch pad from his pocket and had begun to scratch something on it, while the elder, William, stood back a bit with his hands in his pockets, watching the whole group with a shrewd eye.

"Amazing," Isabelle said, standing beside him and looking up at the walls in awe.

"Seems an incredible waste for just one person," he said, looking at the sarcophagus that sat alone in the room.

"But an amazing feat, nonetheless," she insisted.

He inclined his head slightly as his only concession. He tried not to think about the fact that he stood in the bowels of the massive stone structure and focused instead on the members of the expedition. Maude drew his attention simply by her focus on the wall in front of her. Her brow creased in a frown and she placed her finger lightly on the picture she studied.

Curious, James motioned to Isabelle and they approached her. "What have you found?" he asked.

The older woman jumped a bit. She glanced at James and Isabelle and then turned her attention back to the hieroglyph. "I'm not sure," she said. "I believe I've seen this image in one of my books, but I can't remember."

James looked at the spot on the wall where her finger absently traced an oval that had been carved neatly into the rock. It was one of three identical shapes that were surrounded by a rectangle.

"It must be fairly uncommon then," Isabelle said. "I imagine it would come directly to mind were it something recognizable."

Maude nodded. "Indeed. I am very curious."

"Mr. Deveraux," Isabelle said and drew the Frenchman's attention. She motioned to him, and when he approached, she added, "I wonder if you wouldn't mind looking at this for us." She pointed at the images. "Have you any idea what this represents?"

The Frenchman looked at the wall, frowning a bit and moving closer. They shifted to make room for him, and he traced his finger along the center oval, much as Maude had done. "I am not familiar with this," he said, sounding surprised. He glanced at the symbols preceding the ovals and murmured, "This represents death, and this one here, great wealth. Behind it here is a bird, an ibis from the looks of it. And this," Jean-Louis said, "I believe it's a star." He ran his finger along a small figure to the right of the rectangle. It had been lightly carved into the stone, so lightly it might be mistaken for a random scratch at first glance.

James leaned forward and looked over the man's shoulder. He narrowed his eyes, thinking he must certainly be stupid, but he couldn't stop the shiver that made its way down his spine. "Looks like Phillip's birthmark," he murmured to Isabelle.

He heard her swift intake of breath as she, too, looked carefully at the star. She shook her head slightly and said, "Perhaps we are mistaken. It might not be a star at all."

Jean-Louis looked at her curiously. "Perhaps," he said. "But the lines are very precise. See here?"

They all stared at the carvings in silence for a moment until Jean-Louis was distracted by one of the Stafford brothers who requested his attention across the room. Maude, too, eventually left the wall, leaving James and Isabelle to study it alone.

Isabelle traced her finger along the star with a frown. "There's something I haven't told you yet. Alice has a star birthmark."

James squinted at her.

"It's a five-pointed star to the left of her lower spine, and it is bothering her."

"Bothering her how?"

"Stinging, itching."

James stared at the faint outline of the star on the wall. It was all much too sensational, and he was not the sensational or superstitious sort. "Coincidence," he finally said.

Isabelle snorted. "If you say so."

"Come now, Belle," he said, pulling her away from the wall and toward the entrance of the room. "You don't believe there's something supernatural afoot."

"Ordinarily I wouldn't," she whispered, "but I won't close my eyes to the obvious."

"And what would that be?" he snapped.

"There is something odd about the fact that Phillip and Alice both possess this mythical mark and that said marks are reacting to that *thing* back at the hotel!"

James looked for a retort but found he had none. The fact that the jewel itself hummed on a regular basis was beginning to bother him. But to admit that there was something otherworldly about the whole legend business exceeded his willingness to believe.

He rubbed his forehead and looked out of the chamber and into the Grand Gallery. Beyond that was the narrow, low-ceilinged passageway he was going to have to enter once again if he ever hoped to see daylight. His breathing increased in dreaded anticipation. Powerful jewels, identical birthmarks, the cramped passageways of an enormous pyramid—how in the world had he found himself here?

James was about to tell their guide he was leaving on his own when the group joined him and Isabelle at the doorway, preparing to exit. He breathed a subconscious sigh of relief and steeled himself for the torturous passageway.

* * *

Isabelle blinked in the sunlight as she exited the pyramid and descended the steps that took her to ground level. She marveled again at the sheer size of the structure. When viewed from Cairo, they seemed little more than children's toy blocks. Up close, they were overwhelming. The pyramids soared into the sky, and when Isabelle had first approached the Great Pyramid and looked up, she had grown dizzy from the sight of it against the deep blue above.

She heard James exiting the pyramid behind her, taking appreciative breaths of fresh air. "Better?" she asked him as he joined her on the ground. He was pale and shaking.

He nodded. "Rather pathetic for a man to be so afraid," he muttered.

"Nonsense," she said and looked around for Sally and Alice. "You're only human, man or no. Where did those girls go?"

"There's a crowd of people around the head of the Sphinx," James said, shielding his eyes against the glare of the sun. "I know I'm going to regret this, but tell me again about Alice's birthmark."

Isabelle shrugged. "It's no more than I told you before. She has a five-pointed star at the base of her spine, and it seems to be positioned exactly as you've described Phillip's. When I asked her about it, she told me it's been bothering her."

"Does she know about Phillip's birthmark?"

"I suppose she may have heard us talking about it when we were looking for him in India. The birthmark was the primary reason Sparks sought him out."

"Perhaps she is looking for some attention."

"And fabricating the birthmark?"

James nodded.

"There's a flaw with that theory," Isabelle told him.

"Which is?"

"I've seen the birthmark."

"She showed you?"

"Not exactly. But I offered to lace up her dress this morning. I took the liberty of quickly examining her back."

James looked disappointed, and Isabelle laughed. "I'm sorry to squelch your hopes. The girl most definitely bears the same mark as your brother." She sobered. "I find it an amazing coincidence. Too amazing, in fact."

"I see the girls," he said and motioned with his head. They began walking toward the Sphinx, and Isabelle called over her shoulder to Genevieve.

"We'll await you here," Genevieve answered and turned toward the animated chatter of the Staffords.

"You don't find it coincidental that both Alice and Phillip bear the same mark?" James asked her as they walked.

Isabelle adjusted her hat to better shade her eyes from the sun. "No, I don't."

"You believe it destiny or fate that we met her?"

"Oh, I don't know," she said, wiping at a bead of sweat that trickled down her temple. "I know little of destiny or fate, but I do believe there is something bigger at work than we realize. In my experience, things that seem a bit too conveniently coincidental usually are not that at all. I do find it interesting that one who bears the mark is supposedly one who can find the jewel, and *coincidentally,* the jewel ended up in the possession of Alice's family."

"Who are they talking to?" James asked as they neared the girls.

The girls stood near a man, clearly either European or American, who seemed engaged in pleasant conversation with them. As Isabelle and James grew closer, he looked up and then bid the girls a hasty good-bye.

"Who was that?" Isabelle asked when they reached Sally and Alice.

"Oh, Belle! How was the pyramid? Was it simply amazing? I'm sorrier than ever that I wasn't brave enough to go inside," Sally said.

"Don't be," James said.

Isabelle repeated herself. "Sally, who was that man? Someone you know?"

Sally wrinkled her brow. "Who? Oh! You mean Mr. Jones. He traveled on board the ship with us from India."

"Coincidentally, he also came to Cairo," Alice added. "It was quite a surprise to see him here. We had thought he was set to return to Calcutta."

"Coincidentally," Isabelle murmured.

"What is it, Belle?" Sally asked. "Are we not to speak with certain people?" There was an edge to the girl's voice Isabelle smiled at.

"Not at all. I've become horribly overprotective, I believe. Since your abduction I've been rather on pins and needles. I don't trust many people."

"Well, rest assured, Mr. Jones is harmless." Alice smiled at Isabelle. "He is all that is gentlemanly and gracious. He sounded familiar to me when we first met him aboard the ship, although I couldn't place it. He asked just now about our welfare and hopes we are having a delightful time in Egypt. He is just the sort of man of whom my mother would have approved." Alice wrinkled her nose in thought. "Of course, he did seem to be working aboard the ship to pay for his passage."

"That doesn't make him any less agreeable," Sally told her and opened her parasol with a snap. "Mercy, but the sun is bright." She began walking toward the pyramids, and Alice fell into step beside her, also opening her parasol.

"I didn't say he was *disagreeable*," Alice told her. "But he was obviously short on funds, which my mother would have found undesirable."

"Perhaps he was robbed or some such in India. He obviously has money now; perhaps a bank in Cairo advanced his funds . . ."

Isabelle let out a small sigh and looked at James, who was pinching the bridge of his nose with his thumb and forefinger. "They do go on," he said.

Isabelle pursed her lips in thought and looked in the direction Mr. Jones had taken. He was nowhere to be seen. "He left their company rather quickly," she said.

James nodded and followed her gaze.

"You also find it suspect, or am I overreacting?"

"There was something familiar about him," James said. "I thought I might know him from a prior meeting. The name is prosaic enough; it means nothing to me."

Isabelle frowned as James took her hand and placed it through his arm. *Coincidence*, she thought. *I don't much believe in coincidence . . .*

8

Isabelle and the rest of the entourage were some distance from Cairo, enjoying a procession similar in grandeur to those they'd witnessed in India. Periodically, they were told, there were pilgrimages that involved spectacle and splendor, and these parades were not to be missed. In truth, it was a feast for the eye; everywhere one looked there was something of interest. There were camels draped in lavish fabrics, people garbed in finery and jewels, music and laughter.

Isabelle glanced over her shoulder as someone jostled her from behind. She didn't make more than a moment's eye contact with a man several yards back but continued perusing the crowd casually as though taking in the whole of it.

She again faced forward with a frown and nodded absently at something Sally was showing her. The crowd ebbed and flowed, with people moving randomly and rarely staying in one spot for very long. It was for this reason that she was surprised to find the man still roughly the same distance from her as he'd been for over forty minutes.

Isabelle wondered whom the man was trailing. "Amateur," she murmured.

James leaned his ear down toward her head. "I'm sorry?"

"We're being followed," she said.

He turned his attention to her with a frown. "You jest."

"No. I'm certain of it."

"Where is he?"

"Don't look around."

James briefly closed his eyes. "What do you take me for? Tell me where he is."

Isabelle leaned closer to his ear. "Behind me, roughly ten feet, just to the right." She applauded for a group of passing musicians and pointed as though drawing James's attention.

As their group began the trek back to their carriages at the conclusion of the parade, Isabelle engaged in animated chatter with the girls, laughing and turning to tell stories and amusing anecdotes. If James thought it odd, he kept it to himself.

"Phillip!" She called and beckoned to him with her hand. "The girls and I were wondering just last night which of you is taller. You or James?"

Phillip grinned. "I am, by an inch, although James chooses not to acknowledge it."

Sally clapped her hands together. "I win! Alice, you owe me a dollar."

James looked at the women, one eyebrow cocked. "You wagered on it?"

"Well, of course," Sally said. "What's a wager among friends?"

An hour of steady walking finally found them at their carriages, into which they promptly settled to begin the dusty ride back to Cairo. As James adjusted his long legs in the confines of the vehicle, he muttered to Isabelle, "What was that display?"

"We were being followed by a man, a westerner, and if I'm not much mistaken, he was being followed in turn."

Sally and Alice sat opposite them. Upon hearing Isabelle's pronouncement, Sally leaned forward. "Who would be following us, Belle?" Alice looked at Isabelle with worry clearly stamped across her features.

"I'm not certain," Isabelle said, "but one thing I do know—he was watching Phillip."

* * *

The city of Cairo was divided into different shopping sections. One lane held spice vendors where huge sacks of spices and herbs sat open to view. Another held clothing and fabrics and still another, jewelry.

There were sections of food of every imaginable sort, some with cauliflower the size of large American watermelons.

Genevieve and William had ventured down a side street in search of rugs and linens for the *dahabeeyah,* which was staffed and ready for departure in two days. Isabelle went with Maude, who was on the search for any books or papers that would tell them more about the site they were to excavate. James and Phillip, in their roles as protectors, split up, one going with each party. William looked at Phillip with some annoyance but held his tongue. Genevieve winked at Phillip and linked arms with him, wondering aloud at how it could possibly be that such a handsome young man could be, as yet, unattached.

Isabelle followed Maude with a smile on her face. James walked behind the two ladies, whispering to Isabelle that being a bodyguard had its benefits. "The view is so nice from back here," he said.

"I'm certain true archaeologists would be mortified that we are going into this venture with so little knowledge beforehand," Maude said to Isabelle as she studied the cluttered shop fronts and stalls that filled the narrow street. She stopped at a storefront and showed a piece of paper to the proprietor who stood just inside the doorway. On it was written the name of the site.

The man shook his head. "No, *ostaza,*" he said in heavily accented English. "I have nothing about that. You try Ahmed. He have more books." The man waved his hand down the street.

"Ahmed it is," Maude said.

It took several false attempts to locate the bookseller in question. When they finally found the correct shop, they entered a dim room filled with pipe tobacco and incense. Isabelle blinked at the haze and allowed her eyes to become accustomed to the dark.

Ahmed stood toward the rear of the store in deep conversation with a customer. Rather than disturb him, Maude motioned for Isabelle and James to look at the books and random publications that lined sagging shelves, stacked haphazardly against the walls.

The books themselves were an eclectic collection of works written in several different languages, including French, German, English, Arabic, and numerous others of which Isabelle had no knowledge. "We need Jean-Louis," she murmured as she ran her finger along several dusty spines.

"I'm hoping for something that will offer a bit more information than I have in my book," Maude said, pulling her spectacles from her reticule and squinting at the titles. She glanced at Ahmed in minor annoyance. "My kingdom for a brightly-lit torch," she muttered and continued to peruse the titles.

At length, Ahmed's customer purchased something and left the store. The proprietor then made his way to Isabelle's side, a gleam in his eye. "The young American wishes to make a purchase from me, yes?" he asked.

Isabelle took in the man's stout frame, the expensive cut of his clothing, and the pipe he held in his hand. He was wealthy by Egyptian standards, and she wondered if he accomplished it by selling old, dusty volumes. Perhaps he traded in antiquities; many a Western estate held pieces purchased in Egypt, pieces that had been illegally procured by Egyptian natives.

"We are looking for literature on this site," Maude said to him from across the room as she made her way to him. She showed him her paper and added, "We are due to stay some time at the place and would like to know more about its history."

Ahmed nodded slowly and stroked his gray beard. "I do have a book, a very small book. Small but valuable, of course."

Of course, Isabelle thought.

"It is . . ." Ahmed pointed his pipe absently at the far wall and then tapped his lip with it in contemplation. "I last saw it . . ." He moved away from the women and waddled to a stack in the corner. He riffled through several books and newspapers, replaced them haphazardly, and turned to the next stack.

"Perhaps if you were to tell us what it looks like, we might help you search," Maude suggested, raising her voice to be heard over his shuffling and what could only be muttered Arabic curses.

"No, no," he said, puffing a bit from bending over double. "Ahmed knows where it is." After searching through and nearly toppling a third and then fourth stack, he found a slim, paper-bound book that looked like little more than a pamphlet.

"Ah!" he shouted. "You cannot escape Ahmed!"

"Excellent," Maude said briskly and opened her reticule. "Three will do for a book of that size?"

Ahmed placed a hand over his heart, a look of horror crossing his face. "Madam! A book such as this is worth much, much more! I sell books for years; I sell books with my father and with his father. You do not know the value of such things!"

Maude raised a brow. "Four and not a bit more."

Ahmed frowned. "Six."

"Four," Maude said.

Ahmed let out a dramatic sigh. "Four," he agreed.

Maude counted out her coins and handed them to the amusingly heavy-hearted businessman.

"You rob me," he said, shaking his head and closing his fingers over the coins with an eager snap.

"I think not," Maude said with a wry smile.

"You come back again when you need more books," he said and followed them to the door. "I have everything you need."

* * *

James stood on deck of the *dahabeeyah* and watched the shoreline as the boat made its way up the Nile. Theirs was one of many that traveled the famous waters. *The Cat's Eye* was a beautiful craft reminiscent of those that once carried the pharaohs. It was large, flat-bottomed, and more than a hundred feet long, with two sails and five sleeping cabins. It also contained a small kitchen, a salon that doubled as a dining room, and an upper canopied deck that rested on the cabin roofs. The rooms were all situated at the stern, the furniture was comfortable, the linens fresh and clean, and the cabin walls beautifully paneled and painted a fresh white. The captain, or *reis,* promised that his cook was the best in all of Egypt. There was even a piano aboard for entertainment.

After waving at strangers on the shore who waved back at them with smiles and shouts of goodwill, the group dispersed with plans to meet in an hour for lunch. James chose to sit on the top deck under the canopy and watch the Nile.

How could it be that a blacksmith from Utah who had never traveled much in his life now sat aboard a boat making its way up an exotic river that was the stuff from which legends were born? Phillip soon joined James on the deck and voiced much the same question.

"How is it that we find ourselves here?" Phillip asked as he watched the people who worked along the shore. "We're an awfully long way from home."

James nodded and looked at his brother, pondering for a moment. "Phil," he said, "I need to tell you something that may have you thinking I've gone and lost my mind."

"Surely not that. You're the practical one."

"I'm not certain anymore." James leaned forward, bracing his arms on his knees, and glanced over his shoulder. "Are you still feeling discomfort in your back?"

Phillip frowned. "Yes, but it's sporadic."

James hesitated. "I think I might know the cause."

"You do?"

"Well," James said and looked at his hands. He finally looked back up at his brother. "Isabelle and I have the Jewel of Zeus. Or, rather, I have it. It's in my trunk."

Phillip stared at his brother and then began to chuckle. "James, you've never been one for pranks, but I'd say Isabelle has shaken your sense of humor loose. That was funny."

"I'm not joking, Phillip."

Phillip sobered. "What do you mean?"

"Exactly as I said. I told you that Colonel Bilbey was in possession of what he believed to be the Jewel of Zeus." At Phillip's nod, he continued. "His good wife took the liberty of having it shipped to India with the intention of selling it to Thaddeus Sparks."

"And now you have it."

"You don't believe me."

Phillip eyed his brother and shook his head slightly. "James, I've never known you to intentionally lie, but I'm thinking you must be mistaken about the true nature of this stone. Most likely it's just that—a stone."

James looked out over the water as the boat sailed smoothly along under a brilliant blue sky. "There's something about it that isn't quite right. It . . . hums."

"Hums."

"Yes," James said, feeling a stab of irritation. "It hums. Almost vibrates. When we left India, I was convinced it was affected by the ship's engines. But it does it still on steady land."

"Does this happen all the time? Is it one long continuous hum or vibration?"

"No, and I have yet to discern the reason."

Phillip drew his eyebrows together in thought. "Will you show it to me?"

"Of course." James rose and Phillip followed him silently down the stairs and to their cabin below. James closed the door securely and opened his trunk with a key. Setting aside clothing and personal articles, he retrieved the box that contained the stone.

Lifting the lid, James turned it so that Phillip could see.

"May I hold it?" Phillip asked him.

James turned the box so that the stone spilled into Phillip's outstretched hand. Phillip frowned a bit as he examined it.

"It is most definitely humming. Almost indiscernibly, though."

James nodded.

"There's something else." Phillip took his gaze from the stone and rested it on James. At James's raised eyebrow, he continued. "My birthmark is burning."

"Burning, how?"

"More intense than it has been, but not crippling, by any means." Phillip put his free hand to his back and rubbed.

"Proximity . . ." James murmured and held out his hand. "Let me have the stone, and you go out and stroll to the bow. Come back in half a minute or so."

Phillip handed James the stone and left the room, letting the door close quietly behind him. James watched the stone in his hand with reluctant amazement as the humming faded and then ceased altogether. Sitting on the edge of his bed, he watched as the stone eventually seemed to brighten slightly and begin to hum its quiet tune, achieving higher intensity until Phillip turned the door handle and entered the cabin.

"Well, my friend, it's definitely you." James looked at his brother, who stared at the stone, his features unreadable.

"The sting lessened on deck. Still there, but just barely."

"And now?"

"It's worse, of course." Phillip's eyebrows drew together and he stood by James, looking at the stone with a scowl on his face, his hands in his pockets. "That would explain why the burning sensation is always worse at night." He sighed. "Sparks wasn't crazy, then."

"I'd say that is certainly still debatable."

"But there was most definitely something to his quest. I find that unsettling."

James nodded and stood, replacing the stone in its box and burying it again in his trunk. Neither brother spoke as James locked it and placed the key back into his pocket. Finally, James asked, "What are we to do with this information?"

"We tell Isabelle. Then we learn more about the legend. We need to know how to destroy it."

"Isabelle will be reluctant to do so."

Phillip pointed at the trunk. "If that thing really is what Sparks thinks it is, then heaven help us if it ever falls into the wrong hands."

James nodded slowly. "We could simply smash it with a hammer," he said.

"James, that rock is somehow tied to my back. You'll forgive me for being a bit leery of hasty action."

"You're right." He paused. "There is another piece to this mystery that grows ever stranger."

"And that is?"

"Alice Bilbey bears a mark identical to yours."

* * *

"It really is the oddest thing," Alice muttered to Sally as the girls readied for dinner. "It only seems to bother me when I'm inside certain structures."

"What do you mean?" Isabelle asked, turning to Alice and fluffing her skirts as Alice tied the laces on Sally's corset. "Are you speaking of your back?"

Alice made a sound suspiciously like a growl in the back of her throat. "Yes," she ground out. "That monstrosity. I do so hate it! What will happen to me when I'm married?"

"Why, your husband need never see it," Sally exclaimed. "It's on your back!"

Isabelle bit the insides of her cheeks.

"I suppose that's true," Alice said, somewhat mollified.

"What do you mean by 'certain structures'?" Isabelle asked her.

Alice finished tying Sally's laces and reached for a lace-edged, white handkerchief she had left on her bed. "Well," she said, "at the hotel, especially as we neared our room, it would burn quite a lot, but then it would subside. It was noticeable, still, but not nearly so much. And now I can still feel that faint itching, as though . . ." She flushed and looked at the handkerchief she'd crumpled in her hand. Exasperated, she smoothed it out.

"As though what, Alice?" Isabelle asked.

"As though it's trying to climb right off my skin! It hasn't bothered me this way since I was a young girl visiting home in England for the summer." She flounced onto her bed and looked so dejected that Isabelle made her way to the girl's side and placed an arm about her shoulders. "It is an absolute disgrace," Alice continued. "I shall die of complete mortification should anyone ever learn of it."

"Nobody need know of it," Isabelle said, "apparently not even your future husband."

"You sound very sarcastic," Alice said. "As though a husband would need to know of such a thing."

"Well, he may want to kiss it."

Alice shrieked and jumped from the bed, making her way quickly to the door in a huff. By this time, Sally had donned her dress and made a dash for her friend. "Alice, do wait!" She threw a scathing look over her shoulder. "Belle, *really*!"

"Why do I find the need to do that?" Belle murmured out loud and found her reticule. With a smile, she exited the room and locked the door behind her. She bumped against James, who was leaving his cabin across the small hallway with Phillip by his side.

"Why the hysterics?" James asked her.

"I am scandalous to a fault."

James tipped his head in acquiescence. "That is certainly true enough." He took her arm and motioned for Phillip to proceed ahead of them.

Phillip glanced behind him at the couple as he walked. "You'll tell her, James? I'll be interested to see what you think, Isabelle."

"About what?"

James leaned close. "Phillip's birthmark reacts in close proximity to the jewel."

Isabelle took the news in stride, pursing her lips in thought and looking at Alice, who stood near the open doorway of the dining salon, her pale blue dress billowing perfectly around her.

"Interesting," she said.

* * *

Isabelle awoke with a start then held perfectly still. From the small cabin window that was open to allow the cool evening breeze to enter the room, she heard a whisper of sound she couldn't define.

She held her breath, straining to hear and wondering if she could get out to the deck quickly enough to circle the perimeter of the cabins and spy the source of the disturbance. It wasn't the natural noise of the night, of that she was certain.

"Do you dare . . ."

She remained still, straining to make out the whisper at the window.

"Do you dare to disturb the resting place of a princess?"

Isabelle shivered in spite of herself, the hair on her arms and the back of her neck rising in response to the quiet question.

"A curse will be upon you . . ."

Isabelle sat up as quietly as she could, frustrated with the streak of moonlight that hit across her bed. Grabbing her outer wrap, she made her way to the door and opened it, slipping out and closing it slowly behind her.

The night was alive with stars; they shone brightly down on the sailors who sprawled on deck in slumber, their long, white robes aglow in the light of the night. Isabelle crept along the wall and hesitated at the corner. She considered reentering the hallway and climbing the stairs to the upper deck to look down over the side, but deciding that time was too much a factor, she slowly looked around the corner and down the deck.

There was nobody there, not that she was entirely surprised. As quickly as she could move and still remain silent, she edged along the outer wall and down the narrow deck, pausing briefly at her cabin window. She clearly saw her bed, illuminated by the glow of the moon. Whoever had been there earlier had most definitely seen her leave.

Hoping she might still catch a glimpse of the whisperer, she continued her walk around the outside of the rooms, nearly at a run by the time she had circled the stern and made her way to the front of the cabins. She went to the hallway, which was empty, and promptly made a dash for the stairs.

The upper deck was also entirely vacant, and she sank down on one of the plush chairs, slightly winded, but not from the physical exertion. As she looked out over the peaceful, timeless river and felt the cool breeze against her skin, she asked herself who in their party or among the boat's crew would benefit from her fear.

She unwittingly remembered the girls' abduction and shuddered. Perhaps Isabelle hadn't been the intended target. It might well be that the girls weren't out of danger.

9

THE ROOM IN THE LAVISH hotel looked unchanged since his last briefing. The players all occupied the same seats, wore the same expressions, each of them continually looking to the Egyptian to follow his lead. Currents of air moved gently through the room, courtesy of hotel staff who stood unobtrusively in the corners with large palm fronds. The Italian stood before the Federation, unruffled and composed.

"So you feel you need to move ahead of our Mr. Sparks, then?" The Egyptian eyed the European man with some skepticism.

"I do, sir. Sparks has made absolutely no progress and I don't believe he will."

"Yet even now he follows them up the Nile."

The Italian nodded. "And that's all he will ever do. Because of his past with the younger Ashby, he will never be allowed admittance to their party, I'm certain of that. You would do well to have someone on the inside. Somebody they come to trust."

"And you have the skills necessary to do this thing?"

The Italian smiled. "I come highly qualified, do I not?"

The Egyptian nodded. "You will make contact with our men along the way. I expect to hear of your progress regularly."

"Of course."

* * *

The *dahabeeyah* was docked for the morning, and its occupants strolled through the streets of a small village situated quietly along the Nile. The shore was thick with palm trees that offered shade and respite from the bright sun overhead. Flamingos and ibises flocked in groups along the shore, and the air was filled with sounds of children at play and parents at work. A small café was nestled in the shade of several large sycamore trees, and James and Isabelle sat at a table with Genevieve and her sons. Half of the rest of their party sat at nearby tables, and the others examined the local wares along the small market street.

"Tell me how it is that you came into Pinkerton's employ," William Montgomery said to Isabelle. He slowly stirred his tea and watched her over the rim as he took a cautious sip.

As Isabelle began to explain her past as a Pinkerton spy, James sat back in his chair and observed Genevieve's oldest son. William watched Isabelle with an expression that suggested neither friendly conversation nor avid interest. "Scrutiny" would have been the best way to describe his attention to Isabelle, and it set James's teeth on edge.

When Isabelle finished speaking and William made no move to respond, Eli filled the awkward silence instead.

"Incredibly fascinating," he said to her. "What an amazing career!"

Isabelle smiled at him. "It kept me busy."

"And will you return to it when you go back home?"

Isabelle looked into the distance for a moment before returning her attention to the younger brother. "I don't know that it suits me any longer," she said. "It is all I have ever done, however. I'm not certain what I will do."

"Isabelle has many talents," James said. "She's entirely too modest."

Isabelle looked at him with a raised brow. "Never been accused of that before," she said, and Genevieve laughed.

"She is modest," the older woman said. "Her marks at school were perfect; she excelled at absolutely everything she attempted."

"Why is it that we never did cross paths those many years ago?" William asked.

"You had moved to New York City and Eli was away at school," Genevieve said. "And I never could persuade Isabelle to stay with me for very long."

Isabelle must have finally sensed William's intense regard; she leaned back in her chair, her hands in her lap, and tilted her head as she fixed her gaze upon his face. Her direct examination matched his own, and they sat that way for a few moments before Genevieve cleared her throat and signaled for the café's only server. The moment was broken, and as they each moved to collect their belongings and stand, James glanced at Genevieve, who was watching William.

"We'll be along shortly," Genevieve said. "You go on ahead and examine the marketplace. See if there might be something I would like, Isabelle."

* * *

William watched the younger woman walk away with Mr. Ashby. He studied them as they left the café and rounded the corner, out of sight.

"Is there something on your mind, William?" Genevieve asked.

He thrust his hands into his pockets and turned to his mother, watching as she donned a pair of delicate white gloves. "Miss Webb was quite a fortunate recipient of your charity," he said.

"She showed promise," Genevieve said as she briskly tugged the fabric into place over each finger. "I hated to see it go to waste."

"Funny, isn't it, that you never sponsored any other orphans once Miss Webb and her sister finished school?"

Genevieve retrieved her small parasol and purse from the ground next to her chair and straightened, finally leveling William with a look that was all too familiar. "What are you suggesting, William? You know I detest coy wordplay."

He looked at his mother for a few moments before fixing what he hoped was a pleasant expression on his face. "Nothing. Merely protecting your best interests, that is all."

"You needn't worry about 'my best interests' as it concerns Isabelle. I tried for years to get that girl to accept no more than she deserved and she constantly refused. That she let me fund her schooling was a miracle."

"What do you mean when you say you offered her 'no more than she deserved'?"

Genevieve waved a hand in dismissal and opened her parasol. "She was a good girl who deserved the world. She was determined to earn it herself."

"An admirable trait," William said as he tilted his elbow to Genevieve. They strolled away from the café and around the corner to the market. Rather than push any further, he decided to let the topic of Miss Webb drop for the time being. He was sure it would surface again, sooner or later, whether Genevieve wanted it to or not.

* * *

"I suspect he believes I have abused his mother's charity," Isabelle spat as she walked toward the market street with quick strides and James trotted to catch up with her. She shook her head slightly, a humorless smile playing at the corners of her mouth. "I hate being the object of one's contempt."

"He's a cad, Isabelle," James said and grabbed her hand, forcing it through his arm and slowing her walk to a more sedate pace. "Hardly worth the energy required to think of him."

"A cad, hmm?" Isabelle nodded. "You've also noticed, then?"

James snorted. "I'd be a fool not to. He has a very high opinion of himself and a very low opinion of the rest of the world."

"I thought such was my observation alone."

"Nonsense, Miss Webb. Since when has your astute analysis of a person's disposition and character been anything but amazingly accurate?"

Isabelle looked up at him from beneath her hat. Her face relaxed into a rueful smile and she shook her head. "How very correct you are, Mr. Ashby. Sarcastic, perhaps, but correct nonetheless."

"I was interested to hear you say you're not certain which path to pursue upon your return home." James looked straight ahead at the stalls of food and wares.

He heard her intake and exhalation of breath and resisted the urge to look at her. "That much is true," she finally said. "I don't know what I will do with my time."

"I can think of something that would suit you well."

"Do tell, Mr. Ashby."

He smiled. "I believe I'll keep it to myself. Should you arrive at the same conclusion, I will be satisfied that we are of a mind."

"But how will we know I have arrived at the same conclusion?"

He finally looked at her, capturing her golden gaze with his blue one. "*I* will know."

Isabelle looked at him for some time, her mouth slack. She shut it firmly and looked straight ahead, finding the diversion that she probably desperately searched for. "Oh, look! It's the girls," she said and pulled against his arm, quickening her pace.

James smiled and allowed her to pull him along. It had become his mission to keep her slightly off balance. It kept her from being afraid.

* * *

As Isabelle neared the girls, she watched with some interest an older woman conversing with Alice. It marked the second time that Alice had been approached by a woman of advanced years bent on telling her fortune. She had grasped the young girl by one hand and was speaking earnestly to her, looking up at her face and squeezing her hand to recapture Alice's gaze when she looked in confusion at Jean-Louis Deveraux.

"She is saying you must take the talisman," Jean-Louis was telling Alice.

Alice looked up at the Frenchman. "Why is she accosting me?"

Jean-Louis glanced at the old woman. "I don't believe she means to 'accost' you," he said gently. "She clearly believes that you will benefit by owning this charm."

As Isabelle walked around behind Alice and looked over her shoulder, she saw that Alice held a small, round metal object in her hand, suspended by a chain. The charm was roughly an inch in diameter, and silver. The chain that held it was thin, and the whole of it sparkled as though it had just been polished.

Alice glanced at the old woman and said, "Mr. Deveraux, please will you tell this woman that her gift is very kind, but I certainly cannot take something so precious from her." Alice's voice trembled a bit and she cleared her throat.

Jean-Louis translated Alice's sentiments, and Alice turned slightly to Isabelle. "Why am I attracting batty old women?" she muttered.

Isabelle shushed her as the woman began to speak in a voice that was rough from her advanced years and gesticulated with fingers that were gnarled and work-worn. Jean-Louis nodded at the woman and murmured something in response that seemed to calm her agitation.

"The good woman truly insists that you need this, Miss Bilbey. She is most adamant about it," Jean-Louis said.

Isabelle looked again at the charm as it caught the light. The inscription carved into the metal seemed a hieroglyph of sorts, and it certainly was familiar. It was a rectangle surrounding three separate ovals that stood side by side.

Isabelle's heart tripped over itself, and she bit her lip to keep from exclaiming aloud. She swallowed once and whispered to Alice, "I think you should accept this necklace."

Alice glanced over her shoulder at Isabelle in obvious surprise. "Why on earth?"

Isabelle looked to Jean-Louis. "Will you please tell this gracious woman that we gladly accept her beautiful gift."

Jean-Louis translated again, and the old woman seemed satisfied. She said one more thing to Alice and then released her hand. Turning away, she shuffled back to a stall and disappeared within the building it stood against.

"What did she say?" Alice asked as she looked at the building.

"She said it is your protection for your birthright. That by rights it transfers to the firstborn daughter, not the son." Jean-Louis, too, looked at the lonely stall in some bafflement.

"*This* is my birthright?" Alice looked down at the silver charm, one brow quirked.

"*Protection* for your birthright . . . It's certainly been well maintained," Sally observed and ran her finger over the shapes carved into it. "In order to keep our silver beautiful, my mother had it polished regularly ."

"This is a hieroglyph?" Alice asked the Frenchman.

He nodded. "I'm certain it must be, however I do not know what it signifies." Glancing at Isabelle, he added, "We saw it in the Great Pyramid only days ago."

Sally shook her head as though to clear it. "Well," she said briskly, "you certainly do seem to have your share of ancient admirers." She took the chain from Alice's hand and unhooked the clasp, fastening it behind her friend's neck.

"Gah," Alice protested, "I'm not altogether certain I want to wear it!"

"Nonsense," Sally said. "It's a beautiful little trinket. If it turns your neck green, you can remove it."

The small charm suspended to a point three inches below the hollow of her throat. Alice shook her head and touched it with her forefinger.

"Do you feel magic?" Sally whispered to her with a grin as the girls linked their arms together.

"You are so silly," Alice said. They began to move down the little street in the direction of the river.

"It really is very pretty," Sally said.

"My mother would have found it too plain."

"Ah, but I'd wager your father would have approved."

Alice smiled a bit at Sally and they moved out of earshot.

"What in the world was that all about?" Phillip asked James as the four adults stood in the middle of the dusty road, watching the girls make their way to the café where some of the party still lingered.

Jean-Louis shrugged. "I do find it all rather odd," he admitted.

"In what way?" Isabelle asked.

He frowned. "I've never believed myself to be a superstitious person, but it is a bit perplexing that the young woman seems to be the object of some attention by the older generations of Egyptian society."

"It has happened only twice," James said.

"True enough," Deveraux said. "However, both messages contained warnings and talk of birthright."

Isabelle squinted at him in surprise. "I wasn't aware the first woman spoke of any birthright."

"I didn't think Miss Bilbey need concern herself with all that was said. She seemed rather shaken at the time."

"Please, will you be certain to keep *me* informed of everything in the future that concerns either of the girls?" Isabelle asked.

Jean-Louis flushed. "Most certainly. It was not my intent to keep information from you, Miss Webb. I suppose I hadn't given it much thought until I heard many of the same sentiments repeated here today."

"Upon our return to the boat, would you mind repeating to me the things you remember hearing from both women? I'd like to write it down."

He nodded.

"And the hieroglyph? You truly do not know what it means?" Phillip asked the Frenchman.

Deveraux spread his hands wide. "I am at a loss. I looked in one of my guidebooks after we encountered the symbol in the pyramid, but to no avail. It is not recorded in any of the materials I possess."

Isabelle frowned and took James's offered arm as the four turned to follow the girls. She didn't care for strange coincidences. It was only then that she realized she hadn't told James about her ghostly visitor from the night before. She opened her mouth to mention it and then closed it, thinking the better of it. Phillip was in conversation with Deveraux a few steps ahead, and she was reminded of the fact that she shared close quarters with people about whom she knew very little.

10

The tranquil cruise up the Nile passed smoothly, day after day. The party of twelve enjoyed themselves by spending time together, chatting about what they might find at the site, and going ashore every now and again to visit local villages along the way. Isabelle reflected often upon the fact that it was an idyllic setting, that they were all experiencing something that happened only once in a lifetime. As curious as she was about the site they would eventually excavate, she was reluctant to leave the quiet peace of life upon the *dahabeeyah*.

Maude had memorized nearly every word contained in the small pamphlet she purchased in Cairo. Isabelle had given it a once-over, partially out of genuine curiosity but mostly out of kindness to Maude, who was eager to engage in conversation about what they might discover.

The night before they were to arrive at the site, the whole group was seated in the outdoor salon. Water lapped against the sides of the boat, and there was a cool, gentle breeze that lifted tendrils of hair off the neck and carried pleasant fragrances of the blossoms along the shores. The gentlemen sat bareheaded in the company of the ladies, and the ladies were without gloves and bonnets, a testament to the level of familiarity that permeated the group.

Isabelle was seated next to Alice and Sally. The girls were in quiet conversation and turned to include Isabelle. "Why is it that we have no need of a dragoman?" Alice asked her.

"We have Mr. Deveraux," Isabelle said, "otherwise we most certainly would need one."

"A dragoman translates?" Sally asked.

Isabelle nodded. "He is rather a guide of sorts."

"Mr. Deveraux fits the bill nicely," Alice said and she turned to look at the Frenchman who was in conversation with Eli Montgomery. "I believe him to be the smartest man I've ever met."

Sally exchanged a glance with Isabelle and tamped down a smile. "He's rather handsome as well," she said.

Alice turned back to Sally in some surprise. "Well, I suppose that's true. Why, do you have designs on the man?" The bite to her voice was obvious, although she clearly tried to disguise it with a nonchalance she couldn't manage.

Sally laughed. "I myself do not. But I wonder about you."

Alice rolled her eyes. "Pish-posh," she said. "Now you are nothing short of silly."

Maude crossed the deck and made her way to an empty chair next to Isabelle. "Is Mr. Ashby returning soon?" she asked Isabelle.

"I don't believe so," Isabelle said and motioned to the seat. "He is writing a quick letter to his mother and a friend at home who is caring for his business in his absence."

Maude took the seat with a sigh. "I confess, I will miss life on this charming boat."

"It may be that we will choose to simply return to it each night. The site is only a mile from shore, isn't that correct?" Isabelle asked.

"True. However, if we yearn for the true archaeological experience, we should pitch our tents and sleep on cots." Maude smiled. "I would like to try it, at least until these old bones convince me it is folly."

"Have you come across anything interesting in your reading of late?" Isabelle asked.

Maude nodded. "I'm not certain the Antiquities Department is aware, but I'm fairly convinced there is something of significance about this site."

"How so?"

"You know that all we've read concerning it is little more than a footnote in history. I came across a reference in one of my books that speaks specifically of the site as the final resting place of the disgraced eldest daughter of Imhet III."

"Disgraced, how?"

Maude shrugged. "I don't know. It doesn't say, but it states that they buried her apart from her mother and siblings deliberately, and it definitely implies that the intent was that everyone forget about her and show nothing of honor or respect for the tomb. She was supposedly buried with none of the traditional trappings considered crucial for accompanying one into the afterlife."

"So I don't suppose we'll uncover piles of gold at her resting place." Isabelle smiled. "The girls will be most disappointed."

"Why will we be disappointed?" Sally asked, interrupting her comments to Alice.

"The tomb in question at our site will likely have nothing in it but a mummy. A disgraced mummy."

Alice wrinkled her nose in distaste and Sally nodded. "That is disappointing."

"In truth, girls, I wonder whether or not we'll actually even find that particular tomb," Maude said. "It is supposedly rather hard to locate. We have approximately three-quarters of a mile of rock and caves to explore. It could be anywhere along that stretch, if, indeed, it really is there at all."

"Surely the locals will have found anything of significance by now," Isabelle suggested.

"One would suppose; however, teams all over the country continue to find interesting things that tell us all about the lives of the ancients."

"What kinds of things are they finding?" Sally asked.

"They learn much from the bones of the mummies themselves."

Alice and Sally looked at her with bland expressions that had Isabelle laughing. "Perhaps we'll find an ancient golden headdress or bangles fit to decorate the arm of a queen," she told them. "And if not, well, how many young women can say they've been on an archaeological expedition and a cruise up the Nile?"

They nodded in unison but were prevented from further comment by a soft laugh that came from the Frenchman's direction and had Alice turning her head. Phillip Ashby climbed the stairs and strolled to Sally's side, asking if the seat next to her were taken. Sally's mouth went slack for a moment before she recovered herself and stammered that it was most certainly vacant and available for him to use however he wished.

Isabelle looked at Maude, who by now had given her a nudge in the arm. Maude was all smiles and Isabelle couldn't help but join her. The entire voyage had held the promise of mystery and romance—a brutal combination for young hearts. She hoped the girls would escape with theirs intact.

* * *

James sat in his bed, Phillip in his, and the two read in companionable silence. James found his mind wandering, thinking of the woman across the hall and wondering what their odd courtship would be like if they were at home, living their normal routines. He smiled. Probably not nearly as fulfilling, he decided, and tried to read the page in front of him for the third time.

A soft knock at the door had him glancing at Phillip in some surprise. Phillip moved as though to answer, and James waved him back into bed. "I'll see who it is," he told his brother as he found his robe on a nearby chair and put it on.

"Belle," he said as he opened the door a crack. He took one look at her somber face and opened the door wider. He looked around trying to decide whether to let her in or go out into the hallway when Phillip beckoned.

"She can come in here," he said. He rose and retrieved his robe as well.

James pulled her inside and closed the door softly behind her. "What is it?" he asked and guided her to a chair. He perched on the foot of his bed, Phillip likewise on his own.

"Would you like some privacy?" Phillip asked Isabelle.

She smiled a bit and waved a hand at him. "No, as you're the other half of the security team, you should hear this." Isabelle rolled her eyes and looked at James. "It's probably a silly prank, but I thought I should mention it."

"Isabelle, there are no silly pranks when it comes to you and the sorts of people you attract." James felt a familiar stirring of apprehension crawling up his spine, and he braced himself for her words.

"A few nights ago, someone whispered into my window, something about daring to disrupt a princess's sleep or similar nonsense. I gave chase, but couldn't find anyone," she said.

Phillip interrupted her. "You gave chase alone?"

"She often gives chase alone," James answered while still keeping his eyes on Isabelle's face. "It's her biggest flaw."

Isabelle narrowed her eyes. "At any rate," she said, "tonight when I went into my cabin with the girls, I found this on my pillow." She withdrew a paper from her pocket and handed it to James.

He unfolded it to see an image that looked similar in design to the ancient hieroglyphs they'd seen in the pyramids and on countless brochures, advertisements, and documents since arriving in the country. It depicted a pharaoh with an animal head who was in the process of stabbing a sacrificial offering through the heart. The victim lay prostrate on an altar or table and was unique in that she was dressed in clothing clearly depicted as western in origin, very like the dresses Isabelle and the other women aboard wore.

"It's obviously meant to be me," Isabelle said.

"Possibly," he said. "I suppose that's logical, considering it was left on your pillow."

"That and the fact that there's a cane on the ground next to the altar."

James squinted and tilted the small paper toward the light. She was right; a cane had been drawn in the picture, as though to indicate it had been dropped there by the sacrificial victim.

Phillip cleared his throat and shrugged. "It could be anyone," he said lamely.

"Who else in this party carries a cane with any sort of regularity?" She asked. "I appreciate your reassurance, but truly, it is clearly meant to be me."

"Maude uses a cane on occasion," Phillip offered.

"Do you suppose someone is trying to warn me for Maude?" she asked, one brow raised.

"Who would have drawn this?" James murmured as he examined the picture.

Phillip held out his hand for it. "May I see?"

James handed it over and looked at Isabelle, who sat as composed as ever. "Eli is an artist," he mused.

Isabelle nodded slowly. "He is, but . . ."

"But he is a likeable sort? So was Ari, if you'll recall."

Isabelle snorted. "Ari was obsequious and transparent from the very beginning. Eli has a sense of gentleness about him . . . I don't know."

"I rather think that William fellow is a bit of a tyrant," Phillip said as he examined the picture. "Perhaps he shares his brother's artistic talents."

"Or there's always Deveraux," James said. "He knows hieroglyphs . . ."

Isabelle rubbed her forehead. "We might as well throw Genevieve into the pool of suspects. Or Maude. Or one of the giddy Stafford brothers. This is insane."

"Insane, perhaps, but the fact of the matter is that someone within this circle obviously has an issue with you, with the girls, and who knows who else? Maybe Phil or I have an enemy who seeks to drive us away by scaring you." James shook his head. "Perhaps we should abandon this little adventure."

Isabelle shook her head. "It's an attempt to frighten me. Could even be one of the crew who dislikes western treasure hunters or something."

"Do you remember anything specific about the voice the other night?" Phillip asked her.

"No, it was just a whisper, barely a thread of sound. I couldn't discern an accent. Plus, I was so foggy from sleep I may have misunderstood him altogether."

James ground his teeth. If only he and Isabelle were married, he could legally and morally be by her side all night long. As it stood now, he hated to let her out of the room. He felt the drama and intrigue of India returning and was extremely unsettled. What could he say, though? *Marry me now, Isabelle, so I can keep you safe.* She would run for the hills, screaming.

Isabelle would never be one to marry for her own protection, and that was but one small part of the reason he wanted her for his own. He could hardly pursue the issue now, however. As they left India, she had shown signs that she might be comfortable with the idea that he would push for her hand in the future. He felt as though they'd now taken a huge step backward and it frustrated him.

"Well, I just thought you should know," Isabelle said and stood to leave.

James nodded. "I will see you back to your cabin."

"It's three steps across the hall."

"Isabelle, don't be difficult," Phillip said, and when she looked at him, he winked. "Let the man see you to your cabin."

She shook her head and smiled a bit. James followed her to the door and stepped just outside it as she crossed the short distance to her cabin. When she turned back to tell him good night, he stepped into the hallway and grasped the back of her neck with his hand, pulled her close, and kissed her.

"If you hear so much as a squeak tonight, I want you to scream for me," he told her.

She looked a bit shaken, but in the end acquiesced with a nod. "I'm truly convinced it's nothing more than someone trying to frighten me," she said.

"Doesn't matter. I can't for the life of me imagine why someone would want to frighten you. It makes me angry. Tomorrow I'm going to take a very close look at the crew, the cooks, everyone. I wish you'd have told me right away about the other incident."

Isabelle laid a hand aside his cheek and smiled. "I certainly don't mean to insult, but I doubt you'd have been able to find him any better than me."

He turned his face slightly and kissed the inside of her palm while still holding her gaze. "You wound me," he said against her skin.

She shivered. "I will tell you immediately if anything else occurs." Turning the doorknob, she pulled her hand away and entered the room where Alice and Sally lay sleeping. "Good night," she whispered to him and softly closed the door.

* * *

The next morning, Isabelle stood in the small village square along the coast where the *dahabeeyah* had docked an hour earlier. The Stafford brothers had the situation readily in hand and were in the process, through Jean-Louis's translating and their own limited stabbings at Arabic, of hiring a team of workers to help the expedition set up their site, provide meals, and help with the actual physical labor associated with an archaeological dig.

There were many men of varying ages who were eager for the work, and securing a labor force soon proved to be rather easily accomplished. Harry and Henry were clearly living the dream of a lifetime, and their enthusiasm was infectious. Even the irascible William seemed caught up in the excitement of the moment.

Going down a list in a small, leather-bound journal, Harry Stafford procured food stuffs, people to prepare it, materials for their sleeping quarters, and donkeys and carts to carry all in the party plus luggage from the *dahabeeyah*. The boat itself was at their disposal for the two months they planned to stay at the site, and many of the crew had also signed on to help at the dig, ecstatic at the prospect of earning more money.

Isabelle turned to Genevieve, who stood at her elbow. "The Staffords are as efficient as army generals," she said.

"Are they not delightful?" Genevieve said, beaming at the brothers. "They are worth their weight in gold, if for no other reason than they keep spirits high."

"Were you expecting they would lag?"

Genevieve made a face. "One never knows when it comes to certain people." Isabelle figured she was too polite to openly complain about her son. "The negativity can become wearying."

Isabelle nodded but made no reply. Instead she said, "Tell me about Eli. Has he been an artist for many years?"

"Oh, yes. You may not remember, but the paintings in my home are almost exclusively his work. He was gifted from the cradle and still continues to amaze me."

"And has he never married, then?"

Genevieve's face clouded. "Yes, he is married. He has two daughters as well. They are eight and six years old."

Isabelle couldn't help but prod. "And does his family miss him when he is gone?"

"Not nearly enough," Genevieve muttered and turned her eyes to her younger son. "But I misspeak. His daughters miss him, certainly. His wife is a bit . . . unhappy that he pursued a career as a professional artist."

"Mmm. Perhaps doesn't make enough money to suit her needs?" Isabelle asked, although mentioning such a thing in polite conversation was vulgar, at best.

Genevieve looked askance at her. "Oh no, he makes plenty of money. He's one of the lucky few. She simply hoped he would be content to live on family money as a true gentleman of good breeding and status. That he works for a living is galling to her."

Isabelle rolled her eyes. "She lives in the wrong country, then, truly. Working for a living is what Americans do. Most do it with a fair amount of pride."

Genevieve visibly clenched her teeth. "She is a thorn in my side. I mean Eli's side, of course." She winked at Isabelle. "I am working to cut the apron strings. Eli cut them long ago. I keep tying them back together." She paused. "He is a good man, a sincere person. I would very much like for him to be with someone who would love him and his talents."

"Surely you wouldn't want to see the marriage dissolve. That would be scandalous."

Genevieve looked at her for a moment. "Surely I wouldn't want that." She looked back at her son, who stood near Harry Stafford and nodded in conversation. She sighed and winced. "I want him to be happy," she said. "There was a young woman once who adored him, but she was swept to the side when the current wife wormed her way into his life."

"Has he told you he has regrets?"

"Not in so many words. He would never say so, even if it were true. He does love his children, though, and they think the sun rises and sets in him." She smiled. "Something wonderful did come out of that union. I need to remember it more often."

Isabelle looked at the younger brother and felt a wave of sympathy for him. Everyone had a story, and nobody escaped from life unscathed by something. She looked at William and was about to ask Genevieve about her older son when Henry Stafford quickly came to them with a smile that split his face. "It is time," he said with a flourish, "to go to our site!"

11

Belle sat on her cot and looked around herself at the cozy tent. It was roughly ten feet square and housed her and the two girls. There were eight tents total that made up the small camp. They were situated in two rows with a path in the middle, making the whole of it resemble a small street. On one side was the tent the Montgomery brothers shared, followed by Maude and Genevieve's tent, then Belle and the girls, and finally James, Phillip, and Jean-Louis.

On the other side of the "street" and across from the Montgomery brothers stood the artifacts tent, then the dining tent, followed by a canopy that was open at the sides and meant for socializing, and finally the Stafford brothers' tent sat at the end across from James, Phillip, and the Frenchman.

The bulk of the day had been spent in setting up tents, organizing tools, and scouring primitive maps of the area that had been provided by the Antiquities Department. Their location was south and east of the Valley of the Kings, which was situated nearly three-and-a-half kilometers off the west bank and across the river from Luxor and the Temple of Karnak. Even though their site was near noteworthy discoveries and a rich cache of mummies and treasure, it was of little consequence according to Genevieve.

"I do hope my brave little band won't be too disappointed if we don't find a single thing," she had confided to Isabelle as the bulk of the party assembled in the artifacts tent to review tools and methods of excavation. "I'm relatively certain the Antiquities Department allowed us to do this thing here simply as a diplomatic nod to an old American lady with money."

Now, Isabelle looked around herself at her tent in satisfaction as the gentle glow of the lanterns played on the soft, warm tones of the tent fabric and the gold, brown, and green designs in the large rug that spanned the entire floor. The cots were set against three walls with the fourth wall unobstructed for easy access to the tent opening. Each woman had a trunk at the foot of her cot that contained the basic necessities of daily life and a few practical outfits—mostly those of Indian style that Isabelle had purchased in Calcutta.

The light material of the Indian clothing and absence of corsets and petticoats was a welcome relief in the dust and dirt of the Egyptian desert. Isabelle had been obliged to assure Alice that wearing the clothing on a daily basis was not going to harm her reputation as a good woman. ("But *Isabelle,* only *fallen women* go without corsets! It was another matter entirely when Sally and I were hiding from Ari and his henchman—we were incognito!") The rest of the party's belongings stayed behind on the *dahabeeyah,* which was accessed easily enough should the need arise.

The hour grew late and the girls were still in the dining tent. She could hear their laughter mixed with masculine voices and the occasional comment from Maude or Genevieve. It had been her intention to fetch the girls and insist they go to bed; the sun rose early on the desert and she wasn't certain camp life would be amenable to young girls with proclivities to sleep the morning away. They sounded so happy, though, that she was loathe to disturb them.

Isabelle thought longingly of the nightdress folded neatly at the top of her trunk, but instead she opened her satchel that sat next to the trunk and pulled out the small book she'd laid atop her other belongings. She'd perused Maude's small guidebook before but now settled onto her cot and opened it again with the objective of familiarizing herself as much as possible with the area's history and terrain.

She read the story that Maude had told them the night before, about the fallen daughter of the pharaoh. Thumbing through to the last page, she looked again at the hieroglyphics that were printed tightly, small and crammed together, as though the author had much to say and wanted to fit it all on one page.

Her eyes ran over the symbols and she thought of asking Jean-Louis to translate it for her in the morning. She yawned and felt her eyelids close of their own volition. When she began to sway forward, her chin falling toward her chest, she jerked herself awake and decided to collect the girls. The pamphlet had begun to slip out of her hands and she clutched at it, glancing down as it slid to the ground.

Isabelle leaned over and picked up the booklet, beginning to close it when a small symbol toward the upper third of the page caught her eye. There, sandwiched in between other hieroglyphs was a rectangle with three oval circles inside. She frowned and held it up to the light. Pursing her lips, she tried to think back to the reason the symbol had caught her eye in the Great Pyramid, and then again when seeing it on Alice's necklace. There was something about it that had seemed familiar, as though she had seen it somewhere before.

She continued to stare at the small rectangle. As she tilted her head to one side, she had a flash of a memory, a scene that flipped through her mind and she had to fight to hold on to it. "The temple in India," she said aloud and stared at the wall of the tent. That was it. The temple where James had learned of the meaning of the birthmark his brother bore and Isabelle had spoken with an enigmatic guide who seemed to know more than he was willing to share.

The symbol had been there, inscribed on the wall, she was certain of it. It had seemed odd at the time because it was so unlike the other Hindu symbols and drawings—rather plain in comparison. That must certainly have been the reason it struck her again when she saw it with James in the Great Pyramid.

Now Alice wore a necklace with the symbol etched into it. And two old women had approached the young girl out of nowhere, each warning of similar things. Alice bore the legendary birthmark of one who had the power to seek out the legendary Jewel of Zeus, and not only that, her family currently owned the jewel.

But *why* . . . What did the symbol signify and how did it relate to Alice? And what of Phillip, whose birthmark also burned when in close proximity to the jewel? Suddenly it seemed imperative that Jean-Louis translate the page for her, if only so she could settle the recurring thought that she did not believe in coincidence.

* * *

Alice was restless. She tossed and turned on the small cot until she despaired that her thoughts would drive her mad. Sometimes she missed the familiarity of her life in India and the constancy of her father so much that it hurt like a physical pain in the center of her chest.

She rose from the bed and pulled her robe on over her nightdress. Needing to see the stars, she quietly glanced at Sally and Isabelle, both of whom were sound asleep. She unfastened the tent flap as quietly as she could and slipped out into the night. Taking a few deep breaths, she looked up at a night-blackened sky alive with sparkling stars.

She had thought that all she really needed was some fresh air, so when her throat began to burn and tears filled her eyes, she found herself surprised. She glanced back at her tent and decided she couldn't go back in there. Isabelle or Sally would awaken and wonder why she was sad. It would have been hard to tell them why when she hardly understood it herself.

Alice walked toward the dining tent and entered it, sitting at the table alone in the dark. She hadn't been an attentive daughter; she had been selfish and demanding, and it was only when she had been abducted with Sally that she began to realize it. By then it had been too late. Her father had been murdered before she had been put aboard the ship to Egypt, and her mother even before that. She couldn't even remember having said a decent good-bye when her mother left India for the quick trip to England that would be her last.

The tears flowed unchecked down her face, and she felt her shoulders begin to shake. Her mother had been insufferably high-strung, her father quiet and serious. But they were familiar. They were her parents. And now she felt hopelessly adrift. If not for Belle and Sally, she would be utterly terrified. Her direction had been unalterably changed, and she had no idea where life would take her.

Alice despised feeling helpless. Even with her parents, or perhaps because of their idiosyncrasies, she had always been in control. She knew how to manipulate situations to her own advantage, how to charm or storm her way into whatever she wished. Now she was at the mercy of a world that didn't much care that she was the daughter of a colonel and peer of the realm. When word reached her brothers at Eton that their parents were dead, they would undoubtedly all be called back to the ancestral estate where a distant cousin of their father's would act as guardian until her oldest brother came of age. She wondered if he even knew yet that he was now Lord Banbury. Daniel had always been serious, like their father, and she had never understood him. Charles was closer to her in age, and they had fought like cats and dogs when they were younger.

Her seventeenth birthday had passed the day before, and she hadn't even told Sally or Isabelle. It suddenly seemed silly to shed such light on herself. A month before, she would have been livid at the thought of her birthday coming and going without significant fanfare. Suddenly all thoughts of a celebration seemed pointless.

Daytime was usually good; Alice was able to lose herself in the company of the others and pretend that her life was normal, that she was just a girl on an adventure. When it came time to close her eyes at night, however, the fears and terrible sense of loneliness crowded in and she felt as though she were suffocating.

The tent flap rustled and Alice sat up straight and wiped her face. "Who . . . who is it?" she asked, hating the quaver that was so apparent in her voice.

"Miss?" a man answered, and she saw his face illuminated by the flare of a match that he struck and held to the wick of a lantern hanging by the door. "Oh, Miss Bilbey," he said and made his way to the table with the light.

"Mr. Deveraux," Alice said and felt herself blushing furiously. Where was her handkerchief? She fumbled in her pocket to no avail.

"May I join you?" he asked. My, but the man was handsome, and his French accent was divine. She was absolutely mortified to the depths of her soul that he would see her in such a state.

"Of course," she answered.

"Here, Miss," he said, and she looked up to see he offered her a white handkerchief.

"Thank you." She took it and surreptitiously wiped at her eyes and nose. She closed her hand around it, not wanting to return it.

"May I join you?" he asked again.

She nodded and indicated the seat across the table from her. "Certainly."

"I can see you are distressed," he said to her, his warm brown eyes looking at her in concern through his round, wire-rimmed spectacles. "Is there anything I can do to be of service to you? Shall I fetch Miss Webb or Miss Rhodes?"

Alice shook her head. "No, thank you. I don't want to disturb them. I was merely . . ." She shrugged. He was virtually a stranger, and she didn't know what to say.

"I see you're wearing the talisman from the villager," Deveraux said, pointing to the chain she wore around her neck.

Alice glanced down and ran her fingers across the smooth charm. She smiled a bit and nodded. "It seems silly, I'm sure," she said.

"Not at all. It's a beautiful piece."

"I wish I knew what it meant and why these old women are so insistent." She shrugged and tried to laugh, wishing the floor would open up and swallow her whole. She must look a fright!

The Frenchman's brows drew together. Subtle auburn highlights in his amber-colored hair glinted from the light of the lantern, and she wondered if the slight wave in it would curl if it were allowed to grow longer. "I confess," he answered her, "I am baffled that I do not know the meaning." He actually seemed to flush a bit and he hastened to add, "I do not profess to know all hieroglyphs. I have made quite an exhaustive study of it, however."

She nodded and wished to ease his discomfort. "I should love to learn some of the symbols," she offered. "Do you have paper and pen in your pockets?"

He looked surprised. "I do." He reached into his inner coat pocket and withdrew a small journal and pen. "Would you truly like for me to show you some?"

"I would!" Any distraction from her former thoughts would be welcome, and said distraction coming from the handsome young Frenchman was most welcome indeed.

Mr. Deveraux moved to her side of the table and sat down, pulling the lantern closer between them. He kept a respectful distance, taking care not to brush his leg against hers or touch her in any way. The very fact that they were alone, late at night, was scandalous enough, but she found herself oddly unconcerned. She was at ease in his presence.

"The world has known the meaning of Egyptian hieroglyphs for roughly one hundred years," he told her as he opened the book to a blank page and uncapped his fountain pen. "Are you aware of the Rosetta Stone, the translation of it?"

"I'm afraid not," she said, wishing she had more of Isabelle's masculine knowledge of the world.

"The Rosetta Stone," he said, writing it as he spoke, "was found in 1799 by Napoleon's army, but it wasn't deciphered until around 1819 by a man named Jean-Francois Champollion. It is a stone tablet with text written in three different forms—hieroglyphs, Greek, and demotic."

"And you have learned all of the hieroglyphs?"

Again, he seemed to blush and she found his modesty charming. "I certainly have more to learn, but I have made an exhaustive study of it."

"Do you speak any other languages?"

He nodded.

"And they are?" she prodded.

"Besides French and English, of course, I also speak Italian, Spanish, German, and Arabic. I understand hieroglyphs and am currently studying Greek and Hebrew."

Alice felt her eyes widen as his list grew. He held her gaze for a moment before looking down at the book and clearing his throat. "So," he said. "That is all."

"That is all?" Alice stared at him. "When do you find the time?"

He shrugged. "I work at a university in France as a professor of linguistics and have some spare time to devote to studying."

"You're a professor? I always envisioned professors as old men with white hair."

He laughed softly. "I am the youngest of the staff, to be sure."

"And how did you come to be here on this expedition?"

"I made an acquaintance with Harry Stafford," he said. "I presented a paper on hieroglyphs in England last summer and he was in attendance."

"Without his brother?"

At this, Deveraux laughed harder. "Yes, if you can imagine such a thing. At any rate, when he was chosen by Mrs. Montgomery for the expedition, he told her of my linguistic abilities and suggested I would be able to serve as both translator and hieroglyph expert. I received a sabbatical from the university, and here I am."

Alice nodded, feeling suddenly young and very naïve. She wanted to impress him with something witty, but nothing came to mind. She looked at him, registering somewhere in the back of her mind that her tears had dried up and she felt a sense of calm. "Can you show me how my name would look in hieroglyphs?"

"Yes, of course," he said and looked back down at the book. "Bilbey, then."

"No, please, will you show me how to write Alice?"

He looked back up at her face. "Certainly. Alice."

* * *

In the early morning hours, just before dawn, Isabelle turned in her sleep. The whispering near her ears was somehow familiar, something she'd heard before. It was so quiet, so unobtrusive that she found herself lulled backward into the former stages of sleep. Just as her dreams began to pick up where they'd left off, her consciousness prickled in alarm.

A whisper sounded again in her ear, as though someone were leaning over her. Her breathing increased in rhythm, as did her heartbeat, and she opened her eyes. Her cot lay against the back wall of the tent, and she awoke to find her face mere inches from it. Turning over and then jerking herself upright, she looked around, seeing only Alice and Sally, both of whom still slept on their cots. There was nothing else in the tent to indicate a disturbance of any sort.

Isabelle looked at the wall of the tent and wondered if she'd see footsteps outside in the sand. Shaking her head at the folly of the thought, she realized she'd see dozens of footprints from those who had erected the tent the day before. She lay back down on her back and pulled the quilt up to her chin. She tried for sleep that didn't come as the sun began to peek over the horizon, bathing the tent in a warm glow.

12

James finished his breakfast well before the rest of the camp and took the opportunity to observe not only those in their party but the crew that had accompanied them from the ship. To the casual eye, none seemed overly concerned with either Belle or the girls. He ran a hand through his hair and wondered if it was even worth staying with the expedition. Belle had seemed wary that morning, and when he'd quizzed her about it she'd admitted she thought there might have been someone outside her tent before dawn.

James winced as one of the crew brushed past with a tray of food and jostled his shoulder in the process. He put his hand to it and gently massaged, ignoring the stab of pain. He had been shot in India only a couple of days before boarding the ship for Egypt, and he found the wound acting up a bit. Of course, it hadn't helped that before leaving India, he'd hung from the rafters in a warehouse while trying to apprehend the man who'd abducted the girls. Ever since, his shoulder flared up at the most inconvenient times. Just when he thought it was truly healing, he either strained or stretched the wrong way.

James wandered around outside while the rest finished their breakfast. It wasn't long before one of the Staffords emerged from the dining tent. He figured him for Harry as he scribbled in a notebook while he walked.

"Good morning to you, Mr. Ashby!" the man said. "Have you seen Antar, by chance?"

"I'm sorry, I don't recall who he was . . ."

"Our foreman, our leader of the other workers. I have instructions for him. We are going exploring, and I would like him to accompany us."

James nodded. He looked beyond the tents to a small gathering of local men and boys, noting a man who stood a head taller than the rest. "Is that Antar?"

"Indeed, indeed!" Stafford motioned toward Antar, who left the others and made his way over.

"Good man," Stafford said when Antar reached his side, "we have an exciting day before us!"

James listened with some amusement as Stafford enthusiastically told the Egyptian villager about their plans to explore the site and his desire that Antar come along. Antar nodded politely and answered in broken English that he would be honored. "I live here all my life," Antar told them. "I show you all I know."

The rest of the group filed out of the dining tent and gathered around Maude, who consulted the small map in her guidebook. The others chatted and looked around, the women opening parasols against the sun. Isabelle was talking to Deveraux, and, much to James's chagrin, he felt a stab of jealousy when he saw her laugh at something the Frenchman said. For the millionth time, he wished he could whisk her away somewhere private where he could have her all to himself. It surprised him; he had never been prone to possessiveness or bouts of jealousy.

Unable to contain his curiosity any longer, he made his way to Isabelle's side, hoping he appeared casual and unassuming. Isabelle was explaining something to Deveraux about Maude's guidebook.

". . . symbols so densely packed together I could hardly distinguish one from another," she was saying. "Of course, I don't know what I'm looking at, but I wonder if you would examine it later and translate for me?"

"Of course, I would be delighted," Deveraux said. He glanced up as he heard his name and acknowledged Henry Stafford's request for a translation. "Please, find me later, Miss Webb, and I will gladly look at the hieroglyphs."

"*I would be delighted,*" James muttered in a faux-French accent when Deveraux moved out of earshot.

"Pardon?" Isabelle asked as she watched Deveraux begin conversing with Antar. She seemed to realize what James had said a moment later, however, because she tore her gaze from the others and looked at him with wide eyes. "You have something against the man?"

James shrugged, feeling more than a bit sheepish. "He's just . . . well . . . French," he said, trailing off.

Isabelle's eyes narrowed. "You have a dislike for the French? And when did this come about?"

"You and I don't know everything about each other yet," he said, sinking deeper into his self-made hole. "Perhaps I do have a particular problem with the French."

"Do you?"

"No. Not particularly."

She laughed. "Are you feeling out of sorts?"

"My shoulder is paining me a bit," he said, grateful for the diversion.

"Oh!" Her face was one of instant concern. "You ought to have said something sooner. You never do, you know, and I find myself relying on Phillip's reports of the pained sounds you make when you think nobody else can hear."

"Pained sounds," he said. "I'm going to have a chat with Phil."

The group finally moved forward on foot, and the official exploration began. The desert floor where they camped ran along the base of a vast hilly, rocky, and cliff-peppered valley that spanned into the distance as far as the eye could see. Within the sides of the rock walls were multiple caves, accessible by meandering paths that crisscrossed their way from the valley floor to the tops.

Antar motioned to the Staffords as they walked along and said, "I know of many caves that have mummies."

Maude exchanged a glance with Genevieve and then Isabelle.

"What was that?" James asked Isabelle, and she shifted her parasol, lacing her hand through his arm.

"Many of the sites have been plundered—they were plundered in antiquity, in fact—and those things that weren't taken by the ancients have since been stolen and sold by locals and fortune hunters. Maude said that she's been warned about locals insisting there are treasures to be had in abundance. At some sites there seem to be, and yet others . . ."

"Well, either there are or there aren't. The locals cannot very well fabricate what doesn't exist any longer."

Isabelle shrugged. "But they can send foreigners searching for the impossible and thereby extend the length of their own employment. Perhaps that is part of the reason for their duplicity. Of course, much superstition abounds among the villagers concerning burial sites. Many are said to be laced with curses, and the locals do not seem to want entanglements with the netherworld."

"Antar seems a genuine sort," James said and looked at the man. "I hope he is all he appears to be."

Isabelle looked ahead at their guide and James caught her scrutiny. "What do you think of him?" he asked.

She drew her eyebrows together. "Too early yet to tell, I suppose."

"What of the crew from the ship? Have any of them caught your attention at all?"

Isabelle shook her head. "Nothing out of the ordinary. They are pleasant, for the most part. The cook seems to be taken with the girls, but he is all things solicitous. There are three sailors who seem rather surly most of the time, and when they do design to speak it is only to each other. I haven't felt anything particularly threatening from them, however."

"I believe I know the three of which you speak. They may be harmless . . ." James was prevented from further comment by Alice's approach.

"Isabelle," Alice said as she joined them, leaving Sally up ahead with Phillip. "I need a few things from my trunk that we left behind on the *dahabeeyah*. Do you suppose we will return in the next few days?"

"We can," Isabelle replied. "Are you willing to wait until tomorrow or the next day, perhaps?"

The girl nodded. "I realized I left my diary behind. I've been keeping it since our adventure aboard the ship from India—the captain gave it to me—and I should like to continue writing in it. I had thought it was in the trunk I brought to camp. Oh," she said, her eyes dancing, "and I am learning hieroglyphics!"

Isabelle raised a brow. "You are indeed? You are to be commended, Alice—that is a worthy pursuit. Are you studying one of Mrs. Davis's books?"

"Oh no, Mr. Deveraux has begun to teach me. We will continue our lessons tonight after dinner, provided he has no other obligations to the Misters Stafford."

"When did you begin these lessons, Alice?" James asked her.

She squirmed for a split second—so briefly that he wasn't sure if he'd imagined it. "Yesterday. After dinner, really."

Isabelle nodded. "We will return for your diary. I will tell you when the time is convenient, and you may come along with me. Do you have an aversion to walking the distance?"

"No, not at all. I would enjoy it."

"We shall set out early one morning, then," Isabelle said, smiling.

"Oh. Yes, well, I suppose we must." Alice wrinkled her nose. "All of this early rising . . ."

"For the birds, is it not?" James asked her.

Alice laughed and turned, trotting to catch up with Sally. Isabelle watched her go with an unreadable expression on her face.

"What are you thinking?" James asked her.

"The girls are bound to communicate with everyone in the party," she said, her voice low. "As much time as we've all spent together, it shouldn't surprise me that Alice has formed a friendship."

"With Deveraux?" James asked under his breath.

Isabelle nodded.

"You seemed to like him well enough earlier," James said. "Reservations now? Jealousy, perhaps?"

"Oh, for pity's sake," Isabelle muttered. "Of course not. I haven't decided yet whether or not I trust him. I'm thinking of the note left on my bed . . . Deveraux has such a thorough knowledge of hieroglyphs . . ."

James was tempted to believe the same thing, but if the Frenchman were the one behind the antics, he was a very good actor. His demeanor as a quiet scholar was perfected completely. He mentioned as much to Isabelle, who sighed.

"I was able to turn different personalities on and off at will," she said. "Some of us are very good at it. I suppose it's why I don't trust many on sight. One thing I do know for certain: if he is playing at something underhanded with Alice, he had best watch his step."

"Feeling maternal toward her, are you?"

Isabelle laughed. "I speak of Sally. She would likely tear him limb from limb."

* * *

It is so arid here, so different than anything I've ever seen, Sally wrote in her diary. *I am enjoying every moment of it, however. I don't know that I'll ever again have the opportunity to travel this way, and I certainly do not know what may await me at home—nothing, most likely.*

Sally glanced up from the chair where she sat outside the tent. Some of the other camp members had done likewise; when the shadows of the day grew long, the relaxing hours just after supper were perfect for catching up on correspondence, diary writing, or reading.

Phillip Ashby now sat under the canopy and was in conversation with Eli Montgomery. Sally watched Phillip, devouring every detail about him with her eyes.

He was just over six feet tall, broad through the shoulders, with deep brown hair and blue eyes. She stifled a sigh as he laughed at something Eli was saying and offered his own remark in return. Phillip was so very charming. He was at ease in conversation with everyone in the party. When she, Isabelle, and James had begun looking for him in India, she had formed an opinion of Phillip. To her delight, he not only met but exceeded all of her expectations.

She felt like a silly schoolgirl in his company and had yet to come up with anything witty to say to him. It was with equal amounts of trepidation and elation that she watched him leave Eli Montgomery and approach her. When he reached her side, he motioned to the empty chair next to her.

"May I?" he asked.

Sally nodded. "Of course, please."

Phillip smiled at her. "Such a pleasant evening, wouldn't you agree?"

"Oh, most certainly. I almost hate to go inside."

He nodded his head toward the diary she held in her lap. "Are you writing about our adventures?" he asked.

"Yes. I don't want to forget anything." She rubbed her finger along the cover of the book. "Isabelle bought this diary for me when we were in London. That was when we met James."

Phillip nodded and looked a bit uncomfortable. Sally knew a moment's panic as she realized he probably didn't want reminders of the reason they were all together. She opened her mouth then closed it again, looking down at the diary and cursing herself a fool ten times over.

Phillip cleared his throat. "I find myself at a loss to explain . . ."

Sally looked up at him, wishing for all the world she'd never mentioned meeting James. She shook her head. "There's nothing at all to explain, really, and especially to me."

"No, there is. You and Isabelle have risked your lives for my sake, and I very much regret having placed anyone in such a position. You were abducted, for heaven's sake. I find it amazing that you can view me with even the least bit of charity." He rubbed his hair, his face slightly flushed.

"Mr. Ashby," Sally said, her heart in her throat, "please, you mustn't. I have admired your gumption, your determination to take on the world and go on an amazing quest, from the moment your brother first told us of it. My only regret is for your sake, that you were taken advantage of in such a cruel fashion. Were I to ever come face to face with Mr. Sparks, I would give him a piece of my mind, and then I would claw his eyes out."

Phillip smiled. "I do believe you would, and I'm honored to be championed so valiantly." He tilted his head to the side. "You would certainly do the world a favor; his eyes are a most unearthly shade of green."

Sally smiled at him, but the smile soon faded. "Green? Bright, intense green?"

"Yes," he said slowly. "Why do you ask?"

She shook her head. "Perhaps it is nothing but a coincidence. Of course, Belle says there is no such thing. There was a man aboard the ship that Alice and I sailed on from Calcutta. His name was Mr. Jones, and he was a charming American man. His eyes were green unlike anything I have ever seen in a human face."

Phillip leaned forward, the tension evident in the set of his shoulders. "What was his physical build?"

Sally pursed her lip. "Hmm, not quite as tall as you are, perhaps a few inches shy of your height. Slim, sandy-colored hair. Handsome enough, I suppose, and yet plain, nondescript. He could easily lose himself in a crowd, except for those eyes."

He sat slowly back in his chair, staring at her. "Where did you see him last?"

Sally felt her heart begin to thump in her chest. "When we visited the Great Pyramid. He was there, in Cairo."

"And he would have docked at Suez, just as you did?"

She nodded. "Cairo is a common enough destination, though, isn't it? Are you suggesting he followed us to Cairo from Suez? Even if he were the same man, he could never have known that you would accompany Belle here to find me. I don't even know how he would have known Alice and I would be aboard that ship. As it was, we were placed there as a matter of happenstance."

"But you forget he had joined forces with Ari Kilronomos. Sparks would have known that Ari had abducted you and where he had planned to take you. We learned from Ari's henchman that you were bound for that ship anyway; when you were placed aboard in the end, he found great mirth in it."

"So," Sally said, her foot tapping a rapid rhythm against the dirt, "Sparks was to have boarded the ship with Ari and us. Ari never arrived, of course, and the henchman was arrested while we were hiding from him. And we happened to hide in the very barrels that were headed for that ship." She shook her head. "It all seems very . . . bizarre."

Sally looked at Phillip, who stared into the distance with a frown. "I wonder if he trails us still," he said. "He may now follow us, putting everyone at risk, because he is obsessed with something he believes I possess."

"Perhaps he doesn't know where we are. Beyond that day at the Great Pyramid, I didn't see him again. What would he do? Hire a crew for his own *dahabeeyah* and say, 'Go wherever that ship goes!' I don't know where he would have procured the money. He seemed to be working for his passage from Calcutta."

Phillip nodded and looked back at her. "He was very short on funds there at the end," he said. "He must have earned enough aboard the ship, though, for train fare to Cairo." He shook his head. "The man is a fanatic. Absolutely crazed."

Sally's eyebrows drew together. "Perhaps we are speaking of two separate people, after all. The man Alice and I knew was all that was gracious and gentlemanly. In fact, I believe Alice saw Mr. Sparks in Bombay the day the two of you met with her father."

Phillip frowned. "I don't remember meeting her."

"Perhaps she wasn't actually introduced to you. She may have observed you coming or going." She paused. "And as I said, Mr. Jones was very charming."

Phillip laughed, but it was short and void of humor. "He does that. Only later does he reveal his true colors."

Sally drew in a breath and exhaled. "Phillip, I am so very sorry. You must believe that I am the last one who would bring you unwelcome news."

"Think nothing of it," he said and looked earnestly into her face. "Miss Rhodes . . . Sally," he amended when she scowled at him, "I desire your good opinion, and I shudder to think that my past foolishness will again affect the innocent."

Her heart tripped in her chest, this time owing nothing to anxiety over Sparks. "You most certainly do have my good opinion, sir."

The sun had dipped behind the western horizon, the light that trailed after it fading. The stars twinkled into sight one by one, and a soft breeze blew across the small camp. Noises from the others in the entourage formed a cozy backdrop, and the voices of native Egyptians filled the air with a sense of another place and time.

Phillip leaned forward. "I am extremely glad that you met my brother in London."

She smiled and wished for something sophisticated to say. In the end, she merely murmured, "As am I."

13

Isabelle smoothed her hair and put on the wide-brimmed straw hat that was becoming de rigueur amongst the members of the expedition. She tied the ribbons loosely beneath her chin and glanced down at herself with a satisfied smile. The lightweight clothing from India and the effectiveness of the hat promised to make for a comfortable day walking around in caves.

"Girls, finish your ablutions quickly. We are to go exploring in less than an hour. I should like to see you both eat a good meal before we leave." With those parting words, she left the tent and looked around. The camp was a bustle of activity, the sun bright and the earth reflecting the light. She noted that already the hat was proving to be more effective than her usual bonnets.

Isabelle was nearly to the door of the dining tent when she glanced up the small road created by the tents and saw James, Phillip, and Jean-Louis in conversation with another man. The stranger was as tall as James, perhaps a bit slighter in build, and wore the trappings of a European.

Her heart tripped in her chest at the sight of James. His dark hair shone in the sun; his tall, broad-shouldered stance was familiar and attractive. For a moment, looking at him there, she felt a surge of euphoria, a lightness in her heart and mind that left her breathless.

As she watched the four men converse, she noted James and Phillip exchange a glance that suggested to her a sense of caution. Her curiosity piqued, she left the promise of a good-smelling meal and walked toward the men instead. James glanced up as she neared them, and seeing her, beckoned with his hand. "Miss Isabelle Webb," he said, "this is Mr. Jackson Pearce. Mr. Pearce joins us from England, although he hails originally from Scotland."

Isabelle glanced at James, wondering what prompted the introduction. She looked at the gentleman in question and offered her hand. She didn't cup her hand downward, expecting a perfunctory kiss, but rather turned it to the side to clasp his in a gentleman's handshake.

"A pleasure to make your acquaintance, Mr. Pearce. And what brings you to our humble dig?"

His expression showed no reaction to her gesture, but he grasped her hand in his own as if he greeted every woman of his occasion thus. His reaction told Isabelle several things to consider for later review. He smiled at her, revealing a strong jawline and a row of even, white teeth.

"The pleasure is mine, Miss Webb. As I was telling your associates, I am a professor of history at Oxford and have been yearning to see this site for quite some time. How fortunate that I happened upon you just as you are beginning to excavate." The Scottish brogue was pronounced and smooth. His voice was a resonating baritone that oozed charm.

"Indeed," Isabelle said. "Most fortunate, for we have yet to even ascertain a good place to begin. How did you come to know of this particular site? It is not well known, even among Egyptology enthusiasts."

"Perhaps not, but to those of us who pursue a more thorough study, it is common enough. There is a legend attached to these caves, one involving a pharaoh's scandalous daughter, among other things. I've wanted to witness something a bit more subtle, something that could yield incredible finds but on the surface appears rather . . ."

"Dull?" Isabelle said.

"Inconspicuous," the man replied with a smile.

"Perhaps you would be good enough to join us for our morning meal?" Jean-Louis asked the man. "We can then introduce you to the rest of the group, and you may explain your wishes."

"And what are your wishes, Mr. Pearce?" Isabelle asked.

"If all in your party approve, I should very much like to aid in the expedition."

* * *

Pearce followed the three men and the woman into the dining tent, comfortable to once again be using the speech and accent of his homeland. The more he kept to the truth, the less fabrication there was to remember. This line of thinking often served him well, but with the Federation he had been obliged to pass himself off as an Italian.

He entered the tent, where the elder Mr. Ashby cleared his throat and made introductions. "This is Mr. Pearce," he said and left the floor to him. He could feel the distrust radiating off the man in waves. The reaction from the younger brother was similar. The Frenchman he couldn't read.

"Well, hello to you all," he said. "I am certain this must seem odd to you, but I am most eager to experience this particular excavation. I have read what little I can find on the region for several years now, and when I heard that a small group had obtained permission to dig here, I was desperate enough to swallow my pride and beg admittance to your little family."

There was a small silence, followed by an exchange of glances here and there across the room. Finally, an older woman stood and made her way to him. She was regal in her bearing, looked to be one who brooked no foolishness, and must have been a magnificent beauty in her day.

"Mr. Pearce," she said, "I am Mrs. Genevieve Montgomery. I am the head of this little family, and I would be most interested to learn more about you. Won't you join us here while we eat, and may we offer you a meal?"

"Yes, thank you, madam." Pearce took the woman's hand and bowed over it. She smiled at him and led him to a vacant spot at the table, where he took a good look around and established a positive identification of the one person he was most interested in seeing. Yes, there she was. The Federation was nothing more than a proverbial hound sniffing up the wrong tree. Several sets of eyes stared at him as he sat and began to spin a tale.

* * *

"This is the one," Antar said, scratching his jaw and pointing to a cave approximately twenty feet up from the ground. "This one has many paintings and hieroglyphs. Come. I show you."

Isabelle looked dubiously at Maude and Genevieve, both of whom had opted to ride donkeys from the camp. They were tired from the walking they had done the day before, and even now seemed to droop a bit. Others in the group must have been of a mind, because they all turned to look at the women. "Perhaps the ladies would rather wait here?" Harry Stafford offered.

Isabelle looked at Maude's fallen expression and made up her mind. "Nonsense," Isabelle said. "The slope is gradual enough, and look, over there to the left is a path that leads right up to the cave. It isn't as though we must scale the mountain." She turned to look at the older ladies. "Would you come up if we were to offer some assistance?"

"Most assuredly, yes," Genevieve said and wiped at her neck with a handkerchief. She and Maude also wore wide-brimmed straw hats and light-colored day dresses. Isabelle might have suggested they leave the undercarriages for their skirts back in the camp except that the hoops, while not as excessively wide as those fashionable in past years, were still substantial enough to hold the yards of material that fell over them and neatly cascaded to the ground. The fashion was lovely enough in polite society, perhaps at Shepheard's in Cairo. On an archaeological dig in the deserts of Egypt, they were less than desirable; to wear the dresses without the hoops, however, would have been cumbersome and heavy, not merely unattractive.

"Impossible to believe I need help," Maude grumbled as she began to attempt a graceful dismount from her beast of burden.

Isabelle went to the woman's side and gestured with her cane. "We all need help in some form or other," she said with a smile and helped Maude disentangle herself from the animal.

"You were shot," Maude said archly and reached for her small bag that contained her pamphlet, a notebook, and pen. "That, at least, is exciting. I am merely old."

Isabelle laughed. Genevieve snorted at her friend as she dismounted from her own donkey with some help from Phillip and Jean-Louis. "Dear friend, if you are old, then I am positively ancient." Genevieve motioned to Isabelle with a slight inclination of her head, a gesture so subtle Isabelle might have thought she imagined it had Genevieve not leveled her with a stare that left no question.

The group bustled around, securing the donkeys and preparing to climb up to the cave. Isabelle walked to Genevieve's side. "Ma'am?" she asked.

"What do you feel about this Pearce fellow?" Genevieve asked under her breath as she searched for something in her reticule.

"Not much yet. I would say he is . . . adaptable. He is one unfazed by surprise or inconvenience. He has learned to go along with whatever the situation demands."

"Rather odd traits in a professor of history, wouldn't you say?"

"Not necessarily, I suppose," Isabelle said and shrugged, tipping her head to keep the sun from shining directly into her face. She helped Genevieve hold the small bag as she continued to fish through it. "Are you missing something?" she finally asked the woman.

"Of course not! I am doing what you do."

"And that would be . . ."

Genevieve waved a hand absently as she searched for the right word. "Espionage. I am appearing to search for something, while in reality I am engaging you in a secret conversation."

Isabelle laughed and Genevieve shot her a silencing look that had her biting the insides of her cheeks. "True enough," she said to the older woman. "You are a natural."

By now the group had begun to move to the left, toward the beginning of the path that twisted its way up the side of the rocky hill to the cave entrance. Isabelle and Genevieve followed at the end.

"At any rate, I do have connections," Genevieve said.

"Indubitably," Isabelle said and offered Genevieve her arm. "What sort of connections are you thinking to employ?"

Genevieve lowered her voice and, after glancing up at Mr. Pearce, said, "I have associates in Cairo who are intimately acquainted with staff and general goings-on at Oxford. I dined with two recently retired department heads the night before we set sail."

Isabelle raised a brow. "Ah."

"We shall know soon enough if Professor Jackson Pearce is all he appears to be."

"Clever," Isabelle had to admit. "And in the meantime, we keep watch."

The trail was gradual enough that climbing to the cave entrance was simple, even for the older women. Examination upon entering proved that it had, indeed, once been a place of burial. Lanterns illuminated paintings on the walls; Jean-Louis explained that the hieroglyphs depicted a journey into the afterlife for the one who had inhabited the cave as a final resting place.

"Clearly, any mummies once here have long since been removed," Harry Stafford remarked. "You did say, Antar, that there are caves requiring actual excavation?"

"Of course, of course. This way." Antar made his way to the front of the group and exited the cave, passing James, who had hovered near the entrance the whole time.

The procession followed Antar back down the path to the valley floor. As they continued northward along the base of the rocky incline, Isabelle hung back to wait for Genevieve and Maude. Sally conversed more easily with Phillip, she noted, and Alice exchanged comments with Jean-Louis. All things told, the entire entourage seemed to be having a good time, with the possible exception of William Montgomery, who muttered to Eli, "I don't know why we all have to come traipsing along." The pair moved out of earshot before Isabelle could hear Eli's reply.

They stopped at three more caves, with the Staffords making notes as the group continued down the corridor. They had progressed roughly a half mile from the campsite when Antar stopped the caravan and pointed to a cave entrance that poked in from the rock face and was situated as high on the hill as the first cave had been. The grade was a bit more gradual, but the trail leading up to it was narrower.

"This is the tomb; this is the one," Antar said, scratching his beard and eyeing the rock face with a look of something akin to reverence and perhaps a smidgen of fear. "I show others before you, but they all want a pyramid. Or a permit to dig in the Valley of the Kings. This," he continued, shaking a finger at the cave, "this cave, my father and his father, many fathers, they say this is the one."

"Well, my good man," Harry Stafford said after clearing his throat, "lead on! If this is indeed 'the one,' we have little time to waste!"

Antar began the climb up the narrow path. The Staffords ascended next, followed by Jean-Louis, Mr. Pearce, and Eli Montgomery.

"See one cave, you've seen them all," William Montgomery said and looked at the group that filed upward into the cave.

Sally glanced at the man with barely disguised disdain before motioning with her head. "Belle, are you going up?"

Isabelle nodded and looked at the older women. Maude said she would attempt the climb, but Genevieve opted to remain behind with William. Phillip, meanwhile, offered his arm to Sally, who took it with a blush. Isabelle fought the twitch at the corners of her mouth.

"And you, James?" Isabelle asked.

"I would be happy to escort Mrs. Davis," he said, offering Maude his arm, "but I doubt I'll enter."

Maude made a motherly tsk and looked at him in sympathy as they began to walk. "Of course you shouldn't enter if it is uncomfortable for you. My late husband was much the same."

Idle chatter continued as they climbed the narrow path, sometimes having to walk single-file. Once at the cave entrance, Isabelle entered to find a cavern approximately ten feet deep, after which a mountain of rubble blocked any further progress. The walls were adorned with a fading but unmistakable mural.

Eli Montgomery looked at the mural, his fingers reverently hovering just over the surface. By this time, both of the Staffords had opened small books and were making quick notes, moving closer to the entrance for the light. "You'll sketch the mural, of course?" Harry Stafford asked Eli, who nodded.

"We shall need the men we hired to begin clearing the rubble," Henry said. "Once we've cleaned it out a bit, we'll be able to see how far back the cave extends. Perhaps we may find something worthwhile!"

The Britons' enthusiasm was contagious, and Isabelle felt a thrill at the prospect of digging through the dirt and rock to see what ancient things might lay beyond. Mr. Pearce also seemed in awe of the place.

"This is splendid!" he said. "Imagine if this were the tomb of the disgraced daughter!"

"I wonder what she did to cause such disgrace," Sally said. "Do you know, Mr. Deveraux?"

Jean-Louis shrugged. "I do know more now than we did. I was able to translate that segment of the pamphlet you mentioned, Miss Webb."

The young princess's father was a pharaoh who was said to have ruled with an iron fist. She had other sisters, and her mother died under mysterious circumstances. He had no more children, despite being married a second time."

"Would she have inherited the throne?" Alice asked.

Jean-Louis nodded. "I believe she was to inherit. But some sort of scandal ensued, and she was sentenced to die. She was spirited away in the night by loyal family members, but beyond that, not much is known about how long she may have lived. It is believed she is buried somewhere in this region, although she hasn't yet been found."

"If she was truly disgraced and sentenced to die, then her tomb wouldn't be full of treasures," Sally said, a hint of disappointment in her voice.

Harry Stafford smiled. "Perhaps not, but the mummy itself would be an incredible find. But we don't know what sort of 'treasures' her family may have managed to send with her." He sighed. "Unfortunately, that's all we've been able to learn. If Mrs. Davis's pamphlet hadn't contained most of the information, we would know little of it at all."

Isabelle looked at Jackson Pearce. How had he learned of the disgraced daughter? She considered questioning him right then and there but instead held her tongue. A better time might present itself. She hadn't had enough time to study him.

Alice pointed at the mural and turned to ask Jean-Louis a question about one of the symbols. Isabelle noted the easy way in which they conversed, not certain if she should feel concern. As she watched the pair, she noticed that although Alice nodded and appeared to follow the Frenchman's explanation, a slight frown had appeared between her brows and one of her hands went absently to her back, where she lightly scratched at the spot where her birthmark lay.

Isabelle found herself riveted for a moment before shaking her head. The birthmarks, the proximity to the jewel—it all had to be nonsense. Just the same, she looked for Phillip, wondering if she would find him also scratching at his back.

The young man in question stood near the entrance, talking to his brother. If his back was bothering him, he wasn't paying it any attention. Isabelle wandered to Alice's side, pretending to study the mural.

Alice dropped her hand, only to lift it again and rub it against her spine.

"Fascinating," Alice said to Jean-Louis with a smile. "Will you remind me of these symbols tonight when we study? And I would dearly love to learn more French, if you don't mind."

Isabelle raised a brow. The man was teaching her French?

"*Mais bien sûr,*" Deveraux said.

Alice looked at Isabelle with a grin. "I understand that," she said.

"I'm very impressed," Isabelle said. "Have you not had French lessons before?"

Alice shook her head. "Mother didn't feel it important enough for my tutors to spend time teaching me languages."

"She is very adept," Deveraux said to Isabelle. "I am finding Mademoiselle Alice to be a quick learner."

"Good," Isabelle said with a smile. "I expected nothing less."

Alice beamed. "Thank you, Isabelle. My mother and father never thought . . . well . . . that is . . ." The girl faltered, her smile dimming.

Isabelle and Jean-Louis seemed to have similar thoughts as they both motioned Alice forward toward the mouth of the cave, seeking to distract her. "When we have finished with French, we shall move on to Italian, no?" Deveraux asked her.

"You shall be an amazing linguist, Alice," Isabelle said to her.

They moved out of the cave and back into the sunlight. Slowly making their way down the path, they waited at the bottom for the others to join them. Isabelle glanced at Alice, glad she'd been able to convince the girl to wear the lighter Indian clothing. It was then that she noticed the absence of a familiar sparkle that had adorned her neck of late.

"Where is your necklace?" Isabelle asked her. "The talisman?"

Alice's hand went to her neck. "I forgot to put it on this morning," she said. "Odd. I felt as though something was missing."

14

Thaddeus Sparks looked over the shoreline from the deck of the small *dahabeeyah* and considered his options. The Ashbys and their friends had established camp roughly a mile from the river, and from what he'd been able to observe from a distance, they seemed settled down for a while. He pulled his hat forward to shade his eyes from the sun, cursing the reflection of the bright light onto the desert floor and wondering why people chose to vacation in such a place.

It was time to put his plan into action. There were a score or more men from one of the villages along the river who were working daily at the dig, and it was his intention to become one of them. Gnawing on his lip, he thought of the brief missive he'd received from the Federation. They expected news, and soon, of his progress. How he was ever going to bring Phillip back into his good graces was a laughable question that plagued him daily, but he was immersed deeply in a brew of his own making, and he knew the Federation did not have a limitless supply of patience.

Feeling a sense of urgency that began to tear at his nerves, he made up his mind. Spinning on his heel, he walked with purpose toward his cabin.

* * *

The work that ensued over the next several days kept everyone at the site busy. The campers had settled into a comfortable routine; they awoke early in the morning hours, spent time helping the hired workers carry out rubble at the dig site, and explored the valley itself. Often,

Isabelle and the girls walked to the river and back, taking time to visit small villages and settlements within a few miles' radius of the camp and up and down the coast, as far as they were comfortable walking in the course of a few hours. In the evenings after dinner together, the campers frequently separated into couples or smaller groups, reading, writing in journals or correspondence to loved ones and friends, and relaxing in the warm glow of pleasant conversation and physical exhaustion.

Isabelle had kept Jackson Pearce under close scrutiny and was forced to admit that, for the moment, at least, he seemed to be as he appeared. He conversed readily about ancient Egypt, the history of the Nile, and was at ease with the members of the expedition as well as the native Egyptian workers who had been hired to excavate the tomb. If he had ulterior motives or a hidden agenda, she hadn't yet uncovered it.

The cave itself was taking shape, extending back much farther than anyone imagined it would. The workers had cleared an impressive amount of rubble, uncovering an additional forty-five feet of space that formed a corridor that twisted and turned backward into the body of the mountain. The mural that was visible from the entrance snaked back along the walls and continued in a long, unbroken panorama of images and stories that blended together and intertwined ever onward. Eli worked feverishly for hours on end, sketching the work, often continuing well into the night by the lamp of his bedside table as he added color and depth to his copies.

Jean-Louis was also busy, transcribing and translating hieroglyphs into notebooks. Alice and Sally frequently kept him company during the day, asking him questions and absorbing the ancient culture like sponges. They had devised several scenarios as to the true story of the pharaoh's disgraced daughter. Depending on the day, she was either a crafty villain or a misunderstood princess figure. Isabelle hoped they wouldn't be unduly disappointed if the cave yielded nothing regarding the young woman, who may not even have existed at all.

Isabelle felt a measure of relief as the days passed and there were no further mysterious whisperings outside the tent walls, no strange pictures drawn on scraps of paper and left on her pillow, nothing out of the ordinary to give pause or alarm. She wondered if whoever had played at the game had decided to give up on it.

She found herself looking forward with anticipation to each moment spent with James. Her heart quickened when he came into view, she felt a thrill at the slightest of gestures—for all that she'd never been a giddy schoolgirl, she wondered if fate were determined she experience her fair share of the drama.

How was it that despite an alarming increase in heart palpitations, she was somehow more relaxed when with him? He excited and calmed her simultaneously. She loved the look of his face, his various expressions, his hair she knew to be soft to the touch. She lost herself in his eyes, which were somehow even bluer in the waning light of day. On the occasions where he held her hand, threaded their fingers together, she felt she could spend an eternity touching him and it still would not be long enough.

There was a part of Isabelle's brain that warned her to take a step back and remove herself slightly to steady her feelings and remain sane. That was the safe way to live, and by staying detached she was guaranteed to avoid pain. It was as though she weren't entirely in control of herself; there were times when she opened her mouth to try to gain some distance and perspective, only to say things she had no intention of uttering.

Isabelle found herself reluctantly confessing some of those feelings to Genevieve one night as they sat under the canopy in comfortable chairs purchased from the village. Everyone else had retired for the night, if not for sleep, then for some peace and relative solitude. Light from a lantern that stood on the table next to the women's chairs made for a cozy atmosphere; the darkness beyond lent an intimate feel to the setting, as if nobody else in the world existed.

"It seems very natural, Belle," Genevieve murmured to her and took a sip of tea. "In the years I knew you as a young girl, he is exactly the sort I would have chosen for you."

"I . . ." Isabelle stopped, frustrated, and looked into the blackness that stood just beyond the reach of the lantern's glow. She took a deep breath, afraid to say the words aloud. "I don't want to give him my whole heart."

Genevieve smiled gently. "Why not?"

"He might drop it."

The Benefactress chuckled and set her teacup and saucer on the side table next to the lantern. "There is always a risk, I suppose. However, I do believe there is less risk of such a thing happening with this man than with any man on the face of the earth."

"I don't understand why he is interested," Isabelle admitted, looking at her hands and feeling foolish, vulnerable, and alone. When Genevieve was silent, she finally glanced up to see the woman's face slack in apparent disbelief. Genevieve then laughed out loud, and Isabelle shushed her with a frown.

"Isabelle Webb," Genevieve said, shaking her head slowly. "I do believe that pigs might just fly, because that is the most absurd thing I have ever heard a body say."

This is what happens when you bear your soul! Isabelle thought to herself, fuming. Genevieve must have read her mind, because she leaned forward in her chair and captured Isabelle's gaze with her own.

"I have not done well by you, child," she said, sobering, "and well I know it. I will never forgive myself for not finding you sooner."

Isabelle looked at her, saying nothing.

"Isabelle, you are the woman of any man's dream, and more than most men could handle. You have beauty and talent and wit and enough compassion to fill a church, although you would rather die than admit it."

"I did not mean for you to feel obligated to compliment me," Isabelle mumbled.

"I do not feel obligated, but apparently I ought to have said it more frequently through the years. You have always seemed so self-assured, and so distant at times, that I feared overstepping my bounds with you. Isabelle, if I had a daughter," Genevieve said, her eyes clouding, "I would want her to be you."

Isabelle looked at the older woman in shock, partly because she had never seen her cry, and partly because she felt a stab of pleasure at the statement.

"I am not at all surprised that a handsome gentleman of substance and character would pursue you. I know you have had admirers in the past," she said as Isabelle snorted lightly, "and I think we both agree they have been beneath your regard. I do not pretend to know all you experienced through the war, and I know much of your time was spent in highly stressful circumstances where you played a game that terrifies me. I don't know how you did it."

Isabelle closed her eyes. She had made a career out of playing parts and extracting information from people.

"I am proud that you did it," Genevieve said, an earnest tone to her voice. Isabelle opened her eyes to find the older woman looking at her with an unblinking gaze. "I am proud as a Yankee, proud as an American citizen, proud as your . . . your . . ." Genevieve shrugged, at a loss.

"Benefactress," Isabelle finished with a smile.

"Yes. Your Benefactress."

"Did you know we called you that?"

Genevieve smiled. "I did." She nodded, her eyes clouding again. "I did. And I was happy to be that for you."

* * *

"I'll join you shortly," James said to Isabelle as they stood outside the food tent the next day after lunch. "I'm to help Maude and Genevieve retrieve a trunk from the *dahabeeyah*."

Isabelle smiled. "You're a good man. What is Phillip doing this fine day?"

"Phillip is obliging Mr. Pearce by showing him a number of caves we opted not to excavate."

Isabelle frowned. "Why would he want to see those?"

James shrugged. He adjusted his hat to block the sun from his eyes and rolled back his shirtsleeves. "I haven't the least idea," he said under his breath. "I am still not certain about the man's authenticity."

"Genevieve is waiting to hear from her friends in Cairo. Have the Staffords gone to Luxor?"

James nodded. "They are looking for supplies or something. We are all scattered today."

Isabelle nodded. "Well, at any rate, the girls and I will be at the dig site when you return, if you fancy an afternoon stroll."

"I fancy anything that puts me in close proximity to you."

Isabelle looked at him, expecting to see a teasing grin. The seriousness in his expression had her swallowing audibly. Her own unsettled state rankled. "I am not a blushing schoolgirl," she muttered.

He raised a brow. "I didn't suggest that you were."

"I know," she said, waving a hand at him and turning to see if Alice and Sally were finished eating. "I find myself irritated, of late."

"With me?"

"With myself."

"Hmm." James cupped his hand around the back of her arm and slowly let it trail down to her fingertips. Kissing her ungloved hand, he smiled at her. "I am relieved."

She turned her face toward his, wishing for a moment that they were alone. Thinking he might kiss her, she closed her eyes as he leaned toward her. When a moment passed without contact, she opened her eyes to find his face inches from her own. "Miss Webb, you will cause a scandal."

"Mr. Ashby, you could only hope," she whispered, leaning closer for a fraction of a second and knowing a moment's satisfaction as his eyes darkened and his breath quickened. She leaned back and pulled her hand from his grasp. As she turned to reenter the tent, she heard a soft chuckle.

She fanned her face and motioned for the girls to join her at the door. "Are you ready to go see the cave?" she asked them.

"We are," Alice told her. "Belle, you should bring your journal. Jean-Louis will teach you the hieroglyphs as he works on his own transcriptions. He really is the most amazing teacher."

"Well, then, it's fortunate I brought it with me." Isabelle motioned to the small bag she carried over her shoulder. "I also have a bit of water and some matches and candles."

The girls nodded in approval and lifted their own small packs. They chatted as they walked, and Isabelle noted with pleasure the health that bloomed in their cheeks.

They reached the cave in a ten-minute walk and waited at the bottom of the trail for workers to pass with baskets full of debris they deposited some distance down the path in a large pile that grew day by day. Once inside the cave, Isabelle waited for a moment while her eyes adjusted before moving farther into the interior. The girls, however, marched forward without hesitation and weaved their way past the workers.

"How goes the work, Jean-Louis?" Alice asked when they found the Frenchman.

He turned with a broad smile. "Well! Very well today! I have found something that may be of interest to the two of you." Gesturing to the wall, he pointed at a specific section of symbols that were encircled with an oval and ending with a straight vertical line that indicated a proper name. "I believe we may have found the scandalous daughter."

"Truly?" Alice gasped. She looked at Sally, whose mouth had dropped open.

"What makes you believe it's her?" Sally asked him.

"This." Jean-Louis pointed at the symbols within the oval. "It indicates her to be of royalty. And this one represents an ibis, which is unlike any I've seen in combination with the other symbols. If it does not indeed represent the daughter, it is the name of someone about whom I have yet to learn."

"It would be so wonderful," Sally murmured. "You must keep reading! Oh, and I shall copy her name into my journal."

The girls fumbled in their bags and withdrew their journals and pencils. Isabelle smiled and marveled at the fact that two once-spoiled young women were a world away from their homes and becoming academics in spite of themselves.

"Show me again, will you?" Alice said to Jean-Louis and squinted up at the wall. He grasped a lantern by the handle and held it up against the hieroglyphs so the girls could see them better.

"Just here," he said and pointed to the symbols. He ran a finger down each one and glanced over his shoulder at Alice's work. He nodded slightly in satisfaction and Isabelle tipped her head to one side, observing him. He honestly seemed to care about the fact that Alice was learning.

Jean-Louis continued along the wall, explaining the hieroglyphs and writing notes in his notebook. He was an entertaining storyteller, making the symbols and their stories come to life. Isabelle found herself swept along in the tide of his enthusiasm and lost all sense of time. Before long, she pulled her own journal out of her pack and began making notes about some of the strange symbols that were beginning to make sense under the Frenchman's tutelage.

Workers continued to haul debris, and Eli Montgomery was a silent presence along the wall near the entrance of the cave where he continued to sketch the large mural that depicted a scene of a solitary white ibis that stood along the shore of the Nile, surrounded by large palms and reedy grasses. In the distant background were three pyramids.

"I believe it is time for luncheon," Jean-Louis said after some time. Isabelle looked up from her journal in surprise. The time had flown, and she was reluctant to leave the mysteries of the cave.

"Oh, certainly not already!" Sally said. "I want to stay and finish copying some of this."

"I'll stay with you, Sally," Isabelle told her. "I also have a few more things I'd like to scribble."

With a fleeting glance at Jean-Louis, Alice echoed Isabelle's comment. "I really am not hungry yet, either," she added.

Isabelle assured Jean-Louis that they would be careful in the cave and would join him shortly back at the campsite. They continued studying the wall in silence as workers carried baskets full of rocks and dirt out of the cave.

"We tell Mr. Stafford immediately," Isabelle heard Antar say as he followed several workmen out of a corridor at the back of the cave.

"Pardon me?" Isabelle asked him, turning as he approached them. "Have you found something of significance?"

The foreman looked at her with an expression she couldn't define; it was equal parts excitement and dread. "Another chamber, *aanesa* Isabelle," he told her. "It is blocked by stones."

"The Staffords will be thrilled," Isabelle said. "A pity they aren't here now."

Antar looked troubled. "They say I tell them right away when we find something . . ."

"I don't know how long they will be gone," Isabelle said. "Harry said they may even be late for supper."

Antar scratched his beard. "We stop, then," he said. "We wait until they see the room before we continue."

Isabelle nodded. She had heard the instructions multiple times from the brothers. Should anything of interest be unearthed, they were to be notified immediately. For both of them to be gone during the course of the day was an oddity; one of the Britons was always on hand at the cave.

"You will wish to mention this to Mrs. Montgomery, of course," she said to Antar.

He looked uneasy. "The Staffords, they in charge. The woman . . ." He rubbed the back of his neck.

"What about the woman?" Isabelle said, careful to keep her voice neutral.

Antar glanced at the workers who continued to wind their way out of the corridor with their baskets full of debris. "The men—they no like."

Isabelle raised a brow. "The men don't like Mrs. Montgomery?"

He waved an impatient hand. "The men," he lowered his voice, "they think . . . women bring, how you say, ill luck."

"Bad luck? Women bring bad luck to a tomb?"

Antar looked startled, as though he only just realized he was speaking to a woman. "I—you—" He took a deep breath and motioned for her to join him farther into the shadows, away from the parade of laborers.

"These men are not happy we dig a cave of the pharaoh's daughter. They say she ill luck. And you here," he said, waving a hand at the girls, "they are . . . afraid."

"Perhaps you should tell them that a woman is paying their wages." Isabelle studied him. "And you? Why are you not afraid of excavating this cave? You led us to it, even. Does the fact that it may house the pharaoh's daughter not bother you?"

Antar grinned at her. "I never worry. I like to find things."

I'll bet you do, Isabelle thought. *You like to sell antiquities on the black market, no doubt.*

Antar's smile faded as he looked again at the workers. "Some, they may leave."

"A pity. They are well paid."

Antar nodded in agreement. "Fear means more than money," he said.

"To some," Isabelle said.

"Yes. To some."

15

Isabelle stood outside the door of her tent, listening to the sounds of . . . nothing. Satisfied, she quietly stepped away into the night and began walking toward the cave. She wore her dark Indian clothing that both served to hide her from prying eyes and allow her ease of movement. It was likely foolish in the extreme, but she wanted to see the newly discovered chamber.

The Stafford brothers had arrived back at camp well after dinnertime, only to be whisked away by an eager Antar. He had shown them the secret room in the cave, and they had arrived back at the dining tent brimming with excitement.

"It is an empty room," Harry had said. "The entrance is walled off with large, smooth-fitting stones stacked atop one another very like puzzle pieces. And on the outside of the entrance is a mass of dirt and rock. It was very well hidden," he finished, giddy.

"The room is empty, yes," Henry had continued, "but on the wall is a painting of an ibis! And at the back of the room there appears to be another archway, piled high with rock. We will all go and see it first thing in the morning! The newly uncovered room may well be an antechamber."

Maude had looked delighted, exchanging glances with Genevieve. The girls clasped their hands together, laughing. Isabelle alone caught Antar's expression of concern. Whether it was worry over the fact that his men might quit the job or worry that too many people might keep him from acquiring treasures for himself was anybody's guess.

Later, when all the other women had left the tent, Isabelle took the opportunity to share with the men the things Antar had told her.

"Ridiculous!" Harry Stafford looked appalled. "Women as bad luck." The other men in the room murmured their assent.

"It is ridiculous," Isabelle said, "yet I wonder if it will cost you the bulk of your workforce."

Both Staffords opened their mouths to argue and then closed them, thinking. Isabelle pitied them their dilemma.

"Ultimately," Jean-Louis said, "the fact remains that this whole project is being funded by a woman. To insult her would be the grossest of errors. Surely Antar must see this."

Isabelle shrugged. "One would think so."

William Montgomery stood with a gruff sound of dismissal. "I will do my mother the honor of *not* telling her about this conversation." He shot Isabelle a dark look, and she bit her tongue to keep from telling him he shouldn't shoot the messenger. He left the tent, muttering something under his breath about having taken on too many interfering people.

"He worries about our mother," Eli Montgomery said. He tapped his ever-present drawing pencil against the table. "He often seems . . . stern."

Isabelle wanted to tell him not to make excuses for his rude brother but again held her tongue.

Jackson Pearce, who had until that point remained silent, added, "There are other villages nearby. If we lose the workforce here, we can replace them easily enough. Money is a powerful motivator for the Egyptian poor."

Henry Stafford nodded. "It's settled, then. We spread the word far and wide that our women," and he beamed at Isabelle, "are good luck charms!"

Isabelle had snorted and bitten the insides of her cheeks.

Much later, after everyone had retired for the evening, Isabelle had lain in her cot, thinking. She wanted to see the chamber for herself; it had been ages since she had done anything remotely out of the ordinary, and she didn't trust Antar not to make a scene the next day about the women being in the cave. Her leg pained her less each day, and she was almost feeling like her old self.

James had a splitting headache from spending half the day without his hat to shade his eyes, and Phillip had fallen asleep quickly, as was evidenced by his snores. She couldn't ask one of them to go with her, and as long as everyone else was asleep, the danger of wandering around alone at night was minimal. Besides—she had a gun.

Isabelle felt the familiar shape of the weapon inside her shoulder bag as she walked along in the darkness. Her feet made little noise on the dusty path, and she felt a rush of excitement at the prospect of being alone in an eerie cave. It was just the sort of thing she enjoyed. The thought of innocent fright without the threat of real danger was appealing.

In addition to the gun, she had brought matches to light one of the larger lamps that were always left at the entrance to the cave, two small candles, and her items from earlier in the day, which included her notebook and pencil, handkerchiefs, and a small goatskin filled with water.

The night was lit with a canopy of stars, numerous and bunched tightly together. The moon was bright overhead, making the sandy earth glow. Before long, Isabelle reached the cave and quickly climbed the narrow path that led to its entrance. She paused, once there, and peered into the blackness within.

Taking a deep breath, Isabelle picked up a lantern sitting at the mouth of the cave, lit it, and ventured inside. The air was considerably cooler within the thick walls, and she shivered. The light from the lantern splayed across the interior, casting elongated shadows and lending an already eerie scenario an even spookier feel.

The silence was so profound that it hummed. Isabelle smiled to herself, nearly ready to turn back but figuring if she did, she'd have to admit to herself she was getting old. She took a steadying breath and stepped farther into the cave.

She passed the wall where she and the girls had spent time with Jean-Louis earlier in the day. Making her way toward the corridor entrance at the back, she paused for a moment, listening. She shook her head, figuring her imagination was playing tricks on her, and continued walking.

The corridor itself was narrow and pitch black. Whatever lay beyond the reach of the lantern light was a mystery until she came upon it. She fancied meeting a mummy or seeing the ghost of a long-dead pharaoh and considered plastering her back flat against the wall as she walked.

She shook her head in disgust and as if to show the supernatural she had no fear, picked up her pace, and made her way aggressively to the end of the corridor. Once there, she saw the pile of rock the Staffords had mentioned leading up to an opening roughly three feet high and five feet wide.

Clambering up the rock pile, she reached the opening and lifted the lantern. Wrinkling her face in disappointment, she considered the empty room and conceded she had secretly been wishing to find something inside. "Are you in here, disgraced daughter?" she murmured aloud, and her soft voice echoed through the room with a chilling effect.

Isabelle heard a sound at the end of the corridor and jumped, yanking the lantern outward in an attempt to see what was there. A tiny glow manifested itself in the distance and grew in circumference until she heard familiar voices.

"Girls," she said as the light grew nearer, "I've half a mind to beat you both with a stick. A large one."

"Belle!" Sally's eyes were wide as she and Alice approached arm in arm and smashed so closely together they could hardly walk without tripping each other. "What are you doing here?"

"Sally Rhodes, I might ask the same of you," Isabelle said, still perched atop the rock pile.

"When you snuck out, we could hardly let you go alone," Alice said, sounding miffed. "What would people think, with you walking around in the middle of the night in Egypt, of all places?"

"Well, as everyone I know here is safely abed," Isabelle said, "the odds of my reputation coming to harm are rather slim! Girls, I cannot believe you followed me."

"Oh, Belle, we want an adventure too," Sally said.

Isabelle shook her head. "As if being abducted in India and shipped off to Egypt wasn't enough of an adventure," she muttered.

"Can we at least climb up there with you and look inside?" Alice asked tentatively, wincing a bit.

Isabelle considered the pair for a moment and relented. "Fine. Just take care." Her lips twitched. "I see you copied my form of dress as well."

Sally grinned as she set the lantern down on the ground, and she and Alice released their hold on each other to navigate the rock pile. "It hardly seemed appropriate to dress to excess when sneaking about at night. Besides, the Indian clothes are so much more comfortable."

The girls stumbled and clawed their way to the top of the pile where they lay down like Isabelle and peered inside the room.

"It's empty," Alice said.

Sally sighed. "They told us as much," she said, her voice flat with disappointment.

"I know," Alice said. "I suppose I was hoping they had missed something sitting in a corner."

"I'm afraid not," Isabelle said as she peered inside again.

They looked in silence for a moment, taking in as much detail as the lantern would allow.

"Can we go in there?" Sally asked in a whisper. "I see something."

"What do you see?" Isabelle asked her.

"A mural on this wall to our right. We can't see it clearly from here, but if we were to go inside . . ."

"It will be excavated soon, and then we will be able to see it well enough," Isabelle said.

"I agree," Alice echoed.

"Well," Sally said, sniffing, "I might have expected something like that from a *lesser* woman, perhaps a more *conventional* woman."

Isabelle glanced at her from the corner of her eye. "The last thing we need, Sally dear, is to be stuck in this cave overnight."

"How would we be stuck? We simply drop in from up here, look at the mural, and then you hoist Alice and me back through the opening. We will then pull you up and through," Sally finished.

"I know I will regret this," Alice muttered as Isabelle looked at her with one brow raised.

"You do not have to come in, Alice," Isabelle told her, feeling rather pathetic that it took so little convincing on the part of a seventeen-year-old girl to make her throw all good sense to the wind.

"If you think I'm staying here by myself, you're insane," Alice told her.

Isabelle moved first one leg and then the other into the opening and allowed herself to slowly drop down into the room. As she stretched to full height, she was able to just reach the bottom of the opening with her fingers. She considered it carefully before allowing the girls to follow her down.

"Yes," she nodded, satisfied, "I can boost you through, and then if you can pull me up enough, I can swing my leg up and catch the opening, or perhaps you can hoist one of the larger rocks up from the bottom of the pile, drop it in here, and then I can stand on it . . ."

"Excellent," Sally said and thrust the lantern through the opening before putting her own leg through and beginning her descent.

Isabelle helped her and then Alice to the ground. They stood in the small room the Staffords called the "antechamber" and looked around in awe.

"Do you suppose we're the first people in this room in a thousand years?" Alice whispered.

"Something like that," Sally answered as she moved closer to the mural she'd been so anxious to see.

Closer examination of the room showed mostly smooth-surfaced walls that displayed the mural and hieroglyphs. There was a large arch-shaped opening at the back of the room that was similar to the opening they'd crawled through. It was blocked with large rocks that were fitted tightly together from floor to ceiling.

"Another chamber behind there, perhaps?" Sally asked, following Isabelle's gaze.

"Could be, I suppose," Isabelle said. "If this room was only just uncovered today, I wonder why it's empty."

"Perhaps robbed in antiquity," Alice said. "And then the entrance again buried."

"Or perhaps this room was never intended to hold anything. It may be that there are things on the other side of that enclosure." Isabelle set the lantern down against the side wall. It cast an upward spray of light that illuminated a white ibis in the painting.

"This cave certainly seems to be dedicated to someone or something specific," she said, her finger hovering just above the ancient picture. A thrill skittered down her spine at the thought that it was possible they were the first humans to see it since the artist had finished it.

The hair on the back of her neck stood up, and she whirled at the whisper of sound in the opening. *"You dare . . ."* came the voice from the darkness. *"You dare to disturb the resting place of the princess . . ."*

She heard Alice's swift intake of breath as both girls moved closer to her. Isabelle lunged for the lantern just as something sailed through the air, hitting the wall just above the light. Two more objects followed in rapid succession, and before she could shout a warning for the girls to flatten themselves along the wall near the opening, she heard the sickening sound of rock against flesh. Another hurtling object struck the lantern, and the cave plunged into blackness.

16

"Sally!" Isabelle heard the girl hit the floor, and she scrambled to the spot where she'd last seen Sally standing. Alice shrieked into the darkness, and any further whispering of their disembodied ghost was drowned out in deference to Alice's noise.

"Alice, hush!" Isabelle snapped at her when she heard a sound that alarmed her far more than the ghost had. Someone was piling rocks onto the opening by what sounded like the basketful. She stood and ran to the entrance only to be stopped by a shower of rock and dirt that fell from the opening and onto her head and shoulders. A particularly large rock glanced off her shoulder, and another grazed the side of her face before she had the presence of mind to jump back out of the way.

Several of the large rocks that had originally formed the barricade were shoved back in place, buoyed up by smaller rocks and dirt. It was as though time was reversing itself, and the work undone earlier in the day by the Egyptian villagers was finding its way back into its original form with the aid of large, unseen hands.

"I will find you!" Isabelle yelled at the entrance as she scrambled toward the spot where she'd dropped her shoulder bag. A sense of fury engulfed her as she ripped it open and closed her fingers around the gun. "Do you hear me? I will find you!"

There was a faint amount of light from the lantern in the hallway, but Isabelle was unable to make sense of the shadowy form that worked feverishly to barricade the opening. She fired a shot into one of the few remaining spots of light in the opening and listened with satisfaction as she heard a muttered curse.

Jumping up, she caught the top of the wall with her fingertips only to slip as her hand pulled away rock. By the time she recovered her balance, another shower of rock and dirt rained down on her head and arms.

"Stop!" Alice screamed, and Isabelle winced as the girl ran into her full force. "Stop! How can you bury us alive?" she yelled at the wall as Isabelle steadied her and held her close. Alice trembled and her knees buckled.

"Oh no, you don't. Do not faint," Isabelle said as she lowered the girl to the ground. "Bend your knees up and put your head between them."

"For pity's sake," Alice shouted, her voice muffled. "I am so angry! How I wish my father were alive! If he were here, the persons responsible for this . . . this . . . *travesty* would suffer severely! I cannot bear another thing! I have been abducted, I have been hungry, I have slept in filthy alleys and spent considerable time in a *barrel* in the hold of a ship. Now I am to die in a godforsaken *cave* that was the final resting place of an ancient pharaoh's *sinful* daughter!"

"Alice, breathe deeply. In and out. There's a good girl. No more talking." Leaving Alice sitting, Isabelle crawled back toward the spot where Sally lay as the last sounds of rock settled into place and the corridor fell silent. "Sally," Isabelle breathed, swallowing hard as she felt the girl's prostrate form. "Sally, please."

Finding the girl's head, she lifted her by the shoulders and pulled her upward until she lay sprawled halfway across Isabelle's lap. She placed a hand on Sally's throat, grateful to feel a pulse and sense a steady intake and exhalation of breath. Isabelle's eyes burned as she felt along Sally's head until she located a sticky lump on the side that had already begun to swell.

"Sally, please wake up," she said, rocking the younger woman back and forth. "Please, please, you must wake up."

Alice's breathing was ragged but becoming steadier. Isabelle heard her scuffle across the floor until she reached Sally's legs. The girl felt along her friend's inert form until she reached Isabelle's arm.

"Belle," she whispered, her voice a broken thread of sound, "is she dead? Please, please don't let her be dead."

"She's not dead," Isabelle said and reached to pull the other girl close. "She has a bump on the head, that is all."

"You are afraid for her. I can hear it in your voice." The sound of Alice's quiet terror and grief tore at Isabelle's heart.

Seeking to distract her, Isabelle put her to work. "Alice, I need you to get your handkerchief out of your bag. I will find mine, too."

Alice sniffed and began rummaging through her bag. "Thank the stars we decided to bring these," she said. "When we saw that you had yours . . . ah, here it is."

Isabelle felt Alice pressing cloth against her arm, trying to find her hand. Taking the handkerchief from her and combining it with her own, Isabelle created a makeshift bandage for Sally's head. She put slight pressure on the wound, and before long, the girl moaned and began to stir.

Isabelle breathed in and out, slowly. "Alice," she said, "will you please see if you can light one of your candles?"

Alice sniffed in the darkness, and Isabelle heard her again pawing through her bag. After much fumbling and many false starts, Alice managed to light a small candle. Isabelle squinted at the flare of the match and caught a glimpse of Alice's tear-stained face.

"We will be just fine," Isabelle told her and put a hand alongside her cheek. "We will get out of here."

Alice nodded and swallowed. "Who did this?" she whispered.

Isabelle shook her head. "I don't know."

"Do you have even the slightest idea?"

"Not yet. But give me some time. I will find him."

The ghost of a smile played on Alice's lips. "I almost pity him."

"You should."

Isabelle turned her attention to Sally and motioned for the light. Alice held the candle aloft and looked on as Isabelle examined the lump on Sally's head, which was trickling a slight amount of blood that was already beginning to congeal. Sally winced and brought her hand to Isabelle's, which still held the cloths against her head.

"She will be fine," Isabelle said, although she was uncertain if it was Alice she was trying to convince, or herself. "She will have a headache for a while, I should think, but otherwise . . . see, the blood isn't flowing rapidly from the wound. It's but a scratch."

"A very large scratch," Alice said. She looked at her friend, her eyes again filling with tears. "I . . . if anything . . ."

Isabelle brushed Sally's hair out of her face and watched as she slowly came awake. "Alice, do you see the lantern, by chance? Is it broken or was it just knocked over?" Isabelle asked.

Alice lifted the candle to expand the feeble circle of light. "Broken," she finally said and brought the light back to Sally. "Belle, what's wrong with her eye?" Alice muttered in Isabelle's ear.

"I've seen it before. It will go away," Isabelle said. One of Sally's pupils was large, nearly obscuring the blue. "It's as I suspected, though. You will have a bit of a pain in your head for a while, Sally."

"What happened?"

"A rock, I suspect. Someone tried to scare us."

"And he succeeded," Alice added with a sniff.

"Where are we?"

"In Ibis's chamber." Isabelle smiled at her. "We wanted a better look at it, after all."

"I've had my fill," Alice muttered with a shaky breath and shifted to stand. "I think I should begin pulling the rocks down."

"What do you mean?" Sally asked, her eyes widening. She sat up, exclaiming in pain as she did so. "Are we barricaded in here?"

"Alice, I will work on that. You come back here and sit with Sally for a moment. Is there another candle in this bag?" She handed Sally's shoulder pack to Alice.

Alice nodded and retrieved the candle as Isabelle helped Sally hold the cloths against her head. "My kingdom for another handkerchief," Alice said with a furtive swipe at her nose. "Never did I think I would see the day I would be caught wiping my nose with my hand."

"I have two handkerchiefs in my pack," Sally murmured as Alice sat with her, gently laying her friend's head on her lap.

"We may yet need another one to stop the blood." Alice shook her head and looked up at Isabelle. Her eyes flashed, even in the dim light. "I am the daughter of a Lord and colonel in the British military," she said. "Somebody's head will roll for this!"

Isabelle smiled at the level-headed anger in the girl's voice. It was so much more productive than the nonsensical screaming. Her smile faded a bit as she took the extra candle over to the opening and studied the mess. Whoever had covered it had been quick but thorough. As she experimentally pushed at the newly added rocks, she realized they weren't going to budge. When she stretched to her full height with her fingers reaching up toward the top of the opening, she still found herself well shy of it.

"Sally, how are you feeling?" she asked her charge.

"My head hurts and I feel nauseated."

Isabelle lifted the small candle up toward the opening. "What have we here?" She smiled. "A gap. They made a noble effort but didn't have enough time to make it truly impressive. Alice," she said, turning toward the girls, "I'm going to need your help. Please get Sally as comfortable as possible and then come over here. Sally, do you think you can hold one candle?"

"Yes, I can."

Alice moved out from underneath Sally's head and placed the pack there instead. "It's not much," she said to Sally, "but I suppose it's better than the dirt. What do you need me to do, then, Belle?"

"I need you to sit on my shoulders and start pulling some of these rocks out."

Alice looked at her for a moment before nodding.

"I will hold the candle. It won't give you much light up there, but it will be better than not having any at all. Just begin pulling the rocks at the top out with your hands and toss them over to this side, the farthest away from Sally. Oh, and please do try not to drop them on my head."

Alice took a deep breath when Isabelle bent over. She climbed gingerly onto Isabelle's shoulders and flailed for a moment, trying to gain her balance as Isabelle stood. "Belle, I fear I will crush you," she said as she steadied herself with her hands against the rock.

"Nonsense." Isabelle blew her hair out of her face and tried to stand still. "You're as light as a feather." She glanced at the other circle of light. "Sally, perhaps we should extinguish your candle and preserve it for later."

"How long do you think we will be in here?" Sally asked as she blew out the candle.

Alice grunted as she began groping with her hands, attempting to dislodge the rocks near the top. A small rock dropped near Isabelle's head and she closed her eyes. "Well," she said, "one never really knows, now, does one?"

"This will take an eternity," Alice muttered, and Isabelle had to secretly agree.

"Alice, you do as much as you can, and then if you think you could bear it for a few moments, I will switch with you."

"Very well," Alice said as she grasped a rock larger than her hand and sent it flying. The momentum disturbed her balance and she teetered backward, forcing Isabelle to stutter-step backward also. Isabelle leaned forward, attempting to regain her balance, but instead dropped to her knees and released Alice, who stumbled forward into the wall.

Alice sobbed once and turned and slid down to the floor. "We are buried alive!"

"Alice," Isabelle said firmly, "the Staffords will be here with the workers first thing in the morning. We'll be here for the night, that's all. We will get out of here and I will send you home. I will send you home, and you will be safe."

"Nooooo," Alice wailed. "No, I don't have a home! I don't have anything, anywhere to go." The sobs came in earnest and her tears rolled down her cheeks. "I don't want to be anywhere but with the two of you and yet we are always in *danger*!"

Isabelle laughed, which surprised Alice into silence. "Alice," she said, "we are going to take precautions from this point forward. And really, haven't all these adventures made for some marvelous journal entries? How many other young women of your age and status can lay claim to such rich experiences?"

Alice drew in a shuddering breath. "I am sorry, Isabelle. I don't mean to complain. I don't want to go home, truly, I don't." She paused. "I am so frightened."

"Alice," Sally murmured, "Isabelle can do anything. We shall be fine."

Alice bit her lip and then stood, wiping her face. She took a breath and looked back at the entrance, frowning. "How did they pile the rocks on so quickly without all of it falling inward?"

"I don't know," Isabelle said. "I remember several larger rocks sitting to the side next to the baskets that were waiting to be emptied. I suppose they hefted those up and then piled baskets of smaller ones at the top. This makes me suspect that this whole show was to frighten us, not bury us alive."

"You really are most clever, Belle," Alice said as she looked at the wall. "I shouldn't wonder at the fact you are unmarried. Mother said gentlemen prefer a wife who holds little by way of strong opinions and doesn't bother with thinking things of consequence."

Isabelle squinted at the girl. "Thank you, Alice." She made her way to Sally and sat on the floor next to her. "How are you faring?" she asked her.

"Well enough." Sally attempted to sit up, and Isabelle pressed her shoulders back down.

"Just be still for a bit," she told her. "We may as well enjoy our night in the daughter's antechamber."

Alice walked over to them and sat down, her hand on her lower back. "We don't know that it's the daughter's chamber, really, although it would be rather amazing if it were true."

"Alice, does your back hurt?" Isabelle asked.

Alice frowned. "I . . . yes, I suppose it does." She glanced down at her arm, looking surprised to find herself rubbing her lower spine.

"When did it begin to hurt?"

"I don't know." She paused. "I don't . . ." She looked up in confusion at Isabelle. "I suppose only just now, although I do remember it bothering me a bit as we climbed up the rock pile. Once we were in here I was distracted, and then there was the excitement of being buried alive and all. Odd."

"Hmm. It is odd," Isabelle said, narrowing her eyes and thinking. "Why would it be hurting you here?"

"Oh, Alice, where is your necklace?" Sally asked her, looking at her friend's neck. "What a shame if you've lost it somewhere in here."

Alice's hand flew to her throat and she looked stricken. "I was becoming rather attached to the thing."

"We can look in here," Isabelle said. "The room isn't very big. I'll light another candle and we can examine the floor."

She and Alice walked the perimeter of the room and then crisscrossed the whole of it twice. They paid special attention to the barricaded opening where she had climbed atop Isabelle's shoulders, but to no avail. The necklace was nowhere in sight.

"I'm sorry," Isabelle said. "Perhaps you lost it on the other side as you were climbing up to the opening. In the morning, we'll see if we can't find it out there."

Alice nodded and flounced back down next to Sally. "The next time Isabelle goes off on an adventure, my vote will be that we stay behind."

Isabelle laughed, but Sally didn't crack a smile. "What if we hadn't followed her? She might have come across the evildoer as she left the cave, and he might have done much worse to her."

"True enough," Alice said. "I suppose we should keep a closer eye on you, Isabelle."

"That's very thoughtful," Isabelle said, still walking the room.

"I didn't know you had a gun," Alice said as Isabelle placed her hands along the back walled-in entrance. "I wonder if your shot found its mark."

Isabelle had been thinking much the same thing. If someone in their party had a wound, she would know who the villain had been. If, however, it was one of the many workers, he could disappear back into his village and she would never be the wiser.

"I wish we could see what's beyond this doorway," Isabelle said. She tugged experimentally at one of the smaller rocks toward the top, but to no avail. "We need tools."

"Muscles wouldn't hurt either," Alice muttered. "Had I known we would be in for hard labor on this trip, I might have done something to prepare for it."

Sally laughed and winced. Isabelle came back to her side and looked again at her eyes. The larger pupil seemed to be shrinking in size, but she couldn't be sure. "Sally, you need to stay awake."

"Why? I'm not sure I could sleep in here anyway, but why do you say so?"

Isabelle sat next to her. "During the war, I saw head wounds that resulted in symptoms similar to yours. The doctors would insist that the patients be kept awake for a certain amount of time to be sure . . ." *To be sure they wouldn't fall asleep permanently,* she thought.

"To be sure . . ." Sally prodded.

"To be sure the wound is properly healing. So what shall we discuss? How about Phillip?"

Sally looked at her in surprise. "What of Phillip?"

"Or perhaps Jean-Louis?" Isabelle said, turning to Alice.

"What of Jean-Louis?" Alice asked her.

"Come now, girls. Tell me everything."

17

James felt his heart beating in his throat by the time he reached the cave. If Isabelle and the girls weren't inside, then he figured he'd allow himself the luxury of becoming well and truly frantic.

"They've always made it a point to tell us where they're going," Phillip said as he matched James stride for stride.

"Not always," James told him. He shook his head. "Isabelle has gone off on her own more than once. She doesn't tell me if she thinks I might argue with her about it."

"But would she involve the girls?"

James shook his head. "I don't know. I wouldn't have thought so."

"The three of them together," Phillip murmured as though trying to reassure himself. "They ought to be safe . . ."

They reached the base of the path leading up to the cave, and James stood rooted to the spot. How on earth was he going to go inside? Phillip must have sensed his hesitation, because he placed a hand on James's shoulder.

"I'll go in," he said. "You wait out here."

James shook his head. "No. I'll be fine."

They climbed the path and entered the cave. Phillip pulled matches from his pocket and lit one of two lanterns sitting inside the entrance. Holding the light up, he looked at James. "Are you sure?"

James nodded. He followed Phillip into the cave and took a deep breath. As they walked deeper into the interior, he felt certain the walls were closing in on him. He concentrated on Phillip, looking neither left nor right.

He heard the sound of rapid footsteps behind him and turned to see the Staffords running toward them with Antar on their heels. They all continued down the corridor, and James followed closely behind Phillip, looking at his brother's shoulders. Before long, Phillip came to a halt. "This must be where the excavating stopped," he said.

Harry Stafford moved around James with a sound of dismay. "But where is the opening? Someone has covered it!"

James heard a faint sound and held up his hand. "Listen," he said and managed to look at the wall in front of him.

Phillip cocked his head to one side. "Hello!" he shouted.

"Help!"

"Isabelle!" James yelled. He looked at the rock pile and tried to determine the swiftest course of action. He turned to Antar. "We can work faster if you get your men to help. At least some of them."

Antar looked at them with wide eyes. "They will not come in here. They will think there are spirits in there."

James wanted to throttle the man. "They aren't spirits. It's Isabelle and the girls. It will take Phillip and me much longer to tear this down alone than it would with help from the workers."

Henry spoke up. "We are ready to assist you as well, James."

James hesitated. "Yes," he said looking at the slight man.

Phillip glanced at Antar as he set his lantern down and began to roll up his shirt sleeves. "If you can find any men brave enough to help three women, bring them."

Antar looked as though he wanted to retort, but he held his tongue and left.

James looked down the corridor at the man's retreating back and felt the walls shrink again. He took deep breaths and stifled a curse.

"James," Phillip said, "I'm going to climb up and fill this basket. I will hand it to you, and you set it aside. All we need to do is create an opening large enough to pull them through."

"And what would you have us do?" Henry asked, rolling up his sleeves as Phillip had done.

Phillip looked at him for a moment. "Yes, well. James will hand you the basket, you hand it to Harry, and Harry will set it down."

The Brits looked pleased at their assignments, and for a moment

James forgot his discomfort. He managed a smile at their enthusiasm and turned to Phillip, who had already perched himself atop the pile.

"James?" The call from the other side of the wall was faint.

"Isabelle!" He answered back and took a full basket from Phillip. "We'll have you out soon!"

" . . . go outside!" came the muffled response. " . . . don't like caves!"

"I'm fine," he shouted back and concentrated on handing Phillip an empty basket. She said something in reply, but he couldn't make it out.

Phillip pulled enough rocks from the top that it wasn't long before the voices on the other side became clearer. It also wasn't long before his brother's natural charm surfaced. "What on earth are you doing in there, Isabelle? You might have waited for the rest of the expedition," he said as he handed James another basket.

"We are having a picnic," came the response. "It's good of you to join us. We were growing weary of one another's company."

"Quite a clever way you had of closing the door behind you," Phillip said. He motioned to James and the Staffords to move out of the way, and he pulled a large stone free and sent it tumbling down the rock pile. When it stopped at the bottom, Harry Stafford rolled it to the side of the corridor with a grunt.

"I wish we could take credit for the handiwork," Isabelle was saying to Phillip. "As it happens, someone came along and did it for us."

Phillip rolled another large rock down the incline. Another followed, and then another in rapid succession. He told Isabelle to stand back and shoved a couple of the larger rocks into the smaller chamber. "You can stand on these," he said. Before long, he created an opening almost large enough to crawl through. He put his head and shoulders through to the other side. "Are you all well?" he asked, the teasing quality of his tone gone.

"Well enough," was the answer. "Sally has been hurt a bit, though. We need to look at her in better light."

Phillip pulled back through the opening and went to work on another large rock. "What happened?" he asked, his voice terse.

The answer was hushed, and James couldn't hear it.

"I'm sorry?" Phillip asked, pausing in his efforts. He put his head into the opening again. "Just James and the Staffords," he then said quietly. He paused, and James saw him nod.

There was activity in the corridor then, and James turned to see approaching lanterns. Antar had recruited Jean-Louis, Jackson Pearce, Eli, William, and a handful of workers. The added presence of so many extra people in the already tight space made James feel light-headed. He moved slowly until his back came up against the wall.

"James, we have enough help now," Phillip said to him.

"James, get out!" he heard Isabelle shout from the inside room. "Wait for me outside."

He shook his head, mortified at his own weakness and hating the fact that his breaths were becoming shallower and quicker.

"James, go!" Phillip said and motioned with his head.

James fought his way down the corridor, his head swimming as he bumped into the others. When he made it to the larger chambers in the front, he saw light at the cave entrance and felt his chest muscles relax a bit. He stumbled to the opening and sat down, blinking at the bright sunlight and taking great gulping breaths of air. Shaking his head, he rubbed his eyes with his hands, resigning himself to the fact that he was never going to like dark, tight spaces. It had bothered him as a child and would likely bother him forever.

Some time passed before he heard noise in the cave behind him. The group filed out, Isabelle walking just in front of Jackson Pearce, who attempted to help her by placing a hand under her elbow, Alice leaning on Jean-Louis's arm, and Sally in Phillip's arms, her head resting on his shoulder. The rest followed behind Phillip.

James stood, looking at Isabelle. She had a few scratches and a bruise near her temple but otherwise looked well, if disheveled, filthy, and tired. Alice was pale and looked exhausted. Sally concerned him. She had an arm around Phillip's neck, but the other lay limp in her lap. She opened her eyes as they neared the entrance and winced as if in pain.

"I can walk," Sally said as she lifted her head, still wincing.

"I will return with a donkey cart," Jackson Pearce said and Phillip nodded.

"It's a long walk with a pounding head," Phillip said to Sally. "We'll wait for the cart."

"Why don't you all wait," Jean-Louis said. "We will return with two carts. You can stay in here, out of the sun."

James expected Isabelle to insist she was well enough to walk, and that she didn't caused him concern. Instead, she nodded her agreement and sat near the entrance. Phillip carefully let Sally down to the ground near Isabelle. Alice moved to Sally's other side and sat near her, holding her hand.

"What happened?" William asked, looking at the three women.

"It's been a long and interesting night," Isabelle said, looking up at him.

"Might I suggest it would have been simple and uninteresting had you stayed in your tent?" William said.

Isabelle narrowed her eyes slightly. "You might."

The man scowled. "Really, why were you in the cave at night?"

Eli shifted his weight. "Why don't we wait until we are all back at the camp and the women have had a chance to freshen up and eat before we decide what has happened here?"

William clamped his mouth shut and followed the others who left the cave in an awkward silence, beginning the descent down the narrow path.

"Mr. Ashby, we will bring the carts back," Eli said to Phillip. "You remain here with your brother and the ladies."

Phillip nodded his thanks and sat near the opening. James watched the men file back to camp before sitting and leveling Isabelle with a stare.

"You had a headache and were in no position to accompany me," she said without preamble.

"So you thought you'd take these two?" he asked. His frustration rose as he took in her rough appearance.

"We followed her," Alice spoke up, rubbing her forehead and trying to stifle a yawn. "It wasn't her fault."

"We can discuss the particulars later," Isabelle told him.

James felt his temper flare. As much as he was tempted to press the issue immediately, he took a look at the others seated around them and held his tongue.

"Let's have a look at that head."

Sally moved fully into the light and Isabelle lifted Sally's matted, red-splotched hair to examine her scalp. James looked over Isabelle's shoulder, noting the angry cut that marred the young woman's head.

"It's not bleeding anymore, Sally," Isabelle said. "I'm sure it will be sore for a bit, though. Let me see your eyes."

Sally turned her head and looked at Isabelle, squinting at the light. Isabelle nodded. "Good," she said. "Back to normal."

"Have any of you slept?" Phillip asked them.

"We couldn't," Alice told him. "We had to keep Sally awake to make sure she didn't fall into an eternal sleep."

18

"You didn't recognize the voice at all?" James quietly asked Isabelle. It was early afternoon, and they had just finished lunch. She sat inside James and Phillip's tent with them. She felt James's fury smoldering just below the surface.

She looked at him for a moment and then shook her head. "It was a whisper, hardly discernible. I hesitate to say much around the others. It was likely one of them who did this."

"And you went exploring the cave in the middle of the night why?" James asked her. He looked down at his hands, picking at a hangnail, the muscle in his jaw flexing.

Isabelle felt her own temper surge. "I don't recall needing your permission to do much of anything, Mr. Ashby."

James looked up at her then, eyes blazing. "Isabelle, I understand your desire to see the inside of the cave! What I don't understand is your willingness to compromise not only the future of the excavation but the safety of the girls as well!"

"James, someone willing to try and bury me alive at midnight is up to no good. I am not the one at fault! And the girls followed me of their own accord."

"At which point you should have turned right back around and marched them straight to their beds!" James paused at Phillip's request that he lower his voice. "The people here are superstitious enough as it is," he continued, more subdued. "We'll be fortunate if any of the workers will be willing to set foot in the cave now."

Isabelle fought to keep her own voice down. "So you agree with the sentiment, then, that women should be kept away from the expedition?" The words tasted like sawdust in her mouth. Such a betrayal from him had her heart beating rapidly in her chest.

His expression tightened as he shot her a look of what she could only interpret as disgust. "Of course not," he hissed. "Isabelle, I want to see you *safe*. Since we met in England you have been accosted at the docks, fallen from a roof while spying on someone, and shot at and beaten up in a jungle. Now you are receiving threatening notes and hearing whispering in the night. *Why*," he continued, "you would even find it remotely appropriate to wander the caves of Egypt alone at night is utterly beyond my comprehension. *You are not invincible!*"

Isabelle heard a ring of truth to his words and it made her feel sheepish, which did not sit well with her. She was more comfortable feeling that he was trying to stifle her freedom, so she clung to that instead. "I have never insinuated that I believe myself invincible," she said evenly. "How you interpret my actions is your business, I suppose, but I'll thank you to keep your opinions to yourself."

He looked at her then, fractions of emotions crossing his face. In the end, he sat up straight and gave her a nod. "As you wish," he said quietly.

Isabelle felt her heart sink, but pride kept her mouth closed tight.

Phillip cleared his throat, and Isabelle glanced at him. She felt heat rush into her face at all he had been witness to. She knew he had been worried about her and the girls' disappearance, and he had run his hand through his hair during the course of the morning so much that it was disheveled in the extreme. He did it now again and stood, pacing the few available steps from his cot to the tent opening and back again. "Isabelle, you mentioned anyone may be involved. I'm wondering about someone outside the camp altogether."

Isabelle took a deep breath and steeled herself against looking at the expression on James's face. "Are you thinking of Sparks?" she asked Phillip, rubbing a weary hand across her brow.

At his nod, she continued. "How would he have known about the chamber or that I would go visit it in the middle of the night?"

Phillip had told them of his conversation with Sally regarding the man she knew as "Mr. Jones." The odds that it was indeed Sparks seemed fantastic, but given the group's recent history, too great to ignore entirely.

"If I might offer a suggestion," James said, his tone flat. "Perhaps he has disguised himself as one of the workers."

Isabelle ignored his dig. "It is possible," she said without looking at him. "There are well over thirty—he could easily blend in if he kept his head down and mostly covered."

"I can think of no other reason someone would do such a thing," Phillip said and resumed his seat on his cot. "Who else would have a motive?"

"But what motive, really, does he have against me or the girls?" Isabelle said.

Phillip shrugged. "A desire to finish what he and Ari started with the girls, perhaps?" He shook his head, his eyes troubled. "Once again, I've put you all in harm's way."

"Phillip, we are not going down this road," Isabelle told him. "I will not have it. It is a useless argument and one that you will never win with me. There does seem to be, however, some sort of . . . interest in either me or one or both of the girls. I wonder if I should take them home."

"It is a valid concern," James said. "It would be unfortunate—they have had such a good time of it until today—but their safety must be paramount. Do you believe Sally needs medical treatment in Cairo?"

Isabelle shrugged. "I'm not certain, although my instincts tell me she will be fine. I have seen head injuries much worse than hers, and her eye has returned to normal. Alice and I will monitor her through the night and see how she fares in the morning. If her situation seems dire, I will take her to Cairo. Right now she's resting well enough. They were both sleeping when I left the tent."

James nodded. "In the meantime, I believe either I or Phillip should be with you at all times. Do I have your word?"

"My word?"

"Your word that you will not go off anymore by yourself. Regardless of your feelings, Genevieve has hired Phillip and me to do a job. I intend to do it well."

Isabelle's nostrils flared slightly. "Very well."

"I also believe you should continue to keep your firearm close by."

Isabelle nodded and turned to Phillip. "I don't suppose anyone around camp has been nursing a wound? Even a superficial one?"

He shook his head.

Isabelle pursed her lips. "I was hoping I had hit someone. Perhaps he was merely startled."

Phillip grinned uneasily and glanced from her to James, clearly feeling the uncomfortable undercurrent. "Maybe next time you'll have a cleaner shot."

"One can hope."

* * *

Thaddeus Sparks rubbed his shoulder and winced. Thankfully the bullet had only grazed his skin—otherwise he'd have been in a world of hurt. The light was fading from the landscape, and he lay in one of several tents that housed workers who traveled from neighboring villages to work at the site. It would have been considerably more comfortable to rest on the *dahabeeyah,* but he was trying to blend in; that meant he needed to stay with the others and maintain the charade.

There were others who had asked questions, of course. Why would a white man, an American, seek to pass himself off as an Egyptian laborer? He had paid off those with the biggest mouths, and for the moment, they were silent.

He had made an ally in the expedition, which was extremely fortuitous despite the fact that said ally was the reason he found himself nursing a superficial gunshot wound. In addition, he had been furious to learn that the Federation had sent the Italian to infiltrate the group. Did they not trust him enough? Did they tire of his lack of progress? He knew now more than ever that he would never be able to gain Phillip Ashby's trust again; the Federation, however, did not know this. So why send their own man? If it wouldn't have brought him out of hiding, Sparks would have betrayed him to those in the expedition.

It was for this reason that he now sat with a paper and pen, attempting to write a quick missive to the Federation despite the pain that burned in his shoulder.

You should know that I have seen your man in action at the excavation site. It might interest you to be aware that he seems to be acting in a manner most self-serving. If you are supposing he is there to serve the purposes of the Federation, I believe you would be mistaken. He acts as a man who is looking out for his own interests. I shouldn't be surprised to find that he is looking for the jewel for himself.

As for my own activities, I am happy to report that I am working my way back into Mr. Ashby's good graces. I will be his confidante before long, as he is at odds with his brother concerning the jewel. He is still desirous of finding it—the elder Mr. Ashby is not. I will update you soon concerning my progress . . .

* * *

Maude walked slowly beside Isabelle, Alice, and Sally. They took a leisurely pace to the cave the next morning; Isabelle wanted the girls to get back up on the proverbial horse. They had enjoyed the cave so much up until their overnight adventure, and Isabelle didn't want to see them lose their joy in it because they were afraid to return.

Isabelle turned at the sound of footsteps to see Phillip trotting to catch them. "James will take Mrs. Montgomery back to the *dahabeeyah*," he said when he reached them. "I'll stay with you."

Isabelle nodded. Genevieve wanted to go back to the ship to get some things she had left behind. James enjoyed the older woman's company; she imagined it wasn't a chore for him to accompany her. Besides, Isabelle wasn't sure he would ever venture within twenty feet of this or any cave ever again.

Isabelle was beginning to wonder if he would venture within twenty feet of *her* ever again. She had been so angry with him, her emotions so torn, she wasn't altogether certain she knew what she wanted herself. That he questioned something she had done, that he had made her feel foolish about it, angered her more than she cared to think about. Under the anger, though, was hurt. She had thought he was different, thought he was beyond the mentality of men who believed there were places a woman shouldn't go, things she shouldn't do.

She wanted to talk to him, to clarify things, but she would rather die before being the one to offer the olive branch. She had nothing for which to apologize. What she did was her own business, not his.

Phillip spoke gently to Sally, and it pulled Isabelle from her thoughts. "Are you sure you don't want me to go back and return with a cart or a donkey for you, Sally?" he asked.

"Oh, thank you, but I'm fine," Sally said, smiling back at him. "I suspect the walk will do me well."

Isabelle wasn't certain she agreed. Sally was pale and tired. She had slept well enough through the night, but the dark circles under her eyes gave her exhaustion away. Sally refused to stay in the tent all day, though, "wasting time." Isabelle was forced to admit she understood how the girl felt. Enforced confinement wasn't high on the list of things she enjoyed.

They reached the cave and climbed the path, entering the familiar outer chamber with its mural and hieroglyphs. Jean-Louis was happy to see them and wasted no time in showing the girls the things he'd translated that morning. Before long, they settled back into their routine without any discomfort.

Maude examined the walls, occasionally referring to the symbols in the back of her pamphlet. She wandered the length of the room and then returned to Isabelle. "Will you show me the chamber you had the fortune to examine at some length?" she said with a smile.

"Of course." Isabelle led the way to the corridor at the back of the room and down its length until they reached the end, dodging a handful of workers. There were noticeably fewer than there had been before. She tried to get a decent look at the faces of those they passed, but it was dark enough to prevent a good examination. She had asked Antar earlier if any of the men were injured. He told her that he didn't believe so, but that roughly half of the men had informed him they wouldn't be returning to the cave for work.

"This is it," Isabelle said with a gesture when they reached the room. The excavating had progressed to a point that the rock and debris had been removed to chest height, the pile removed, and only large stones remaining in a vertical wall. The Stafford brothers and Eli Montgomery had climbed inside and were examining every last surface.

"Astounding," Maude said as she looked inside. "I wonder what its purpose was."

"The painting is a companion to the one in the main chamber,"

Eli remarked, jotting notes in his sketchbook as he looked at the picture. "The themes seem to focus around an ibis motif." He turned and smiled at Isabelle. "But then, you would already know that. Are you feeling well?" he asked her, his smile and enthusiasm fading a bit. "I don't imagine it was a comfortable night in here."

"I am well, thank you. I rested comfortably last night." She motioned to the mural. "It was likely the same artist who did both murals, wouldn't you say?"

Eli looked back at the wall. "I certainly think so. The techniques are the same."

"What do you think of the back wall?" Isabelle asked, turning her attention to the Staffords. "It seems bricked in much in the same fashion as this opening."

Harry nodded at her. "Yes, yes indeed. I'm hopeful we can have the main opening cleared by nightfall, and then tomorrow we will begin on the back one." His gaze was troubled. "We have lost much of our manpower, unfortunately."

"Cowards, the lot of them," Maude scoffed. "Have you ever heard of such a thing? Superstitions and utter nonsense."

"Mr. Pearce seemed to believe we would be able to find replacements easily enough," Isabelle said, fighting down a sting of conscience.

Henry nodded. "I believe Mr. Deveraux and I will travel to the next village up the river and see what we can find."

"What is that?" Maude asked, looking down at the floor where she and Isabelle stood.

"Where?" Isabelle asked.

Maude pointed straight down. She bent and picked up an object that glittered as she lifted it.

"Oh!" Isabelle said. "That's Alice's necklace! She'll be very happy. She must have lost it when she climbed the pile and it sifted its way through to the floor. Do you mind?"

"Not at all," Maude told her and handed her the necklace. "Take it to her. She'll be thrilled. I think I'll remain here for a bit."

Isabelle smiled at her and, taking the necklace, walked back to the outer chamber. She showed the necklace to Alice , who responded with a squeal and a request that Isabelle put it on her immediately.

Sally was chatting with Jean-Louis, and Alice listened and made comments while Isabelle fastened the clasp. The necklace settled into place against her skin, and as Alice absently rubbed her back as she talked, her face took on a momentary expression of relief. The conversation continued, and Alice turned a page in her notebook, ready to jot some more notes. "That's better," she murmured to herself.

"What's better?" Isabelle asked her, watching her closely.

Alice glanced up, looking slightly startled that she'd spoken aloud. "My back," she whispered, "it stopped burning." She shook her head, her features drawn and irritated. "I hate it! It acts up at the strangest times. So embarrassing." She glanced up at Jean-Louis as though hoping he hadn't heard her.

Isabelle looked at her for a moment and then said, "Hold still." She began removing the necklace.

"Belle, what are you doing? I don't want to lose it again!"

"Just a moment. I'll put it back on."

"But . . ." Alice frowned and paused, looking at Isabelle.

"What?" Isabelle asked her.

Alice's eyes widened a fraction. "It hurts again," she whispered.

Isabelle looped the necklace around her neck and fastened it for the second time. "And now?"

The younger girl's eyes clouded in confusion. "It's better," she murmured.

Isabelle gnawed on her lip for a moment. "Keep the necklace on," she said.

* * *

Jackson Pearce chatted with Eli Montgomery while keeping an eye on the young Bilbey girl. The exchange she had with Isabelle Webb confirmed what he already knew; Alice bore the mark. What Sparks didn't know, what few people seemed to know, was that she was more of a key to the legend than the younger Mr. Ashby.

He smiled at something Eli said and admired the sketches, his mind considering his options. The only thing, really, was to continue as he was. They would never come to trust him if he told them he needed Miss Bilbey to accomplish an end that might well see her dead.

* * *

When Isabelle and the girls finished dinner, Isabelle took Alice into James's tent and performed the same routine with the necklace. When the jewelry was off, Alice's birthmark burned. When it was nestled against her neck, she was fine. On a whim, she made Alice walk with her halfway back to the cave, and then repeated the ritual again.

"Nothing," Alice said, although Isabelle held the necklace in her hand.

"It doesn't hurt at all?" Isabelle asked.

Alice shook her head and shrugged. "No, not a bit." She paused, her eyes troubled. "What does it mean?"

Isabelle wrinkled her brow and looked at the talisman she held in her hand. "I don't know." She sighed. "Alice, there's something I need to tell you—the legend of the Jewel of Zeus."

Alice squinted in distaste and nodded. "Yes, what of it?"

"Your mother had the right of it. The jewel does exist."

"What?" Alice's voice was flat, her eyebrows raised. "Why would you say that now? My mother was crazy over that ridiculous legend, and the one positive thing about not having her around anymore is the fact that I never have to think about it again."

"Alice, James and I found the jewel. It was in one of your mother's trunks that had been sent from England to Calcutta."

Alice's eyes widened. "The trunk she was so angry about . . ." her voice trailed off. "You said she screamed the ship down when it didn't turn up on board when you were bound for Bombay."

Isabelle nodded. "Before he died, your father told us it actually has been in his family for at least two generations preceding him. It had been taken from India and placed in a safe in your family's English estate."

"And my mother brought it back."

Isabelle nodded again. "From her diaries, we pieced together that she intended to sell it to Thaddeus Sparks."

"The man with the green eyes," Alice said, looking off into the distance. "Sally told me Phillip thinks Mr. Jones is actually this Sparks fellow. I remember when he and Phillip came to see my father in Bombay.

I wasn't formally introduced, and I saw them only from behind as they were leaving . . . It would explain why Mr. Jones seemed familiar to me when we met him aboard the ship that brought us here." She shook her head, her expression strained. "My mother . . . what was she thinking?"

Isabelle pursed her lips in sympathy. She didn't have the heart to tell her that her mother wanted money to not only maintain appearances but to also provide Alice with a spectacular London Season.

"But," Alice continued, "how can you be sure it's actually *the* famed jewel?"

Isabelle shrugged lightly, shaking her head. "We aren't, of course, but there does seem to be something . . . odd . . . about it."

"Odd, how?"

"I can't place my finger on it. But interestingly enough, according to the legend, a person . . . sensitive . . . to the jewel bears a star-shaped birthmark on the lower back."

Alice's eyes widened.

"You have it, of course, and so does Phillip."

Alice looked around as though wanting to sit down. Isabelle looped her arm through the girl's and propelled her back in the direction of the camp.

"Phillip's back burns," Isabelle continued, "when he is near the jewel."

Alice gaped. "How can he sleep in that tent, then?"

"I think he is accustomed to the discomfort by now."

Alice shook her head. "It's terribly irritating," she said. "I don't envy him at all."

They walked in silence for a moment, each lost in her own thoughts.

"Wait," Alice said, stopping in her tracks. "How did the old woman who gave me the necklace know I should have it?"

Isabelle looked at her for a moment and then shrugged. "As much as I hate to admit it, Alice, I really don't know. I've seen strange things in my life enough to accept that there are oddities I will likely never understand."

Alice scowled. "And then there was that old woman in Cairo! Honestly, does every old woman in Egypt know something . . . supernatural about me? And why has nobody offered a lucky charm to Phillip, for heaven's sake?"

Isabelle smiled. "You're prettier? I don't know." She gently prodded Alice forward again. "Would you like to see the stone?"

Alice hesitated. "Perhaps later. That wretched thing killed my mother, and likely my father, too."

Isabelle reluctantly nodded. "Indirectly, yes."

"I hate it."

"Understandably." Isabelle walked with her in silence the rest of the way to the camp. When they reached the dining tent, she glanced up the road to see several people approaching. She recognized James immediately, surrounded by three other people on donkeys, one of whom was Genevieve. An Egyptian man led two more donkeys laden with luggage and tent supplies.

The strangers gave Isabelle pause, but perhaps the thing that caught her most off guard was the fact that James walked with a beautiful red-headed woman on one arm and a beautiful blonde on the other.

19

"That *was* a refreshing walk," Isabelle heard the blonde woman exclaim as the group neared the campsite. "After spending so much time aboard the ship, it *does* feel good to stretch a bit."

Her accent was British, her clothing fashionable, her face and figure exquisite. Belle examined the woman with a thudding heart and a mind bent on physical violence. She glanced at James, who wore the courteous, bland expression he reserved for strangers and those who bothered him, so she felt somewhat mollified.

He must have felt her looking at him, because he turned his head and captured her gaze, blinking once, his expression flat.

Before long, the entire camp gathered in curiosity to meet the newcomers. Introductions were made all around; it seemed that a *dahabeeyah* carrying several passengers from Britain and America was docked alongside Genevieve's ship, and the strangers were *most* interested in spending a couple of days at a *real* archaeological site.

The blonde was Miss Adelaide Burns, traveling on holiday with her aunt and uncle, Mr. and Mrs. Burns, of London. The redhead was Miss Adelaide's *dear* friend, Miss Catherine Throckmorton, of the Wiltshire Throckmortons. They had met up with Catherine at Shepheard's in Cairo, and wasn't it just an *amazing* coincidence?

Amidst the hustle and bustle, two tents were erected next to each other at the end of the tent row, and extra places were set for dinner. While James was clearly annoyed with Miss Burns, he was pleasant enough to Miss Throckmorton. Isabelle watched in irritation as the redheaded woman spoke in cultured tones to him as her and Adelaide's tent was erected next to his.

The entire group gathered for the meal, and despite Miss Burns's best efforts, James deftly inserted himself between Isabelle and Sally at the dining table, jostling Sally roughly as he squished in. Sally glared at him with her mouth open, and he gave her an apologetic shrug and pat on the shoulder. Phillip, who sat across the table from them, paused with his fork midair and stared at his brother.

James began to eat without a word to Isabelle, but he placed his hand on her thigh and left it there, occasionally squeezing uncomfortably hard when Miss Burns laughed or spoke.

"I must know about each of you," Adelaide said between delicate bites. "I'm fascinated by the personalities that would pursue such an adventure!" She pointed her fork at William, who glared at her. "You, sir? What is your occupation here at the excavation?"

Isabelle was distracted from his terse response by a grumble to her right. "Awfully aggressive for a British lady," James said.

"Perhaps she's French," Isabelle murmured, her face down toward her plate as she took a bite of roast lamb and winced at another assault on her thigh as the woman laughed.

"She's not French," came the muttered response to her left. Jean-Louis glared at the woman who was extracting conversation from each member of the party, willing or not. "You'll excuse the insult," he continued to Isabelle, "but she seems rather American to me."

Isabelle glanced at the Frenchman, and her mouth tugged into a half smile in spite of itself. "She seems to fit the general description," she whispered. "You know, though, I wonder. Have you read Jane Austen's novels? She has all the social graces of Mrs. Bennet, who was most definitely British."

Jean-Louis dipped his head in semblance of a bow. "I fear I have not had the pleasure of reading Miss Austen's novels. I shall endeavor to do so."

They shared a conspiratorial smile at their mutual mockery of the new guest until the woman herself directed a question at Jean-Louis, who, although his face was turned down toward his plate, moved only his eyes to look at the woman. Isabelle bit her cheeks as he finished chewing and said, "Yes, I am a professor of linguistics in France."

"And you must be Miss Webb," Adelaide said. "I've heard ever so much about you."

"My reputation precedes me," Isabelle answered with a dab of her napkin. "May I ask how?"

"Why, from Mr. Ashby, of course!" Adelaide laughed lightly and glanced at her friend, who had yet to say much of anything but had been quietly observing the group.

Catherine smiled at Adelaide's comment. "It's true," she said. "Mr. Ashby speaks most highly of you."

Isabelle smiled, tightening her eyes a fraction. "He's most kind."

"That he is," Catherine said, smiling at James before turning her attention again to the meal.

Adelaide's attention had shifted again, and she assaulted Mr. Pearce, who explained his reasons for being at the dig. Isabelle watched the newcomers with interest. Catherine especially seemed focused in her regard of each member of the party, and Isabelle wondered what she was observing in the woman's face. Interest? Curiosity? Speculation? Long after Adelaide had moved on to someone else, Catherine's regard remained focused on Mr. Pearce, who seemed oblivious to her observation.

Perhaps she finds him attractive, Isabelle thought as she picked at her meal and continued to watch. Her nostrils flared slightly as she thought of the smile Catherine had bestowed on James. Slight, coy, it had been. Beautiful. She shook her head in an effort to dispel the jealousy. Every now and again she winced at the hand gripping her thigh. She'd likely have a bruise.

Once, before the meal ended, Isabelle noted Jackson Pearce's gaze flickering to Catherine Throckmorton and lingering there for a moment before shifting his attention to Maude and laughing politely at something she was saying. The look he had bestowed on the young Miss Throckmorton wasn't one Isabelle would define as admiration. It was flat, devoid of anything specific, which made her wonder all the more if the two had already met.

* * *

Cursing the fact that she'd had so much to drink at dinnertime, Isabelle crept out of the tent in the early hours of the morning to avail herself the use of the latrine. She had been torn between wanting to stay glued to James's side to assure that Miss Throckmorton wouldn't insinuate herself into his graces and wanting to retreat to her tent to avoid James's enigmatic glances altogether. Beyond his angry gripping of her leg under the table whenever Miss Burns spoke or laughed, he hadn't touched her or said anything at all.

She now picked her way quietly across the camp, crossing some distance into a copse of trees and then pausing at the threshold of the small wooden structure to be sure nobody else was inside.

She entered the latrine and wrinkled her nose, lifting her arms to light the small lantern that hung inside. She heard a whisper of sound outside and quieted her movements, pausing before striking the match. Waiting to hear more, she held her breath.

"You can go back and tell the Federation that I have the matter well under control," said a hushed voice in noticeably Italian accents. "You risk everything by being here!"

There was a murmured response in a female voice, but Isabelle was unable to discern what she said.

". . . need to leave immediately," continued the Italian, and the voices started to fade as they moved away.

Isabelle ground her teeth in frustration. She slowly opened the door and slipped out of the latrine, making her way around the corner. Her eyes straining in the darkness, she spied two forms in the distance as they walked toward the camp. The gentleman stopped at Jackson Pearce's tent and entered without even a backward glance. The woman continued walking down the row of tents until she reached the one on the other side of the Ashby brothers' and entered.

Isabelle pursed her lips, her need for the use of the latrine temporarily forgotten. So Mr. Pearce did indeed know one of the new guests. She couldn't be certain, but she would wager the woman was Catherine Throckmorton. Because the voices had been in whispers, she wouldn't have known the man to be Pearce, especially with the Italian accent.

Curiouser and curiouser, she thought, borrowing a phrase from a fantastical story published just that autumn. At times she did indeed feel like Alice in the rabbit hole. Why were things never as they seemed?

***

"He is who he claims to be, apparently," Genevieve said the next morning as Isabelle visited with her before breakfast. "Mail arrived by steamer just this morning. My friend says that yes, he knows of Jackson Pearce, and yes, he is a professor at Oxford. He was unaware, however, that Mr. Pearce is in Egypt."

Isabelle pursed her lips and sat in one of two small chairs Genevieve and Maude had added to their tent. "I know it was him I saw last night," she murmured to the older woman.

"Do you *know* it was him, or perhaps was it someone visiting Mr. Pearce?"

Isabelle frowned, her brows drawn. "I'm not certain," she finally admitted. "The shadow seemed tall . . ." She sighed. "Who would visit him at three o'clock in the morning? My instincts tell me it was him. I don't know, though."

Genevieve shrugged. "Supposedly the visitors aren't planning to stay with us long. They are an interesting lot, are they not? I would find it all vastly entertaining had someone not tried to bury you and the girls alive."

Isabelle shook her head. "I don't think anything's been intentionally harmful. I tend to believe someone is trying just to scare us. I think the only reason Sally was hurt was because she happened to be standing in the way of the lantern when the culprit threw rocks to eliminate the light."

Genevieve looked thoughtful for a moment. "I don't understand who would benefit from your absence." She shook her head. "I thought all in this little entourage were trustworthy. Someone among us is living a duplicitous life."

"Well, we at least know that Mr. Pearce is who he claims to be. What he has to do with our new visitors is anyone's guess."

Genevieve wrinkled her brow. "In the letter to my friend in Cairo, I mentioned that Mr. Pearce had joined our group and wanted to know what they could tell me about him. He speaks most highly of him, it turns out. He says the man is a wonderful professor and has nothing but glowing praise for him. Says he's known him for years."

"There's something going on here, make no mistake. I don't like it," Isabelle said. She rose. "I suppose we should make an appearance at breakfast."

Genevieve nodded and stood. "What will you do today?"

"Follow people around. Carefully."

* * *

Belle walked alongside Adelaide, Catherine, and Mr. and Mrs. Burns. They were *most* anxious to see the cave and were *thrilled* that they had happened upon a real excavation. Belle bit her tongue to keep from saying that there were excavations all over the country and theirs was especially unspectacular.

"You saw the Great Pyramid in Cairo, I would assume?" she asked the Burnses.

"Indeed, we did," Adelaide answered for them. "It was breathtaking!"

"And do you share your niece's opinion?" she specifically asked Mrs. Burns.

"I do, certainly," the older woman said, bobbing her head. "Mr. Burns enjoyed it as well."

"Quite, quite," the man said.

Isabelle widened her eyes at the lack of further conversation. Were the poor people so brow-beaten by their niece that they hardly knew how to conduct even inane and useless polite conversation?

"What an amazing coincidence to encounter a childhood friend while abroad," Isabelle said to Catherine. "Were you utterly surprised?"

"I was indeed," the woman said. "Could hardly believe my eyes." She smiled at Adelaide, and Isabelle wondered if she imagined the strained look that accompanied it. "It was so fortuitous that they arrived when they did. I had been hoping to take a trip up the river but didn't necessarily want to do so unaccompanied."

"Do you have family in Cairo?" Isabelle asked.

Catherine nodded. "Just my uncle, and he is most jaded as it concerns Egypt. He has seen it all, or so he claims, and has no desire to take yet another trip up the Nile."

"I imagine it would be frustrating. Were you aware of his attitude about travel when you arrived in Cairo?"

Catherine glanced at Isabelle with an assessing glance. "I was not," she said. "I was forced to find things to entertain myself."

"So you see," Adelaide interjected, "we saved her from absolute boredom! I just knew my good aunt and uncle would love to have her join our little group."

Mr. and Mrs. Burns nodded politely with fixed smiles. Mrs. Burns was beginning to look a bit wilted. The heat wasn't as excessive during the month of December as it was in the summer months, but the sun was still bright and taxing for those unused to being about in it all day.

"We are almost at the cave," Isabelle said to the woman. "It is considerably cooler inside."

Mrs. Burns smiled weakly. "I am used to cloudier, cooler skies in London," she said. "And being on the river has its own sense of breeze and coolness."

Adelaide must have decided the attention had been diverted from her long enough. "I was most desirous to have a good adventure," she interjected, "and when Catherine told us of this excavation I was utterly transfixed!"

Isabelle smiled. "Well, I am glad. I'm amazed you knew of this site," she said to Catherine. "It really is most obscure."

"My uncle follows the Antiquities Department and their permits." Catherine smiled ruefully. "He is of the opinion that fewer should be doled out. He feels that soon all of Europe will be crawling around the Nile with a shovel and pick."

"It certainly seems to be the growing trend," Isabelle said. "I'm happy to report that those in this company are thoroughly educated and trained in archaeology and hieroglyphs. It's fascinating to watch."

"You do have an interesting group of people," Catherine said. "Quite a mix of nationalities and trades. I'm curious about how you all came together."

Isabelle gave her the brief version of the expedition's history. Catherine listened politely, nodded at all the appropriate places, and smiled as Isabelle finished her narrative. Isabelle watched her face, wondering what kind of information she was seeking. She didn't seem overly concerned with Mr. Pearce, but she did ask about the Ashby brothers.

"So you say you met them on a whim and joined forces in travel?" she asked.

"Rather, yes." Isabelle smiled at her.

"Oh, those brothers are breathtakingly handsome," Adelaide gushed. "I do especially like the looks of the elder."

Catherine's expression told Isabelle a multitude of things. Her wry smile and flicker of a glance in Isabelle's direction suggested she well knew that Isabelle and James were a romantic item. Isabelle also deduced that the polished Miss Throckmorton thought herself vastly superior to Miss Burns. She looked at her irritating friend as one would observe a pesky fly in want of a good slap.

"They are handsome," Isabelle said. "And remarkably normal considering the fact that they are Mormons."

Adelaide's face clouded. "Mormons?"

Isabelle nodded. "Some members of their religion practice plural marriage. They also avoid coffee, tea, tobacco, and alcohol."

Adelaide winced. "Oh, dear."

Catherine looked at Isabelle and quirked her mouth in a half smile. "I see activity up ahead," she said. "This must be the excavation site."

"It is," Isabelle said. "I hope you enjoy the cave."

20

The excavation buzzed along at a quick pace. The formidable Stafford brothers had marshaled workers who had decided the wages for the excavation work outweighed their fears. She also noted additional numbers as people filed out of the cave bearing baskets and wheelbarrows of rubble. Isabelle walked over to Eli, who was conversing with William near the front mural. "They were able to bring in some extra workers from another village, I take it?" she asked the men.

William nodded. "Before long my mother will be employing the entire country."

Isabelle eyed him for a moment. She hadn't looked kindly on the man since their odd conversation weeks before at the riverside café. "I sense you don't necessarily approve of your mother's hobby," she said. "Not that it should concern me, of course."

He paused for a moment, watching the activity in the cave. Jean-Louis continued to decipher hieroglyphics down the wall of the cave, and one or the other of the Stafford brothers was continually on the move, firing directives and seeing to the smoothness of the operation. Eli was a steady force, copying the artwork of the ancients into his notebooks, and he seemed to be completely in his element. He was relaxed and at peace in the cave. When he spent time with the group, however, he seemed on edge—especially around his brother.

William looked back at Isabelle. "What my mother does with her money is certainly not for me to approve or disapprove."

Isabelle inclined her head and let the subject drop. William looked over her shoulder with distaste. "I see our guests are curious about this place," he said.

Isabelle glanced back to see the three Burnses and Catherine wandering along the wall and stopping to chat with Jean-Louis. Adelaide's laughter rang out, and Isabelle shared a grimace with William and Eli. Eli shook his head and turned back to the mural. William muttered something under his breath about speaking with his mother and made his way out of the cave.

"What about you, Eli?" Isabelle asked. "Do you approve of your mother's diversion?"

Eli glanced up from his work, momentarily startled. He finally shrugged, looking decidedly uncomfortable. "I enjoy the work here," he finally said. "I've also enjoyed the opportunity to travel. Were it not for my daughters, I think I could comfortably travel indefinitely."

"You miss them?"

He nodded.

"Perhaps before long they will be of an age to join you in your travels." Isabelle watched the man who was so at ease with a charcoal pencil or paintbrush and yet so uneasy in conversation.

He nodded again. "Although I'm not certain their mother . . ." He broke off his comment, his lips pursed. Isabelle imagined that if there were enough light in the cave, she'd see his blush.

"Your work is beautiful," Isabelle said as she began to move away and give him some personal space. "I look forward to seeing the finished product."

Eli glanced at her and smiled. "Thank you, Miss Webb."

Isabelle looked to the back of the cave where the newcomers were descending on the corridor. Their presence forced workers to either walk around them or wait for them to pass. Isabelle rolled her eyes. The four awkwardly moved into the corridor, the women in ridiculously large dresses, and followed Harry, who had unwittingly been corralled into showing them the back chamber.

Isabelle murmured her apologies to the workers she dodged around as she, too, made her way into the corridor. Harry was trying his best to act as tour guide, and to his credit he was able to maintain most of his usual charm and enthusiasm. It was clear, however, that he was itching to get back to work in the back chamber. As Isabelle neared it herself, she caught her breath and understood why.

The brothers had overseen the removal of the stones blocking the chamber doorway and had begun to remove the large stones that blocked the entrance at the back wall. She felt her heart trip as she stepped into the room and watched Antar direct the workers to carefully dislodge the obstruction piece by piece. As yet they had removed roughly five inches at the top, but the fact that they would soon see what lay beyond was enough to have Isabelle's head buzzing in anticipation.

Henry Stafford approached her, making notes. "Miss Webb, I must ask you, did you happen to see anything unusual here in the chamber that night? Anything that might be construed as an artifact?

Isabelle shook her head, remorse building. At the beginning of the dig, the Staffords had been clear in their instructions to leave alone anything they came across until the items could be documented and then carefully removed from the cave.

"I am sorry about that, Henry," she said. "Dreadfully sorry. It was irresponsible of us to contaminate the area before you had a chance to examine it thoroughly. I didn't think of it at the time, and I wish I had. It would have saved us a sleepless night, for sure."

The man smiled at her, but it was a shade tight. She was surprised—to see either of the Staffords in a mood other than extreme rapture was a rarity. She deserved it, she supposed. She deserved to be yelled at, in fact, and she told him as much.

"Oh, my, no," Henry said and patted her awkwardly on the shoulder. "I would never yell. But might I ask that you wait, next time, until we've had a chance to look it over first?"

"Certainly. You have my word."

"You know, we can tell the most amazing things from the mere location of certain objects. We like to record exactly where we find things and sketch them, if at all possible."

"Have you considered the use of photographic equipment?"

"Sadly, neither my brother nor I have been trained to use it. Perhaps on our next excavation we shall be able to."

Any further conversation was drowned out by Adelaide's squeals. "You can't mean there might be a mummy behind this wall!"

Harry Stafford nodded at her. "It is why we're here, after all."

Isabelle choked on her laughter and tried to disguise it as everyone in the room looked at her.

"What a remarkable story," Catherine said, eyeing Isabelle. "Imagine a pharaoh's daughter, disgraced and ejected from her home only to find her final resting place here in a humble cave."

"There's more to the story, after all," someone said at the doorway, and they turned to see Jean-Louis standing there. "I meant to tell you earlier, Isabelle, I've been working on the hieroglyphs in Mrs. Davis's pamphlet. It seems the pharaoh's daughter was actually something unique."

Isabelle drew her brows together in question. "In what way?"

"I don't know yet. She was something special, for certain, and I'm wondering if she was a guardian of sorts. There are symbols that suggest it."

"And the symbol for her name? How would we pronounce it?"

He nodded and pointed to the painting of the bird on the wall. "The ibis, of course. It recurs enough throughout that I believe we can safely call her Ibis."

"I wonder why she was a guardian . . . What would she have been guarding?" Henry asked.

"I hope to decipher it," Jean-Louis said as he looked at the ibis mural. "There are symbols I've never seen before. Mr. Pearce is most interested in the story too, of course. We may go into Karnak tomorrow to look for some more reference material."

"Mr. Pearce is delightfully well-versed in Egyptian history," Henry Stafford exclaimed with a smile. "I must ask if he teaches classes in the subject."

Isabelle stored that bit of information for later consideration. "The girls and I would love to join you, if you don't mind," Isabelle said to Jean-Louis. "We've not yet been to Karnak."

"Oh, you must!" Adelaide said. "It's the most *breathtaking* sight ever, you can't possibly imagine it! The pillars of the temple at Karnak are so wide it takes nearly ten men to circle them, hands clasped, and the statues *tower* into the sky!" Mr. and Mrs. Burns nodded with her and smiled.

"It's true," Catherine said into the awkward silence that followed. "They do tower."

"I would love the company," Jean-Louis said to Isabelle.

"Oh!" Adelaide clapped her hands. "Another visit to Karnak would be divine! Imagine how wonderful if we all made the trip together."

Mr. Burns cleared his throat a bit, and Isabelle wondered if he were about to cover for his niece's gauche approach. He remained silent, though, and Mrs. Burns took up the cause. "I don't know, Adelaide, dear, if we will have time. Before long we must begin our journey back to Cairo."

"Nonsense! There is plenty of time, but I'm certain if you'd rather not go again, Aunt, you may relax at the camp or back on the *dahabeeyah* with the rest of our party."

"There are more of you?" Harry asked, pausing in his notebook scribbling.

Isabelle smiled in spite of her best efforts not to.

"My, yes," Adelaide said. "Six others. Americans, all. Rather loud, I'm sure you can imagine, and nouveau money." She glanced at the others in the room, only realizing her rudeness when her gaze fell upon Isabelle.

"That is, I'm certain they . . ." she stammered.

"America is indeed the land of the loud and nouveau money," Isabelle said with a smile. "Undoubtedly some of it is a legacy from the motherland."

Adelaide stiffened. "Quite."

"Perhaps you would be more comfortable in the outer chamber," Jean-Louis said. "It grows rather stifling after a while in the cave."

"Delightful suggestion," Mrs. Burns said and immediately moved to exit the room. The rest did the same, and as she turned to leave, Harry caught Isabelle's arm.

"Most of our countrymen are not so . . . so . . ." he floundered.

Isabelle smiled and patted his hand. "I know." She paused. "I know I have no right to ask, but will you send word when you can see into the next chamber?"

Henry smiled at her and shook a finger. "Only if you promise not to spend the night in there before we have a chance to investigate."

"I promise."

Antar directed a worker to pile rocks into an empty wheelbarrow. He barked at the man in Arabic for a moment and then sent him on his way, giving orders to the next man in line. He paused in his work long enough to look up at Isabelle. "Ill luck," he said to her. "Trapped in a final resting place. You stay away."

"Nonsense," Harry told the man. "I won't listen to another moment of such foolishness."

Isabelle eyed Antar for a moment before leaving. She moved into the hallway with Jean-Louis, flattening herself against the wall so workers could make their way past. As they finally made their way out, she asked the Frenchman what Antar had said so rapidly to the worker.

"He told him to work faster, that there are a number of people who will take his place," Jean-Louis said. "He said that he would grant only so many favors, injury or no."

Isabelle frowned. "I wonder what he meant by that."

Jean-Louis shrugged. "Perhaps the man has a physical ailment and Antar has been patient with him already?"

"Did you get a good look at the man? Did you notice if he seemed to have a disability?"

Jean-Louis shook his head.

"Excuse me," Isabelle said. She rushed ahead and followed the line of workers exiting the cave. She passed each one, looking into their faces as she walked. Most looked at her in curiosity. If they thought she was rude, they kept quiet. She ran out of the entrance and down the path, continuing to run and look at the workers she passed.

When she made it to the large pile of dirt and rock, roughly forty feet from the path that led to the cave, she stopped in frustration. She continued to stand there and look carefully at all of the men who dumped their baskets and wheelbarrows. She watched the way they walked, the way they moved, and especially looked for a pair of unnaturally bright green eyes.

Finally admitting defeat, she slowly made her way back to camp. It had been a long shot, she admitted. What were the odds she'd find Sparks working in the cave right under their noses? Or that she'd find someone who had had a brush with a bullet that had come from her gun?

She sighed. It had been a long day already, and it wasn't even lunchtime. When the noon hour finally arrived, she found herself grinding her teeth in suppressed frustration. Catherine Throckmorton slipped easily into conversation with James, sitting in the only unoccupied seat next to him at lunch before Isabelle could claim it.

". . . would dearly love to visit the Western States someday," Catherine was saying as Isabelle sat across from them, next to Jackson.

"I've grown rather fond of it," James answered her, not showing nearly the amount of irritation Isabelle would have liked. "The desert has its own peculiar beauty."

Catherine nodded. "So I've heard. I've visited the States, but only ventured as far west as Illinois."

"Chicago?" James asked.

Catherine nodded again as she delicately picked at her food with a fork. "Such an amazing city . . ."

The conversation continued and Isabelle felt her temper flare hotter. *What on earth is the matter with me? Do I expect him to never speak to another woman?*

It wasn't just another woman, though. Catherine was one from whom Isabelle felt a threat. She was beautiful, but beyond that, she was intellectually bright. Isabelle knew James was irritated with ignorance whether in a male or a female, and the fact that Catherine was one in whom Isabelle might find legitimate competition made her uneasy.

The fact that she was uneasy made her furious.

* * *

Adelaide had been right about one thing; the statues did definitely tower. Isabelle felt very small as she stood next to the statues that guarded the temple at Karnak. The sights were amazing and overwhelming.

The entire camp had decided to take the day to explore Karnak, and it gave Isabelle ample opportunity to observe everyone together. Small groups broke off, rejoined the larger group, only to reconfigure and split off again in new pairings and threesomes.

Jackson Pearce and Catherine Throckmorton barely exchanged glances. If Isabelle hadn't known better, she would have assumed they were the strangers they claimed to be. William Montgomery kept largely to himself, and Eli spent time chatting with his mother and with Maude. The Staffords floated amongst the entire group, finding something to say to almost everyone, Miss Burns being the notable exception.

Mr. and Mrs. Burns had decided to come along, although they claimed to have seen all of Luxor the first time they visited it. Phillip went out of his way to speak with Sally, pointing to interesting structures and coaxing laughter out of her with very little effort.

Alice and Jean-Louis shared companionable conversation, talking with the ease of two people entirely comfortable together. For all of the Frenchman's amazing intellect, Isabelle had to remind herself that he was in his early twenties. It gave her some comfort as she watched his obvious affection for Alice grow. They were as different as night and day but somehow seemed to . . . fit. Isabelle's contentment with the situation rested on her shoulders uneasily, though. She hadn't forgotten that their troubles had begun when they met and joined up with the expedition.

Isabelle was delighted to find common Egyptian clothing on sale at a side-street bazaar. She purchased robes for herself and the girls, glad to have more time between washings, which were an effort in the dusty camp. Phillip proudly used some of the money Genevieve had paid him for his security services to buy a length of cloth for his mother and another small item that he refused to show anyone.

Isabelle noted an odd exchange, a dance of sorts, between Adelaide and Eli. Adelaide approached him on a couple of different occasions, placing herself in close physical proximity—brushing an arm against his, touching his shoulder after making a comment—and played at a fairly subtle flirtation that Eli seemed quietly baffled by. He didn't openly snub her; neither did he overtly engage. He chatted, smiled, laughed gently, and ultimately seemed to try to place some distance between them by including his mother or Maude in the conversation.

The Staffords carefully poured over reference materials with Jean-Louis in a small museum that was little more than a hut. There were a few books available for purchase, and Jean-Louis found a volume that complemented some of his own materials.

Catherine often made her way to James's side, making this comment or that, laughing at things he said, and rarely including Isabelle in her conversation. Isabelle watched her with narrowed eyes; the woman was too savvy to be innocently claiming James's attention. If Catherine were looking to amuse herself or perhaps feed her own sense of self-importance, she was playing a game with the wrong woman.

James, for his part, was conversant with Catherine and even showed some of Phillip's charm. Isabelle caught a glimpse of how it might have been to try to capture his attention at home in a normal social setting. He had mentioned a failed engagement once—he was far too humble, though. Isabelle wasn't naïve enough to believe he didn't have interested ladies waiting for him at home.

The luncheon hour drew near, and Adelaide announced she must eat or absolutely faint. Jackson Pearce found a small restaurant and ushered them all inside. Attendants split them into smaller groups for comfortable seating around multiple tables. Isabelle watched as Catherine slipped into place beside Jackson Pearce.

Interesting. The woman was forcing his hand; he could hardly sit next to her and not converse. With a deft motion of her head, Isabelle indicated for Sally and Alice to leave the seats they were about to take at Catherine and Jackson's table. It didn't take much doing, Isabelle realized, when the girls noticed that both Phillip and Jean-Louis were at another table.

Amidst much shuffling and rearranging, everyone was finally settled and food eventually ordered. Isabelle wondered how James would fare when faced with authentic, traditional Egyptian food. The camp cook was varied enough in his menus that the expedition members often enjoyed typical Western meals. Other than their time spent in Cairo at Shepheard's, which catered to a European and American clientele, their exposure to Egyptian cuisine had been fairly limited.

Aside from Catherine and Pearce, Mr. and Mrs. Burns were seated at the table, as well as Adelaide, William, and James. "You're a professor, then?" Catherine said to Jackson Pearce.

He nodded and took a sip from his teacup. "I am."

"Born and raised in Scotland, I understand?" she continued.

He bared his teeth at her in a semblance of a smile. "Born and raised."

"I would know it anywhere," she said and smiled at a server who began delivering plates to the table. "Your accent is unmistakable. I have relatives in Edinburgh." she continued. "You said you are also from there?"

"Indeed." Pearce picked up his silverware and began to eat.

Isabelle glanced at him occasionally as she began to eat her food. For some reason, he wanted Catherine to believe he was, in reality, Italian. If so, he was very good. The woman undoubtedly had him rattled, but he hid it well. Catherine either questioned it herself or wanted to expose him somehow to the expedition.

Isabelle wasn't a stranger to affecting different accents of speech. She had done it herself over the course of the war. She had been a Southern woman, a Boston native, a frontierswoman, and occasionally British. It took work to sound authentic, and while she couldn't be certain, Pearce seemed to have the Scottish accent perfected.

"And what of you, Mr. Ashby?" Adelaide said to James. "You hail from the Western States, do you not?"

"I do." James nodded and picked at his food, eating a few bites and then trying something else on the plate.

"And do you have a profession?" she asked.

"I do."

Isabelle smiled and waited for Adelaide's jaw to drop.

"I am a blacksmith," James told her.

Isabelle wasn't disappointed. The jaw dropped and then hastily closed.

"How, how very . . . very impressive." Despite her obvious shock, her gaze took on an element Isabelle didn't appreciate. Adelaide's eyes widened slightly, and she tilted her head to a charming angle, one curl of her elegant blonde coiffure gently resting on her shoulder. "You must be quite strong, I would imagine."

James glanced up at her. "Yes."

"I find your line of work fascinating."

Isabelle looked at Catherine, who closed her eyes and rotated her head slightly on her shoulders as though trying to ease tension.

James was not naïve, and Isabelle knew it. He smiled at the woman and put his fork down. "Do you, now?"

"I do. You must be able to craft the most amazing things with your hands."

Isabelle narrowed her eyes.

"I pride myself on my work, it's true," James said. "I haven't ever had an unsatisfied customer."

Adelaide breathed in, visibly gripping her fork and knife. William cleared his throat and took a drink, throwing Adelaide a look of annoyance. Isabelle watched the woman in wide-eyed amusement, wondering if Adelaide was going to launch herself into James's arms that very moment and throw convention to the wind.

"Your wife must be a fortunate woman indeed," Adelaide said.

"She is. They all are, in fact. I believe I can say that without conceit. I take good care of them." James lifted a piece of meat to his mouth, chewed, and swallowed.

Adelaide's fork clattered onto her plate, and she hastily picked it up. "They, them . . . ?"

James winked at her and smiled.

"Oh!" Adelaide's laugh was shaky. "Oh, you jest with me!"

"Do I?"

Isabelle kicked James under the table.

"I do indeed. My heart belongs to only one woman. She is the sun and the moon and the stars."

Isabelle rolled her eyes.

"And someday I'll forge a beautiful horseshoe just for her because that's what we blacksmiths do for the women we love."

Catherine laughed. "Well, then, heaven bless women everywhere that we will be so fortunate as to find a good blacksmith."

James raised his glass in salute and winked at Catherine as well.

Isabelle decided she had seen more than enough winking for one afternoon.

21

Isabelle was angry with James, and he found himself at a loss. He knew he had upset her with his censure about the late-night cave visit. He couldn't honestly say he regretted his comments, though. She worried him with her proclivities to get herself into dangerous situations.

He did have one regret, though—he wished they had been on better footing before the disagreement. She had been pulling away from him ever since meeting Genevieve at Suez, and he wished that there wasn't now another reason for her to further distance herself.

Her comments to him all day had been clipped and she had avoided his gaze. They were now back at the camp, dinner finished and the dark of night quickly descending. Isabelle had gone into her tent to fetch a shawl and see that Sally was comfortably abed. The girl had developed another headache and needed to sleep.

Isabelle appeared at the tent door and settled it into place behind her. She glanced up at James and then moved to cross the tent row and enter the canopy, where Phillip and Alice sat relaxing by the glow of two lanterns.

James caught Isabelle's arm. "A moment, please," he said to her, and she looked up at him in some annoyance. "I am not at peace with your anger toward me."

"I'm not angry with you," she said, her eyes widening slightly.

"Yes, you most certainly are. You haven't been angry at me since the night we met and I rescued you from the docks of London."

"You did not rescue me, and I am not angry."

"Isabelle, really. I thought you were one for telling the truth."

She sighed. "I am also one for hiding the truth."

"Not with me. We'll not have that between us."

"What is 'us,' James?" She looked up into his eyes, her own luminous, as though she held back tears. "I am not the sort to ever succeed at a relationship, and furthermore, you find me . . . reckless. Irresponsible. Once the novelty of our companionship grows dim, you will find these traits burdensome and irritating. It's as I mentioned in India. We are doomed to fail."

"Isabelle," James said, grasping her arm and gritting his teeth, "you are bringing about your own fears and doing a tremendous job of it!" He shook her lightly. "I do not find your uniqueness burdensome or irritating. I *worry*, Isabelle. I am *concerned*. This is what people do when they love one another!"

She shook her head. "I am not good at love, James." A few tears escaped her eyes and trailed down her cheeks. Her voice, already hushed, dropped to a whisper. "Your affection would be better spent on someone less jaded."

James pulled her close and bent down. "Do you hear yourself?" he hissed. "These are not the words of a woman who served her country during a war, who took in a motherless child! You are telling yourself you are incapable of love, that everybody will desert you, but look at me! I'm still here, Isabelle!"

"You were disappointed in me! I thought you were different. You are like every other man who believes I overstep my bounds as a woman."

It took an effort for James to refrain from squeezing Isabelle's arm tighter in his grip. "Isabelle, you are judging me harshly, and if you examine it closely, you will agree with me! I do not believe you should be kept from the cave because you are a woman. You know me," he whispered, giving her arm a little shake. "You also know that the Stafford brothers were prepared to speak with the workers and explain their position regarding their support of you and the other women in the expedition. You are a person of good sense and have an amazing talent for manipulating situations to your benefit. That you would jeopardize the expedition by visiting the cave in the middle of the night defies all good sense and judgment on your part!"

She remained silent, but her eyes flickered away from his and she stared at a point beyond his shoulder. "And that is the *least* of it," he continued. "Isabelle, when I realized you were in the cave, when I didn't know if I would find you alive . . ." His voice broke and he cursed. "I would have been beyond consolation if you had come to harm."

He released her arm and rubbed his eye, grateful that he could still hear the soft tones of conversation between Alice and Phillip. Isabelle wiped at her eyes and turned as if to move without comment toward the canopy.

James shook his head. "I'm not leaving, Isabelle," he murmured to her back. "I suggest you find a way to accustom yourself to that fact."

She paused, her head turned slightly, then stiffened her spine and walked slowly to the canopy. She sat down with a light, if slightly breathless, greeting to the others. He took a seat next to hers, joining Phillip, who was writing a letter to their mother, and Alice, who was working on a stitching sampler Genevieve had purchased in Cairo.

"No lessons with Jean-Louis tonight?" James asked Alice.

"No," she said, tying off a stitch. "He said he isn't feeling well." She frowned. "I wonder if his lunch didn't agree with him."

"My lunch didn't agree with me," James said. "I wouldn't be surprised."

"You've never been one for adventurous fare," Phillip said with a grin as he continued to scrawl on the paper. "Mother always complained that you were happy only with meat and potatoes."

James stretched his legs out and crossed them at the ankles. He leaned back in the chair and closed his eyes, enjoying the cool night breeze, wishing he could ease the tension he felt cramped around his neck and shoulders. "I fail to see a problem with that," he said to Phillip. "Makes for a consistently simple menu."

A scream echoed through the camp and into the hills. Isabelle bolted up out of her chair and ran for her tent.

"Sally!" Isabelle yelled, her voice laced with fear.

James jumped up and followed her with Phillip and Alice close on his heels. A light shone in Sally's tent, and when Belle reached the entrance, she heard Sally scream, "Belle, stop! Don't move!"

Isabelle halted her movements at the opening, stumbling and nearly falling. James ran up behind her, looking over her shoulder. A black snake, no less than three feet long, sat poised in the center of the tent.

"Be still," James whispered in her ear. "Phillip," he said to his brother, who had come up on his right, "how long has it been since you bagged a rattler?" Phillip drew in his breath, and James continued. "It's not a rattler, but it may be poisonous."

Sally's breathing was rapid and she was well approaching panic. "Stay calm," he said to her. "Phillip will think of something."

"Think of something . . ." Phillip repeated. "I'm not sure . . ."

James saw him in the corner of his eye, rubbing a hand through his hair and looking around. By this time, nearly the entire camp had gathered outside the tent and the questions were coming fast and loud.

"There's a snake in the tent," Alice shouted, her voice trembling. "Somebody needs to get a sack and a big stick. I've seen it done in India."

"She's right," Phillip murmured and moved to follow one of the Stafford brothers, who had yelled that he had supplies in the artifacts tent. Before long, he returned with a large cloth sack and a walking staff. The snake remained stationary, regarding them intently with its beady eyes.

James gently, slowly eased out from behind Isabelle and Phillip took his place. Ever so carefully, Phillip inched past Isabelle until he was in a position to try and bag the reptile. The crowd was hushed, and James was unable to see beyond Phillip's back. In a flash that James recognized from watching Phillip as a young teen, Phillip made his move, finally calling out a triumphant, "I've got it!"

Isabelle moved hastily out of the way and allowed Phillip to exit the tent, his arm extended and holding the thrashing cloth bag. "I want to determine what kind it is," Phillip said as everyone gave him a wide berth.

"This way," Harry Stafford said, wearing pajamas and trying to flatten his hair with his fingers. "To the artifacts tent!"

The rest of the crowd dispersed, most of the men following Phillip and Harry. Catherine stood to the side, looking horrified. Mr. Burns was assisting Mrs. Burns back to their tent, practically carrying her. Adelaide, for once, was blessedly silent. She looked at Sally for a moment before turning and going back to her tent. Catherine looked wide-eyed at James and then shook her head as though trying to dislodge something that didn't make sense to her. She then turned and followed Adelaide.

Maude and Genevieve were visibly shaken and followed Isabelle into the tent to talk to Sally. The girl was understandably tearful; James was not fond of snakes himself. He stood at the tent entrance and watched as Isabelle sat on the edge of the cot and hugged Sally, pulling back eventually to wipe the girl's tears and briskly rub her arms.

"Tell me what happened," Isabelle said to her.

"I was asleep," Sally said, her tone miserable. "Something woke me up—I wasn't sure what it was. Then I heard a voice, and the tent rustled, and then I heard the hissing sound. I lit the lantern and saw the snake on the ground, coming around my cot that way—that's when you came running."

"What did the voice say?" Isabelle asked.

Sally's face crumpled a bit. "It said Ibis wishes us to leave."

"This is becoming ridiculous," Maude interrupted, her face taut. "Who would do such things? First shutting them up in the cave, and now this?" She shook her head and looked at her friend. "Genevieve, you know how much I want to be here, but I fear the danger is becoming altogether too real."

Genevieve nodded. "I agree. The safety of the expedition members must be paramount." Her voice dropped, sounding frustrated. "Someone does not want us here. But why?"

Sally looked up, wiping her face with a handkerchief. "Oh, please, let's not leave! I am frightened, but I don't want to go!"

Isabelle looked thoughtful. "When we determine whether or not the snake is poisonous, then we can decide. I believe if it is harmless," she said, her voice dropping, "we can safely say someone is still just trying to frighten us."

Genevieve's jaw tightened in anger. "I do not like this. Not at all what I had envisioned." She looked at James. "What do you suggest?"

He rubbed a hand across his tired face. "Until we decide what we're going to do, I believe we should post guards around the camp as we've done at the cave."

Genevieve nodded. "Excellent idea."

James shook his head. "I'm not much of a security force," he said to the older woman. "I ought to have thought of it before now."

"We didn't think we would need it at the camp," Genevieve said, her brows drawn. She sighed. "Someone among us is . . . not trustworthy."

Certainly an understatement. James inclined his head to the women in the tent and stepped outside. He made his way to the artifacts tent to find that Phillip had killed the snake and was examining its mouth.

"Not poisonous, as near as I can tell," Phillip said.

James nodded and glanced at Jean-Louis, who looked ill. The Stafford brothers also stood by, looking decidedly upset. Eli Montgomery regarded the snake with distaste, and William appeared perturbed.

"Could they have made an enemy of one of the workers?" Jackson Pearce asked. "It's no secret that many of them are superstitious about having women at the site."

James shrugged. "Could be." He was reluctant to say more. "We're going to need to set up security around the camp," he told them. "Phillip and I will take turns at night, paired with at least one or two of the workers we feel are trustworthy."

"I'd be happy to take a rotation," Jackson said to James. "It will grow tiring for just the two of you to take shifts night after night."

"I, also, will help," Jean-Louis said.

James shook his head. "You're needed at the cave during the daylight hours," he said. "You will want to be rested."

"If there are several of us, however, the shifts would be shorter, no? Then you are not left with the responsibility all to yourselves," the Frenchman told him.

"Thank you for your offer," Phillip said. "Let us consider the details and we will discuss it further. James and I really should take the bulk of it, though; Mrs. Montgomery is paying us well to act as security."

William snorted. "Perhaps if you stopped 'acting' and started doing, we wouldn't be having all of these problems."

James tightened his jaw and opened his mouth to retort, only to be cut off by his brother.

"Absolutely correct you are, sir," Phillip said to the elder Montgomery. "Of course you would want to see that your mother's money is being wisely spent. We aim to achieve that end."

William nodded curtly and left the tent. Following an awkward pause, the rest of the men dispersed, exchanging quiet comments as they left.

Eli remained behind. "I would also like to volunteer my services," he said to James and Phillip. "Regardless of what you're being paid to do, it would be grossly unfair to expect you to stay up night after night."

James offered his hand to the man and shook it. "Thank you. We will consider it, although you, too, are needed in the cave each day."

Eli left after saying good night, and Phillip gathered the snake to dispose of it.

"What do you think?" Phillip murmured. "Who is doing all of this?"

James shrugged, frustrated, and shook his head. "I don't know. And we don't know any of these men well enough to know if we can trust them with a shift of their own. It's going to fall on you and me, brother."

22

Isabelle was up early, despite a fitful rest throughout the night. She wore one of the new Egyptian outfits she had purchased at Karnak and reveled in the light feel of the material. The fabric was simple and durable, and as a robe that wasn't designed to show off a slender waist or well-developed décolletage, she was allowed a freedom of movement she enjoyed. She walked the camp, out toward the cave for a quarter mile, then turned around as it would soon be time for breakfast.

Her mind was spinning, trying to grasp upon any one thing that would make sense, that would sort itself out. The girls were shaken but otherwise in good spirits after the episode with the snake. Isabelle racked her brain in an effort to find elusive clues that would point to the one person or persons who wanted to see them leave the camp.

And at the base of everything, there was James. She was raw from their conversation the night before, frustrated at her own fears and irritations, and frustrated with him as well. Why couldn't he just make things simple and leave her alone? Then she could dismiss him as a cad and be done with it. But she knew that regardless of the outcome, his face would haunt her forever.

She was nearing the camp when she saw Catherine Throckmorton pacing slowly in front of the tent she shared with Adelaide. As of yet, the only other people around were the cook and a few workers who were helping him prepare the morning meal.

Catherine turned and paused in her movements when she spied

Isabelle. She stood still for a moment and then approached with determined strides. Upon reaching her, she said, "Miss Webb, may I take you into my confidence?"

Isabelle assessed the woman's appearance. She was neatly dressed, her hair in place; all seemed normal except for the unusually serious expression on her face. "Of course," Isabelle finally offered. "Is something the matter?"

Catherine took in a breath and glanced over her shoulder. She motioned slightly with her head, and together they moved away from the tents. "Adelaide is missing," Catherine said. "She was not in her cot when I awoke this morning, nearly an hour ago."

Isabelle frowned. "And this is unusual behavior for her, I take it? She is not one to enjoy an early morning stroll?"

Catherine snorted. "Hardly. She would sleep the morning away if she could."

"Does she seem to have slept in her bed at all last night?"

Catherine nodded. "After the incident with the snake, we both retired. I was exhausted; I fell asleep rather quickly, and I sleep soundly. When she would have left, I've no idea."

Isabelle glanced at the colony of tents. "Have you told the Burnses?"

Catherine shook her head. "No. I want to be certain that she's truly . . . missing . . . before I alarm them."

"You've been awake for an hour, you say?"

"Yes. When I saw that her bed was empty, I assumed she was making use of the . . ."

Isabelle nodded.

"So I readied myself for the day, walked down that way to . . ."

"Use the latrine?" Isabelle prompted.

Catherine looked at Isabelle evenly before continuing. "Yes. I thought to spare your sensibilities."

"You needn't worry about my sensibilities. Someone is missing—I do believe we can dispense with the formalities."

Catherine's nostrils flared slightly, but she gave no other outward sign of annoyance. "Needless to say, she wasn't there. I've looked all over the camp. Nothing."

"Her clothing? Anything to suggest what she might be wearing?"

Catherine nodded. "She obviously got dressed, because her night clothes are on the cot. I suppose she's wearing a simple day dress that she could manage on her own . . . she has so many outfits I'm not sure I'd even know which one is missing."

Isabelle took in a breath and looked over the encampment. People were beginning to emerge from their tents. "We need to tell the others so that we can begin a search."

Catherine pursed her lips. "I don't imagine that the Burnses will take this well. They didn't want to leave the *dahabeeyah* in the first place, and after the snake episode last night, Mrs. Burns was a bundle of raw nerves."

"Is there any particular person on the boat that Adelaide may have formed an attachment to? Perhaps they arranged some sort of assignation?"

Catherine shrugged. "Not to my knowledge. She may have wished for such a thing . . ."

Isabelle nodded. She looked speculatively at the tents and watched as the Staffords, the Montgomery brothers, Mr. Pearce, Jean-Louis, Phillip, and James milled around, exchanging morning salutations. The Staffords were in conversation with Jackson Pearce; they motioned for James and Phillip to join them.

"I wonder if she spent some time with one of these esteemed gentlemen," Isabelle said quietly.

Catherine glanced at her with a light smirk. "I assume you would take issue with only one of these esteemed gentlemen. The elder Mr. Ashby seems to be particularly . . . unavailable."

Isabelle took her gaze from the men and rested it on Catherine's face. "Miss Throckmorton, you are partially correct. I would take exception concerning one person. I do not, however, like to imagine that any one of this party would be less than circumspect in his behavior. Knowing Miss Burns for only two days . . . well, a liaison would be highly inappropriate."

"But not unheard of," Catherine said.

"No. Not unheard of. Although I just cannot imagine . . ." Isabelle shook her head with a frown. "No. I believe she is most definitely missing."

Catherine took a deep breath. "No sense forestalling the inevitable. I must go tell her aunt and uncle."

Isabelle nodded. "It seems as though everyone is converging on the meal tent. I will go and inform them of this latest bit of intrigue." She looked at Catherine and felt chagrin at her flippancy. "I am sorry," she said to the woman. "I do hope we find her well and whole."

Catherine looked at Isabelle for a moment and then nodded. "Thank you. As do I."

* * *

The mood at breakfast was subdued. James had departed immediately with Jackson Pearce to check the *dahabeeyah*, which was still docked on the Nile. Phillip grabbed a biscuit and left with Jean-Louis to inquire at the two closest villages. Mrs. Burns sat in a chair, stunned and ghostly pale, her breakfast untouched. Mr. Burns sat next to her, looking befuddled.

Sally and Alice ate well, albeit quietly. Genevieve had excused herself and gone to her tent; Maude sat in her customary chair at the dining table, deep in thought. William had excused himself shortly after his mother had and followed her to her tent. Eli toyed with his food, as did the Stafford brothers, who were uncharacteristically quiet.

Isabelle had little appetite. She tried sitting at the table but found herself too restless, and she joined Catherine, who was standing and periodically pacing. "You sent Antar ahead to the cave?" Isabelle asked Harry and Henry.

They nodded. "Mrs. Montgomery wishes to follow our customary routine," Harry told her.

No sooner had they spoken of the man when they heard a shout outside. Isabelle moved to the tent entrance and opened it, watching as Antar ran at top speed for the camp. When he reached the dining tent, Isabelle moved aside to let him enter and he doubled over, panting.

"Misters . . . Misters Stafford, you come!" Antar stammered the words, gasping.

"What is it?" Harry asked as he and Henry rose quickly to their feet.

"The big men, where are they?" Antar asked Isabelle.

"Who, the Ashbys?" she said.

He nodded. "We need them . . . we need . . ." He looked around. "They are not here?"

Isabelle gripped his shoulders. "They are not here. Tell me what is happening at the cave."

His eyes widened and he shook his head. "You cannot come."

She shook him. "Have you found Miss Burns?"

His face crumpled as though he might cry. "In the chamber . . ." he wailed.

Isabelle dropped her hands from his shoulders and left the tent, lifting her robe and breaking into a run. She covered the distance to the cave with a shouting Antar on her heels, her heart pumping in her throat. As she neared the cave, she saw a dozen workers outside, some standing or pacing, some sitting and looking stunned. Running up the path to the cave entrance, it became clear that none of the workers was still inside the cave.

The way to the corridor was lit, but she grabbed a lantern and made her way down the hallway to the antechamber. She heard Antar heaving behind her.

"Miss, you must not!" he gasped.

"Why?" she snapped and quickened her step.

"It . . . she is . . ."

"What, dead?" Irritated, Isabelle glanced over her shoulder at the man. "I've seen dead bodies before."

She rounded the corner to the antechamber and paused inside, lifting the lamp high. The light caught first on a pair of legs, awkwardly splayed, with the skirt of the dress lifted to the knees. Isabelle shifted the lantern a bit and found herself looking at the very still form of Adelaide Burns, head turned to the side and her eyes wide open. A raised, discolored bruise on her right temple had trickled blood that had run across her eyebrows and down her forehead, dripping onto the floor. The blood had dried, leaving a garish line in its path.

Isabelle slowly circled to the left, examining the back of Adelaide's head. A dark mass of blood matted her blonde hair and had pooled on the floor beneath her head. Whoever had delivered the death blow had let her fall without interfering. Her legs were at an odd angle and her left arm was trapped beneath her body.

"Miss," Antar breathed, standing near the entrance but not venturing inside, "you must leave. This place is cursed."

"Antar," Isabelle murmured, "please be still." She rubbed a hand across her forehead and tried to decide who would have wanted Adelaide dead. Could have been any one of a number of people, she supposed. But to murder someone just because she was annoying in the extreme?

A rustle of fabric caught Isabelle's attention, and she turned to see Catherine at the doorway, breathless. Isabelle watched the woman's face closely as she looked down and saw her friend's body. Her eyes widened, and she looked back up at Isabelle.

"What . . ." she breathed and slowly entered the room. She gripped Isabelle's arm and stared at Adelaide.

Isabelle slowly swung the lantern around the room, lighting the corners and looking for anything that might suggest what had happened. Aside from a broken lantern near the entrance, there was nothing there.

"Why don't you go back to the camp," Isabelle suggested quietly to Catherine. "I'm going to stay here and see that nothing is disturbed until the others return."

She felt Catherine straighten her spine. "I'll stay with you," the woman said.

Isabelle nodded. "Very well. Antar," she said to the man still standing in the entrance, "please contact a local authority. We're going to need your police."

"Yes," the man said miserably.

"Oh, and Antar, would you also please send Eli Montgomery to me."

The man murmured his assent and left, only to be replaced by the Stafford brothers, who were out of breath. When they saw Adelaide, they were both clearly dismayed.

Isabelle walked to the entrance of the room, pulling Catherine with her. "I'm going to sit here, gentlemen, until the police and the others return. I don't want anything to disturb this room until they have had a chance to look at it also." She found a crate and turned it on end, sitting on it and hanging her lantern on a hook that had been hammered into the corridor wall.

"Miss Isabelle," Harry said gravely, "I would be happy to take your place."

Henry echoed his brother's sentiments. "This is . . . very ghoulish."

Isabelle managed a smile. "Thank you, gentlemen, but the two of you need to handle the workers. I doubt seriously that any of them will set foot in here again."

Henry's face fell. "What a shame it would be," he said. "We have uncovered half of the back entrance already . . . that is, it's certainly nothing in comparison to the loss of the young woman . . ." He began to stammer, obviously embarrassed.

"I understand," Isabelle said. "Mr. Stafford, we will not abandon this excavation. Now, more than ever, I would like to see it finished."

The men made their way down the corridor and back into the outer chamber. The silence hung heavy in their absence, and Isabelle glanced at Catherine, who had also upended a crate and now sat beside her.

"I don't suppose you would like to tell me what you're doing here?" Isabelle said to her.

Catherine's expression tightened fractionally. "I'm sure I don't know what you mean," she said.

"Why are you pretending not to know Mr. Pearce?"

Catherine glanced at her. "I can't imagine what you mean. I *don't* know Mr. Pearce."

"Don't insult me."

"I owe you nothing, Miss Webb," Catherine said, looking at Isabelle. "I do not appreciate your insinuations, either."

Isabelle shrugged. "Your friend is in there, dead. Are you going to tell me that whatever it is you're doing here has nothing to do with it?"

Catherine's jaw tightened. "I have no earthly idea what happened to Adelaide, and that is the honest truth."

"You don't know why someone would want her dead?"

"Certainly not!" Catherine was quiet for a moment. "She was extremely vexing, but not so much that I can imagine someone killing her for it."

Isabelle frowned. "What, exactly, happened yesterday from, perhaps, the time we returned from Luxor?"

Catherine's brows drew together. She shrugged. "We returned to the tent, put our purchases away, ate a late dinner, retired for the evening."

"And when Sally discovered the snake in the tent? You both came running for that, I remember."

Catherine nodded. "Woke me from a sound sleep. I was quite shocked."

"And Adelaide? Was she also asleep?"

"I would assume so . . . she was in the tent when I shot out of bed. She was already at the door, looking out."

Isabelle nodded. It didn't make sense. Why had the woman come to the cave late at night? She couldn't assume Adelaide was curious about the chamber—she had already seen everything earlier. She frowned. Except for the partial excavation on the back opening in the antechamber. Might that have been the reason for her nocturnal escapade? She was hoping to find something in the other room?

"I wonder what's in there . . ." she murmured aloud.

"Where?"

Isabelle motioned with her hand. "In the other room. There's enough of the wall down to have taken a peek inside. Must be empty or Antar would have said something."

"Perhaps."

Isabelle glanced at Catherine. "Why do you say that?"

"There are many Egyptians who, alongside their European counterparts, make extreme amounts of money on antiquities. Besides," she continued, "I overheard him telling the Misters Stafford that the only thing visible in that room is another hallway that twists around, making it impossible to see beyond ten feet or so."

Isabelle nodded. They sat in silence for some time, and she said, "We may be here for a while."

Catherine took a deep breath and let it out. "I don't mind. I didn't have the courage to tell the Burnses myself. Pathetic."

"Miss Webb?" Eli Montgomery's voice sounded from the end of the corridor, and he approached them, carrying a lantern.

"Thank you for coming," Isabelle said, standing to greet him. "This will sound odd, Eli, but I wonder if you wouldn't mind looking at the scene in here with Miss Burns. You have an artist's eye for detail, and I'm interested in your impressions."

He took a deep breath. "Very well," he said.

Isabelle lifted the lantern off the wall hook and went back into the chamber. Eli drew in his breath as he saw Adelaide and hesitated, moving forward only as Isabelle did so.

"Dear heaven," he murmured. He turned his face toward Isabelle, his eyes large in the dim light. "I'm not certain what you are hoping I can tell you."

"Just look. Does anything draw your attention?" She wanted someone observant to help her sort through the details.

Eli drew his brows together and lifted his lantern over Adelaide's still form. He was quiet for a moment. "Struck from behind, as well as the front," he said, walking slowly around. He kneeled close to the back of her head and trailed the lantern down the length of her body. He held the lantern over her right hand, which lay across her body.

Ever so gently, he used his finger to tip the side of her hand slightly. Isabelle kneeled on the other side of her body, following his line of thought. She nodded. "Seems to be blood under her fingernails."

Eli looked at Isabelle. "That could mean that she either put her hand to her head here," he said, pointing to the ugly cut and bruise on her temple, "or she scratched her assailant."

"So presumably her attacker could bear marks of some sort." Isabelle looked down again at the body. "I don't want to move her before the police arrive, but I would like to see her other hand."

Eli nodded and moved his lantern, trailing it down Adelaide's side. "Dress is dirty along the bottom, several inches above the hem," he said, his voice hushed. "There's also a tear here, as though she stepped on it, or someone else did."

He stood, then, and took a step back as though he'd reached his limit. Turning away, he aimed his lantern along the back wall where it met the floor. Most of the rocks that had been removed from the doorway had been hauled away in wheelbarrows and baskets, but a few remained behind.

"It might be my imagination," he said over his shoulder, "but I think I see a dark stain on this particular rock."

Isabelle joined him. "It does appear that way," she said. The rock was large enough that Isabelle would need to use two hands to manipulate it, but she imagined that a man larger than she could manage it with one. "Why would the murderer just leave it in here to be found?"

Eli shook his head, looking at it. "Perhaps someone who was horrified and dropped it and ran."

"Or someone who didn't care if it were found or not," Isabelle said.

"Or someone who was hurt himself and ran off quickly," Catherine suggested.

Isabelle glanced at Adelaide. "How much damage could she have done?" she murmured.

Catherine wrapped her arms around her middle and turned away from the door. "I don't know," she said.

"Well," Eli said as he turned from the wall and walked toward the front of the room, "I believe that someone, somewhere, is bearing significant scratches." He raised his lantern one more time, shining it on Adelaide's shoes, which were filthy. He suddenly looked up at Isabelle. "Where were the guards?" he asked.

Isabelle shook her head. "I wondered that myself. When the police arrive, I suggest we ask a few questions of the workers."

"Do the Staffords assign the guards?" Catherine asked.

Isabelle shook her head as Eli answered, "No, Antar does."

23

Sparks reviewed the events of the last couple weeks and wondered how things had gotten so out of control. His plan to work for both the Federation and his new contact within the expedition was working nicely—the money was beginning to add up. But the situation within the camp itself was volatile. The extremes to which he and his contact had needed to resort were risky.

The guards had been dispatched easily enough—money bought anything. He was to have frightened the woman. She had been frightened, that much was true, when she entered the cave and saw him standing in a black robe with his face covered. He hadn't counted on her fighting him, though, and managing to uncover his head and do some damage to his face with her fingernails. She'd given him no choice, but when he told his contact that he'd killed the woman, the response had been less than pleasant.

If he could string the Federation along just a bit more, he would have another payment from them. That, combined with what he was now receiving for services rendered, would hold him quite well for a few years. He would finish here shortly, get away, and disappear from the world for a bit, someplace the Federation could not find him. His own search for the jewel would have to wait.

* * *

The local police official gathered simple statements from everyone in the camp and then promised to search high and low for the person responsible for Miss Burns's death. He took his leave after assigning some of his men to carry the body out on a stretcher and transport her to the *dahabeeyah,* following Mr. and Mrs. Burns's wishes.

Isabelle, Eli, and Phillip were in the antechamber when the policeman's people brought in a crude stretcher and white sheet. Isabelle bent and gently straightened the woman's legs, drawing her dress down to cover them. Phillip went to her shoulders and turned her onto her back; her body had lost its rigidity and was pliable.

Isabelle went to her side and carefully pulled the left arm out from beneath her body. The knuckles were bent and scraped, her fingernails again showing signs of blood and also skin. Isabelle glanced at Eli. "It's not her blood," she murmured.

Eli nodded, his jaw clenching. He swallowed and then cleared his throat. He looked at Adelaide's face, his expression pained. Isabelle watched him for a moment and turned back to the body. Placing Adelaide's hands together and tucking her arms in tightly, she moved to allow the others to place her on the stretcher.

After draping her with the sheet, two men picked up either end of the stretcher and lifted it. Isabelle watched the proceedings with a sense of familiarity. She'd seen it more times than she would have liked. Just like that, the body was truly just a body, a shell. Once covered, it seemed all the more final.

As the men moved toward the entrance with the stretcher, Adelaide's left arm slipped free and dropped down, causing Isabelle's heart to skip a beat. She took a deep breath, fixated on the hand that bore the traces of her attacker. She called to the men to stop, and she carefully lifted the arm back onto the stretcher. She pushed Adelaide's hand higher onto her middle, placing it again atop the other hand. As she hovered to be sure it was securely placed, her fingers brushed the corner of something that had slipped free from the sleeve.

It felt like folded paper, and Isabelle pulled it out and slipped it under her own cuff. She removed her hands from Adelaide's slender arm and tucked the sheet firmly against her side. Eli quietly did the same on the other side.

The men moved forward again. Phillip, Eli, and Isabelle stood behind, looking at the quiet room. The ibis in the mural looked on, keeping her secrets. The spent blood on the floor was a hideous remainder of what had once been a life.

"Phillip, I wonder if you would go check on Sally for me? She is still a bit shaken after the episode last night with the snake," Isabelle said.

Phillip looked at her with a question in his expression but said, "Absolutely. I believe she is at the canopy with Alice and the other women."

"Thank you." She waited, and when Eli turned to leave, she said, "A moment?"

Eli turned back. "Yes?"

Isabelle moved closer to him. "Eli, did you ever speak with Miss Burns alone?"

Eli drew his brows together. "Why do you ask?"

Isabelle paused. "It's none of my business, surely, but did you have tender feelings for her?"

"I'm not sure I know what you mean, Miss Webb," he said and moved to leave.

Isabelle planted herself in front of him. "Mr. Montgomery, did you know Miss Burns before she and her party arrived here?"

"I did not know her, certainly not. What are you suggesting?"

"Eli, forgive me, but I sense that her death has affected you very strongly."

He stared at her, his expression flat but giving way to indecision. His gaze flickered away from hers and rested on a spot beyond her shoulder. "I pitied her," he said. "She . . . she caught me alone for a moment when we were at a shop at Luxor. She suggested that I . . . that we . . ."

Eli ran a hand through his hair and stepped back a pace from Isabelle. He looked at the blood stain on the floor and shook his head. "She was lonely. I believe she was desperate for things she didn't have. Companionship. Money. In truth, she reminded me of my wife when we first met." He was quiet for a moment. "Ironic that I seem to draw the same type of woman, clear across the world."

"What did you say to her proposition?" Isabelle asked him softly.

He shook his head again. "I told her no, naturally. She was outrageously forward. I felt enormous pity for her. I knew that if she did find someone who would provide her with the life she wanted, it would ultimately be a loveless match."

Isabelle watched the man, feeling an enormous amount of pity herself. Eli clearly spoke from experience. "Adelaide was very beautiful," she said.

"Yes, she was." Eli put his hands in his pockets and looked at the floor as though seeing her there still.

"Did she approach you after Luxor, last night? Did you spend any time alone with her?"

He snapped his head in Isabelle's direction. "Certainly not," he said. "I did not speak with her alone beyond the one time at the market." He paused. "Do you think I had something to do with this?"

"Not at all. I would like to be able to reconstruct her final hours, though."

He shrugged. "I saw her outside your tent when we had the excitement with the snake."

"Did you and your brother exit your tent together when you came to investigate?"

"Again, Miss Webb, what are you suggesting?" Eli turned toward her and joined her at the entrance. "Are you hoping he will verify that I was with him?"

Isabelle rubbed the back of her neck. "I am trying to fit the details together." She smiled a bit. "Much like a puzzle. My brain will not let me rest when there are pieces out of order."

He sighed. "I awoke to Miss Rhodes's screams. William and I bolted to the door and ran out. We reached your tent moments after you did."

Isabelle nodded and led the way into the corridor and toward the front chamber of the cave. "Will you be so good as to tell me if you remember anything unusual? About anyone?"

He nodded.

"And thank you very much for your help today. I have come to appreciate James's judgment in matters of . . . perplexity. When he was unavailable this morning, I felt I needed observations from someone with a good visual sense." She paused. "I am sorry—it must have been unpleasant for you to see her in such a state, even though she had been inappropriate in her attentions toward you."

Eli shrugged. He opened his mouth then closed it. The pained expression Isabelle had seen earlier flashed in his eyes. "I suppose I was flattered," he admitted. "Flattered but sad."

Isabelle nodded and surprised him by taking the crook of his arm. "I understand." They walked out of the darkened cave to see Adelaide's body in the distance as it was carried toward the camp.

* * *

Isabelle sat in her tent with Sally and Alice. "I understand how much you like him," she murmured to Alice. "I need you to consider the fact, however, that our problems began when we met everyone in this expedition. Jean-Louis may not be all he appears to be."

Alice flushed. "Isabelle," she hissed, "I trust him with my life!"

"I do not. At this point, trusting him with your life may just be what it comes to, and I am not willing to risk it. I'm not telling you to cease speaking to the man. I just don't want you to be alone with him. I don't want either of you alone with anyone other than me, James, or Phillip."

"What of Genevieve or Maude?" Sally said.

"I should think they would be safe enough, but again, our problems began when we met up with them. I've known Genevieve for years . . ." She paused. "I sincerely doubt you've anything to fear from either or them, but I keep thinking about how things have played out since we met them."

"Belle, our problems began much earlier than that. I think Mr. Jones is responsible for all of this. He knew Alice and I were going to be on that ship. He's been following us ever since."

"Nobody knew you were on that ship. You were inadvertently smuggled aboard."

"Aha, but we were *supposed* to be on it. For all Mr. Sparks knew, we *were* on it. Ari had purchased the tickets, and he and Mr. Sparks were to sail with us to Suez, do you not remember?"

Isabelle sighed. "I do remember. It doesn't matter. Trust no one. I'm going to see about getting us back to Cairo and home."

The girls chorused their protests. She held up a hand and said, "We'll discuss it later. Now we need to go meet with the others at the canopy."

Genevieve held a meeting that was short and to the point. She made it clear that any further mishaps would result in the closure of the excavation and hoped that everyone involved would do the decent thing and take care of one another. It was decided that work would continue as planned—the few Egyptian workers still left were offered double their salaries to stay on. The work would continue for another four weeks unless other problems arose.

The Burnses and Catherine Throckmorton left for the *dahabeeyah,* along with Adelaide's body, James, and William. Catherine thanked Isabelle for her help and left without another word to anyone. Isabelle had noticed a rather pointed glance in Jackson Pearce's direction, but if Catherine had spoken to him alone, Isabelle was unaware of it. She was slightly vexed at the thought that she might never know the nature of the connection between the two. She felt an enormous sense of relief that the woman hadn't singled James out for any further attention.

She hardly knew what to do with the man herself. Her pride kept her from fully acknowledging that he was not altogether wrong in his criticism of her midnight visit to the cave. She was forced to admit, however, that the thought that he might have been interested in Catherine, or any other woman, had set her heart racing and her blood boiling. How fair was she being, then? She wasn't sure she could handle him but didn't want anyone else to have him either?

With a sigh, she sat alone in the canopy while others tried to resume familiar activities. She quietly withdrew the small square of paper she had taken from Adelaide's dead body and read it once again.

2:00 AM at the cave.

The ink was black, written in a nondescript hand that betrayed little except for the fact that the letters were traditionally formed, using script that one learned in grammar school. The ink had been smudged slightly upon folding, the corners of the square bent and creased as the paper was hid in Adelaide's sleeve. The handwriting itself could have been penned by any one of the group; still, Isabelle had determined it wouldn't hurt to observe various handwriting samples from the members of the expedition.

"Isabelle," Sally said as she entered the canopy, placing the strap of her shoulder bag over her head and across her body. "Alice and I would like to accompany Jean-Louis to the cave. Phillip has agreed to go with us," she added in an undertone.

Isabelle nodded absently and tucked the small paper back inside her sleeve. She was debating whether or not to arrange travel back to Cairo for herself and the girls. From Cairo, they would go by train to Alexandria and then sail across the Mediterranean, traveling again by train through Europe, across the English Channel to England where they would see Alice settled, and then home to America. She knew James and Phillip had the same route planned for their return journey; she wasn't sure that they were ready to leave so soon, though. The thought crossed her mind that she could use the girls' safety as an excuse to leave James behind. It was logical, after all. The odds of him staying in Egypt if she left, however, were probably slim. The thought of leaving him made her slightly sick to her stomach, and she closed her eyes in frustration.

Isabelle sighed as Sally joined Alice and Phillip. Perhaps the trip home would be enough of a diversion for the young women that they would get over their disappointment of leaving the excavation early. She sat under the canopy, lost in thought.

She looked out over the vast desert floor. The breeze that rustled through the camp was comfortable—neither too warm nor too cold. The fact that Christmas was approaching lent an air of celebration to the setting despite the recent macabre happenings. Isabelle turned her head at the sound of footsteps light in the sand.

"Miss Webb," Jean-Louis said, approaching with Maude's pamphlet in his hand, "I would like to show you something of interest."

"Please, do call me Isabelle," she said and motioned to a seat next to hers.

He nodded, but Isabelle knew she'd probably tell him the same thing again, as she had a dozen times before. "I was reviewing the glyphs in the back of Mrs. Davis's book, and I noticed something familiar."

"Yes?" Isabelle leaned in and looked as he pointed to a spot on the page.

"In the cave, on the hieroglyphs in the main chamber and then again hidden in the painting in the antechamber is this odd symbol— the rectangle with its three ovals—but notice here, this is a symbol

I believe is meant to represent the ibis, and next to it we see a five-pointed star."

Isabelle sucked in her breath as she looked at the symbols he indicated on the page. "You said these symbols are hidden in the painting?"

He nodded. "I happened to be looking in just the right place with a magnifying glass. In the antechamber painting, the ibis is standing in a burial room. The hieroglyphs on the walls in the painting are miniature and nearly indiscernible. There is, however, a clear image of the rectangle with the ovals, the five-pointed star, and the ibis."

Isabelle transferred her gaze from the book to his face. "What do you suppose it means?"

Jean-Louis shrugged. "I haven't the least idea. I was hoping you might know, as it caught your eye in the Great Pyramid. I am most anxious to learn the secret behind it."

"I wish I could tell you what it means, but I haven't a clue either," she said. "It is most interesting, though, isn't it?"

He studied her for a moment before nodding, almost as though in resignation. "It is. Well, I best be on my way to the cave. The young ladies are anxious to continue our work on the walls."

Isabelle smiled at him. "Thank you for your patience with them. I do hope they're not a hindrance to your work."

He returned the smile. "Not in the least," he said.

Isabelle sat for some time in the canopy, thinking. James planned to speak to the guards who were on duty the night before, and she wanted to be there for it. He would be gone for some time, however, and in the meantime, she had a burning question for Phillip.

She wondered if his birthmark bothered him while in the cave. If such were the case, she could come to only one conclusion: there must be more than one jewel.

24

Isabelle made her way to the cave with her shoulder bag, determined to never again be caught without it. The dust kicked up with the breeze, covering her and everything around her with a light film. By the time she reached the cave, she was grateful to be inside.

She found Jean-Louis, Phillip, and the girls in the antechamber. Jean-Louis's face lit up when he saw her, and he motioned her close.

"Look through this," he said, holding a magnifying glass to the ancient painting on the wall.

Isabelle saw clearly the symbols he had referenced earlier. It couldn't be a coincidence that there was a five-pointed star on the wall and that Alice's back hurt without her talisman. She carefully considered the rectangle with the three ovals. There had to be more than one stone, and it must be in close proximity.

She looked at the progress being made on the arched opening at the back of the room. The workers had it three-fourths of the way uncovered, and the Staffords were moving back and forth through the opening.

"We've found another doorway, Miss Isabelle," Harry told her as he stepped through. "It looks to be similar to these other two."

"May I look?" she asked him.

"Certainly." He paused. "Do not touch anything, if you please!"

She smiled. "I shall clasp my hands behind my back." He turned back around and stepped through the opening. She carefully followed, avoiding the lanterns that had already been hammered into the walls.

The corridor stretched roughly ten feet in front of them and then turned at a ninety-degree angle to the right, where it continued for an additional four feet. "We must be quick," Henry said as he scribbled a few notes in his notebook. "There isn't room for us and the workers at the same time. They've nearly finished the other archway, and I will put them to work on this one as soon as possible."

Isabelle stretched her hand forward then pulled it back with a smile at Harry.

"You may touch it," he said. "Once."

She laughed and he smiled at her. The stone was cool and rough to the touch. She placed her palm flat on the stones that barred the entrance to yet another chamber, and she wondered what lay inside.

"May I help haul rocks?" she asked.

"Surely not, Miss Isabelle," Henry told her.

"Truly, I would like to help. I've no wish to copy any more hieroglyphs. I want to see what's beyond this wall."

The brothers looked at each other and shrugged. "If you wish it, then," Harry said.

Before long, she was pushing a wheelbarrow full of rocks and dirt out of the cave entrance and into the bright sunlight. The physical labor felt good, and she used the time to review the events that had transpired since arriving on the shores of Egypt until the present.

She had so many questions. How was it that Genevieve had happened to be in Egypt when Isabelle arrived? While in India, Isabelle had been dreaming of Genevieve and then suddenly, there she was again, back in her life. It didn't make sense, and that bothered her.

Was Sparks on their trail, and if so, how had he managed to track them so completely without showing his face? Was he the one responsible for the note on her pillow, the voice at the window on the *dahabeeyah* and outside her tent, the snake . . .

Who was Jackson Pearce, and what was his business at the site? His proclaimed interest in the dig was flimsy at best. Who was Catherine Throckmorton, and what was her connection to Pearce? What was the "Federation" he had spoken of? Who had met Adelaide Burns at the cave and then killed her? And why?

Was Jean-Louis Deveraux all he appeared to be? Why had he seemed so interested in Isabelle's opinion of the odd symbols on the wall? Why was William Montgomery so miserably surly all the time? Eli Montgomery was layer upon layer of mystery, a man who seemed to have the soul of an anguished poet at the very least.

Antar was an efficient enough foreman but certainly seemed to have an agenda of his own. She had no doubt he had illegally sold antiquities. But was he genuinely superstitious or simply putting on a show in hopes of scaring the expedition away once they had done the bulk of the work for him?

Harry and Henry Stafford had perfected the ideal front for people with a hidden motive. They were happy and innocent in appearance—for all she knew their performance was designed to deceive.

Isabelle made her way in and out of the cave so many times she lost count. Her brain spun with possibilities, options considered and then discarded; she was even beginning to question Maude Davis's sincerity. Surely the old woman was simply that and nothing more? Just a person with a long-abiding interest in ancient Egypt?

After some time had passed, Phillip, Sally, and Alice met her as she was heading back into the cave with an empty wheelbarrow. "We're going to camp for lunch," Sally told her. "Won't you join us?"

Isabelle shook her head. "I'll be along shortly, though. You'll stay with the ladies, Phillip?"

"Certainly." He looked at her closely. "Are you feeling well, Isabelle?"

"I'm fine. I suppose I'm restless." She shooed them off on their way and returned to the cave.

Harry Stafford met her at the antechamber. "Come and see!" he fairly shouted at her. "Leave that here!"

She dropped the wheelbarrow handles and quickly followed him into the smaller corridor and around the abrupt turn. The doorway leading into the new chamber was uncovered to the point that she could almost see into the room if she stood on her toes.

"Here," Henry said and shoved a crate at her feet. "Stand on this and look inside! Hold the lantern high!"

Her heart beating quickly, Isabelle took the lantern from him and stood on the crate. What she saw when she looked over the stone enclosure took her breath away. The room was cavernous and filled with objects. Perhaps the most striking thing, though, was the enormous sarcophagus at the center of it all.

* * *

The rapidity with which the word spread was amazing. It had been only a handful of hours since the discovery had been made, and already the camp was crawling with Egyptologists from the Valley of the Kings and the Valley of the Queens. There were even three European newsmen on hand, asking questions of the Staffords, Genevieve, and anyone else they could get their hands on.

To their credit, the Stafford brothers remained completely in control of the chaos. They dictated who could see the burial chamber and when, and they posted guards outside of the cave and again at the antechamber. They saw to it that once the rest of the opening was uncovered, the artifacts within where carefully documented, sketched where they were found, and then gingerly transported to the artifacts tent where there were posted an additional two guards.

They did accept the services of two experienced archaeologists from a neighboring dig to help with conservation work. Harry stayed in the artifacts tent with them and directed those efforts. Henry remained in the burial chamber itself.

In the meantime, James and William had returned from accompanying Catherine and the Burnses to their *dahabeeyah*. Isabelle found James trying to corner a giddily euphoric Antar and discover who had been on guard at the cave when Adelaide was murdered. Jackson Pearce stood with James and looked ready to throttle the Egyptian foreman.

"I am telling you, I do not remember!" Antar said, his happiness fading and his temper beginning to show.

"I asked you to find two men you trusted," James said to him, "and you told me that was done. Not only were they *not* to be trusted, but now you can't even remember who they were?"

Jackson shifted his weight slightly toward the man, and Isabelle watched with interest. "A woman was murdered in that cave last night," he said, slowly inching his way into Antar's space, "and you may find yourself bearing responsibility for it if you can't tell us who the guards were."

Antar took a small step back. "I will find them," he said with a scowl. "I will bring them to you when I do."

James nodded and turned to Isabelle, looking tired. She approached the two and tried for a nonchalance she wasn't sure she mustered. "How was your little journey?" she asked them.

Jackson rubbed his eyes. "Dusty," he said. "And unfortunate. The poor woman's relatives are beside themselves."

"So something of interest has turned up, I imagine?" James asked.

"Indeed." Isabelle told them about the discovery of the burial chamber and the influx of new people.

"Wonderful," James groaned. "It was bad enough trying to maintain a secure site when there were just a handful of us here."

"I will gladly help you," Jackson told him. "We can take turns on watch."

Isabelle motioned to the artifacts tent. "The Staffords have set up guards there and also at the cave. Supposing they are trustworthy, that should help the cause as well."

The day gave way to evening, and Isabelle was amazed at the progress the Stafford brothers made. The bulk of the artifacts had been transferred to the security of the guarded tent. As Harry came down for a quick dinner, he told Genevieve that he would very much like all the members of the expedition to be present when he opened the sarcophagus.

Nearly an hour later, they all stood inside the burial chamber, excepting James, who stayed behind to help guard the artifacts tent. It was with a hushed reverence that Harry and Henry broke the seal on the massive structure and lifted the lid. Within was another, smaller sarcophagus wearing a burial mask with features undeniably feminine and beautiful.

Lifting the inner lid, Harry and Henry pulled it completely away with some help from Phillip and William. Isabelle felt a chill slip up her spine as she looked upon the mummy of a woman who had been dead for thousands of years. Sally clasped one of Isabelle's hands and one of Alice's.

"Oh, mercy," she breathed. "It's the pharaoh's daughter."

25

Sparks felt his palms begin to sweat as he pulled the swath of fabric hanging from his turban closer about his face. He had been hiding from the expedition all day, tempted to flee. He had heard of the excitement, however, and knew that if he didn't take the opportunity now, it would never come his way again. The jewel had to be there in the cave, perhaps on the mummy itself.

He had been close enough to overhear things. He knew Phillip's back was bothering him. The younger Ashby bore the mark—what else could it be but the jewel that called to him? Sparks knew that tensions ran high and that there was extreme superstition on the part of the locals who believed the cave to be haunted or cursed by the vengeful spirit of a pharaoh's disgraced daughter.

It was clear that he wouldn't be able to make any more money from the Federation; they likely wanted him dead. He hadn't been able to secure a relationship with Phillip Ashby, and they must know it by now. They had eyes everywhere.

He would visit the cave tonight, and he wouldn't leave without the jewel. It was now his only hope for survival.

* * *

"Isabelle, a moment please," Genevieve said.

Isabelle rose from her seat under the canopy where the Staffords were regaling her, James, and the girls with details about the things they had discovered. She joined the older woman out on the small street between the tents and took her outstretched hand.

"What is it?" she asked Genevieve. "What's wrong?"

"Walk with me. I've received word from my friend in Cairo," she said as they moved away from the canopy. "Jackson Pearce *was* indeed a professor at Oxford."

"*Was?*"

Genevieve nodded. "He passed away nearly a month ago. People weren't too terribly sad for him—he'd lived a good life and died at age eighty-seven."

Isabelle stopped walking. "Then who is traveling with us?"

Genevieve looked at her, her eyes large and showing fear. "I don't know."

"*Where* is he?"

"I don't know that either. I sent William looking for him; he can't find him."

* * *

Jackson Pearce paced away from the camp, fighting emotion. He had overheard Mrs. Montgomery speaking to her son, and while it boded no good for him, it also brought him wretched news that formed a lump in his throat.

He walked and then broke into a run. The sun had set and the stars were coming out, twinkling into existence over a tired earth. He reached and passed the entrance to the cave, finally slowing when it seemed as though his heart would pound out of his chest. He turned slowly and walked back, wondering how he was going to explain himself. Surely his ruse was up, and he would be hard-pressed to have them believing anything he said from that point forward.

Catherine Throckmorton had set Isabelle Webb on alert, of that he was certain. Little slipped Isabelle's notice—he had watched the things he said around her so closely that it was a chore. Even though he was used to playing a part, she was quick and he saw her calculating assessment of him in her eyes.

The Federation was on to him as well, and that was quite possibly the worst news of all. A price on his head from that quarter meant he had few options. They had sent Catherine as a warning, and he doubted whatever she reported to them was likely to set their minds at ease concerning him. He had avoided her in Cairo for over a year, knowing full well she might recognize him from his resemblance to his family.

He was at a bend nearing the cave when he heard the shots. Straining to see in the darkness, he caught a flurry of movement. Staying close to the mountain wall, he quietly made his way to the path leading up to the cave.

The two guards lay on the ground, unmoving, stains of red spreading across the chest of one, the face of the other. He pulled his gun out of the back of his waistband and started moving up the path when he heard someone running toward him.

He readied his weapon and squinted to see who approached. He started in some surprise as he recognized Phillip Ashby.

"Did you see someone?" Phillip asked. He was breathing hard and paused momentarily to examine the guards on the ground. He ground out a curse and looked back up, his eyes blazing.

Pearce held one hand up in supplication. "I didn't shoot these men," he said. "Whoever did ran into the cave."

"It's a man by the name of Sparks! I saw him running past the camp." Phillip joined him on the path. "I will kill him with my own hands."

"Are you sure it was him?"

Phillip looked at him. "How do you know who he is?"

"I will explain later. Do you have a weapon?"

Phillip shook his head. "I didn't have time to get it," he said, lowering his voice as they entered the cave.

Another shot rang out, followed by a discernible groan.

"Stay behind me." Pearce led the way into the outer chamber. He crept along the wall to the first corridor, noting a faint, flickering glow bouncing off the wall in the antechamber.

They progressed quickly, quietly down the length of the corridor and paused at the entrance. The guard posted there lay slumped on the floor. The light dimmed and they stepped across the body and entered the room, following the fading light into the second, smaller corridor that led to the burial chamber.

Pausing outside the door, listening and trying to quiet his breathing, he put a finger to his lips and felt Phillip's nod. He heard movement inside the room and a curse as the man inside tripped over something. There was an audible grunt, a heavy scrape, and a thundering crash.

He poked his head slightly forward to see into the room. Sparks was facing the doorway, having just shoved the lid of the sarcophagus onto the ground. Pearce quickly flattened his head against the wall, stilling his movements.

The sound of more movement, scraping, rustling, and swearing came from the area. Phillip edged slowly forward and pressed against Pearce, angry and physically wound tighter than a spring. Pearce shook his head at Phillip and restrained him with his arm, wanting to attempt to catch Sparks with his back to them.

Sparks's frustration grew palpable as his movements caused more noise, his cursing growing more violent. "Where are you?" Sparks muttered. *"Where are you?"*

Pearce risked looking again in time to see Sparks hoist a large metal excavating tool with one hand and strike it against the wall. The man grunted with his efforts, his breath coming in gasps.

Jackson Pearce glanced back at Phillip and nodded. He motioned for him to stay close behind him and quietly entered the chamber. He approached Sparks, moving slowly, his gun drawn. Sparks must have sensed him, because he ceased his maniacal beating on the wall and swung his left arm up, bearing a pistol.

"Drop your weapon," Jackson shouted and squeezed off a shot a fraction of a second too late as Sparks's weapon recoiled and the bullet entered Jackson's side like a javelin of fire.

In a haze, he watched as Phillip Ashby rushed from behind him, taking Sparks to the ground and smashing the man's head against the wall in the process. Ashby straddled him, his hands wrapped around Sparks's neck.

Pearce grasped his side, feeling the blood slide through his fingers. He gulped and coughed, crawling across the floor to Phillip. "You'll regret it," he managed to get out between coughs. "You will always regret it."

The world went black.

* * *

James jogged down the path toward the cave, trying to find his brother. They needed to discuss security shifts for the night, and he had searched the entire camp twice, trying to find him. He was growing uneasy; they had made a point of telling each other where they were going and when they would be back.

"James!"

He turned around to see Isabelle running toward him. "You think he's at the cave?"

"I don't know." He continued running, knowing Isabelle would keep up with him.

"I'll look in there for you," she said.

"I can manage it."

She didn't argue with him, and he appreciated it. He slowed when they approached the path leading to the cave and saw the guards lying on the ground.

"Oh no," Isabelle said and sprinted up the path in front of him. He followed her, his heart beating in his throat.

"Stay right behind me," Isabelle said. She bent to pick up a lantern and lit it with the matches littering the ground.

If he weren't so frantic, he would have been glad just to have her speaking to him. Making their way slowly through the outer chamber and into the corridor, James focused on the back of Isabelle's head and nothing else. She walked quickly through the long hallway and caught her breath, stopping at the entrance to the antechamber. He looked around her and saw another guard on the floor.

He followed her through the antechamber and into another corridor, feeling as though the world was closing in on him. His breathing grew shallow, coming in quick gasps. He felt Isabelle reaching for his hand. She grasped it and held on tightly, pulling him forward.

The cave was still. As they made their way into another room, he heard the first sounds of life. He let Isabelle lead him farther into the other room, where a lit lantern sat on the floor. Coupled with the light from Isabelle's lamp, he saw the scene clearly.

Phillip was in the process of standing up, his hair forward across his forehead, sweat glistening and rolling down his nose and the sides of his face, his breathing ragged and angry. At his feet lay a still form.

Isabelle pulled James toward his brother, setting her lantern down. She released James's hand and touched Phillip's arm.

"This would be Mr. Sparks, I presume?" she asked.

Phillip looked at her and then at James, his eyes huge, crazed. "I think I've killed him."

Isabelle kneeled down and put her hand over Sparks's face. "He's breathing," she said. "And who might this be? Oh, Mr. Pearce. Or *not* Mr. Pearce." She stepped away from Sparks and kneeled down by another body James hadn't even noticed. She looked up at Phillip. "What happened?"

Phillip shook his head. "He knew who Sparks was. I don't know how. Sparks shot him . . . he told me I would regret killing Sparks . . ."

James looked down at the man and winced. "Looks like a shot to his abdomen."

Isabelle glanced up at him. "Do you think you could manage him? He's very nearly your size . . ."

"He's breathing?" James asked.

She nodded. "We need to get him back to camp. I believe one of our admiring visitors from the other sites might be a doctor."

"Many of them have left," James said as he bent over Pearce and pulled him up by one arm.

"Some of them have made use of the Burnses' and Catherine's tents," Isabelle said as she went back to Sparks's side. "I thought I heard one of them say he was a physician. Maude was talking to him about a strained muscle . . ."

James maneuvered the unconscious man up and squatting, he stood with Pearce hauled up and over his good shoulder. He made the mistake of looking to the side and felt the walls of the room begin to slide in toward him. He staggered a bit under the weight and nearly dropped Pearce.

"James, I'll come with you right now. Don't drop him if you can help it," Isabelle said and grabbed her lantern. "Follow me closely. Phillip, can you manage Sparks?"

"Yes," came the response, and James followed Isabelle as she left the room.

The narrow corridor was nearly his undoing, and he stumbled

against the wall, eliciting a barely discernible groan from his passenger. How he made it through the rest of the cave he would never know nor care to remember.

Once outside, he breathed in huge gulps of air and slid to the ground at the bottom of the path. He rolled Pearce as gently as possible onto his back and then removed his own jacket. Ripping Pearce's shirt open, he searched for the wound. It was low on his left side. James then took off his own shirt and folded it, placing it against the gushing wound and wrapping the arms of his jacket around the man's body to hold the makeshift bandage in place.

He looked up to see Phillip exit the cave with Sparks over his shoulder. He, too, laid his burden on the ground, although none too gently.

"I'll come back with help," Isabelle said and ran toward the camp.

"She's amazing," Phillip said wearily and dropped to the ground next to James. "I see now where Sally gets her pluck."

James bent his knees and, placing his forearms on them, hung his head and breathed in deeply. He felt Phillip clasp his shoulder.

"Nicely done, brother."

James raised his head and looked at Phillip. "Now then, would you mind telling me what happened?"

26

The man using Catherine and Adelaide's tent was indeed a French doctor. He took both patients into the tent and sent for his assistant, who was at the Valley of the Kings. "I will do what I can do," he told Isabelle and James. He asked Phillip to stay with him in the tent and answer some questions about the men's injuries.

Isabelle had found the Staffords and asked them to get word to Antar that they again were in need of local police. Everyone had been congregating under the canopy when she had run into camp and breathlessly explained that she was in need of a couple of donkeys and carts. People had scattered after that, some moving to accommodate her request, others peppering her with questions.

Her head was spinning and she longed for a few minutes of peace and quiet to simply sit and think things through. She had many questions for both patients, and she expressed as much to James as they sat in the dining tent.

"I wish they were both conscious," she said as she gratefully accepted a cup of tea and plate of flatbread with jelly.

James nodded, his face still looking a bit pale.

She put her cup down and absently traced circles around the rim. "Something still isn't making sense to me," she murmured. "As far as I can tell, Sparks was not aboard our *dahabeeyah* when I received the note and heard the voice at the window."

James nodded slowly, thoughtfully. "Unless he was disguised as one of the crew," he said. He picked up his flatbread, looked at it, and set it back down on his plate.

Isabelle smiled at him, yearning for the normalcy they'd enjoyed until only recently. "James, it's jelly. You like jelly."

"I don't have much of an appetite yet," he said.

Her heart lurched a little, and she reached for his hand, clasping it in her own. "You were incredible," she said.

He shook his head with a roll of the eyes. "Can't even handle a little cave," he muttered.

"Don't demean yourself. What you did was nothing short of amazing."

Genevieve appeared at the door and gave a soft knock on the table. "May I join you?" she asked.

"Of course," James said, rising and pulling a chair out for her.

"It would appear that our problems are nearing an end," Genevieve said with a sigh.

Isabelle nodded slightly. "I hope so."

Genevieve looked at her. "What do you mean?"

"It seems too good to be true," she hedged.

"Hmm." Genevieve studied her for a moment and then looked at James. "I must thank you for all you're doing—this adventure is shaping up to be an odd one, for certain."

James shook his head. "I've not done anything noteworthy, ma'am. So far, under my competent hand, people have been nearly buried alive, threatened with reptiles, and shot."

"Your being here is a strength to me," she said. "You and your brother have taken good care of both Maude and me. I had hoped Isabelle would meet someone of your good nature."

James nodded his thanks, and Isabelle smiled but refrained from saying anything. He mumbled something about checking on the young women since Phillip was being interrogated by the doctor.

Isabelle waited until he was gone and then turned her attention to the Benefactress. "Why did you happen to come to Egypt right before I arrived?" she asked the woman without preamble.

Genevieve looked at her in surprise then pursed her lips in thought. "I had been dreaming about you, Isabelle," she said. "Ages ago, when in reality you would have still been at home. In my dreams you were far away and you needed comfort. When Maude suggested we go on an adventure and do something fun with my money, it suddenly felt right." She was quiet for a moment. "I knew I would find you here. When we happened upon the girls in Suez just before going to Cairo . . . they talked about you and I knew you were on your way."

She gave Isabelle a small smile and a shrug. "I . . . I don't know. I wanted . . ." Her voice broke. "I wanted to be here for you."

"You have always been here for me, Genevieve," Isabelle said, her throat suddenly feeling tight.

Genevieve shook her head. She opened her mouth and then closed it again. When she finally spoke, it was to change the subject. "You might want to relax a bit while you can. I believe the police are going to be anxious to question all of us about . . . this," she said, waving a hand to encompass the whole area.

Isabelle nodded. Rising, she kissed Genevieve on the cheek and walked with her out of the dining tent. Slapping a hand to her forehead, she realized she needed to speak with the Staffords. "Sparks made a mess in the burial chamber," she said. "I didn't even take a moment to look at the mummy. He was searching for . . ."

She broke off and went in search of the brothers. While she was looking for them, a new influx of people arrived with the doctor's assistant. A reporter snagged her arm and asked her to tell him the story of the cursed cave and what had happened inside. Amidst all the people and questions, she failed to see a member of the expedition who stood in the shadows and watched the tent where Sparks and Pearce lay unconscious, waiting for the right moment.

* * *

James made a quiet visual sweep of the tent row, walking around the perimeter of the camp and taking in the night air and its accompanying sounds. All was relatively quiet, for the moment, anyway. The hour approached three, and he was hopeful that the lack of noise coming from the tents meant that the entourage was finally getting some sleep.

The shadows shifted and threw images with the wind, so he wondered if he was seeing things when he noticed a quiet form slinking behind Isabelle's tent. Squinting in the darkness, he crept toward the tent, quietly making his way around the back side. By this time, the figure had moved on, passed his tent where Phillip and Jean-Louis slept, and stopped at the tent that Pearce and Sparks occupied.

The glint of a knife blade flashed in the moonlight as the figure quietly slashed a long line in the fabric, through which he then climbed. James broke into a run and shouted, making it to the cut in the tent just as the man had lifted the knife high over Thaddeus Sparks. It was dark, but when the assailant turned and looked at James in shock, James saw his face.

The man ran for the tent flap on the opposite side and tore through it, jostling the guard that stood outside. James struggled through the slashed tent fabric, his foot catching in his haste and sending him sprawling across Thaddeus Sparks, who grunted in pain and surprise.

James muttered his apologies to Sparks, who by this time was shouting and grabbing at James's arm. Pulling free with a shouted explanation, James staggered to his feet and made for the tent door in time to see the assailant running away from the camp.

* * *

Isabelle was beginning to wonder if the camp was destined to get a full night's sleep ever again. She heard a sound in the darkness that pulled her awake and had her sitting, disoriented for a moment, in her cot.

"What was that?" Sally asked, her voice groggy. She and Alice both stirred on their cots and also sat up.

"Shh," Isabelle whispered and quietly swung her legs over the side of her bed. She had donned a clean Egyptian robe for sleeping, and it twisted around her middle as she moved and stood. With an impatient tug, she fixed it while she slipped her feet into her shoes. She pulled her shoulder bag over her head and across her body, motioning for the girls to stay in the tent.

"Belle," Sally whispered, "please don't go out there."

A shout broke the stillness of the night and Isabelle ventured quickly outside, senses on alert. She looked to her left and saw Phillip emerge from his tent. He rubbed his eyes and looked from left to right. When he saw her, he said, "Where did it come from?"

A blur behind the tents caught Isabelle's eye, and another darkened form soon followed. She recognized James as the person giving chase, and she yelled to Phillip, "Help him!"

Phillip looked where she was pointing and began to run as Isabelle found her gun in her bag. She soon also ran behind the others, trying to make out the forms in the darkness. She saw James leap and take down the man he'd been chasing. Phillip was soon upon them and helped his brother restrain the prisoner.

Isabelle caught up to them, a gun in one hand and the fabric of her robe in the other. In her haste to see who James had pinned to the ground, she forgot she had lifted the robe up to run. At Phillip's averted gaze, she hastily dropped the fabric and moved closer to James.

"Who is it?" she asked, looking at the back of the man's head.

The man turned his head with a curse and she caught his profile.

"William." She was forced to admit it caught her by surprise.

"Isabelle, will you please go back to camp and find a length of rope?" James asked her.

"Release me now—this is an outrage!" William's face was twisted with fury. "I was on my way to the latrine!"

"By way of the doctor's tent? At the opposite end of the camp? With a knife?" James asked him, kneeling on William's back while the man struggled to be free. Phillip pinned William's legs to the ground, and James wrenched the man's arms up higher behind him. William grunted in pain.

Isabelle handed Phillip her gun. "Just in case," she said. She began trotting back to the tents to retrieve the rope and cast a backward glance at William. "This should be interesting."

Within thirty minutes, William sat in the dining tent with Isabelle, James, Phillip, Maude, and Genevieve.

"I'm hardly likely to run with a gun pointed in my face," William snarled at James. "Perhaps you would be decent enough to untie me."

James studied the man for a moment and then wordlessly motioned for Phillip to untie William's hands. His feet, however, Phillip left bound.

"Perhaps you'd care to explain why you were attempting to kill Thaddeus Sparks," James said.

Isabelle looked at Genevieve, whose face seemed to have aged in a very short time. She was pale and drawn, lines of sorrow and confusion around her eyes. "William, what is the meaning of this?" she asked.

His face was suffused with color. A muscle in his jaw worked and he finally managed to speak. "I will not say a word with these people present," he told her.

"Forgive me, ma'am, for interrupting," James said in Genevieve's direction, "but you don't have that luxury, Mr. Montgomery. "You were attempting to kill Mr. Sparks, and that now involves everybody."

"You must have heard the good doctor tell us that Mr. Sparks was making signs of recovery, that he was mumbling and would likely soon awaken," Isabelle said. "You can't very well allow that to happen if he names you as a coconspirator in his crimes."

"I have had *enough* out of you," William said to Isabelle, his voice low. He leaned forward, his anger palpable. "You are the problem at the root of all of this!"

"William!" Genevieve's voice was harsh. "What have you done?"

The man looked at his mother in rage. "Did you think I wouldn't realize who she is? Did you really believe you could continue to hide it from me? I remember, Mother. I remember what he looked like!" He shook his head. "All those years you were so clever to be sure I never saw her when she was at home with you." William looked at Isabelle as he would a gnat. "You're a fool, Mother—you've been a *fool* to think I wouldn't know!"

Isabelle's heart increased in tempo and she looked from William to Genevieve, who looked stricken and fearful. Isabelle didn't like seeing her that way—it couldn't be good. "What is he talking about, Genevieve?" she asked, pleased that her voice didn't tremble.

Genevieve cleared her throat and looked at Isabelle, then back at William.

"Genevieve?" Isabelle asked again.

"Tell her, Mother." William had the gall to look smug. "Tell her she's your granddaughter."

27

The silence that followed William's pronouncement was deafening. Isabelle stared at Genevieve, stunned. Her mind worked for structure that seemed to have collapsed. Nothing made sense anymore.

She finally found her voice. "Is it true?" Her throat was thick, nearly closing off the words.

Genevieve looked at her through luminous eyes filled with tears that escaped and rolled down her face. She cleared her throat and straightened in her seat. "It is true, Isabelle. Your father was my eldest son."

Isabelle dimly registered several things. James's quiet exhalation of breath. Phillip, who pinched the bridge of his nose between thumb and forefinger. Maude, who stared at Genevieve in a stupor of her own. *Funny,* was all Isabelle could think, *she didn't even tell her best friend.*

"She looks just like him," William said into the silence.

Genevieve's voice cut through the air like a whip. "*Enough* out of you, William," she said. "I'll not hear another word out of you until I'm ready. And then you will answer every question given to you or I will hand you over to the Egyptian authorities myself."

Isabelle wrapped her arms around her midsection and tried to hold herself together. She slowly rocked forward and back once before catching herself and demanding that her body be still. Her foot, however, rebelled and began to bounce her leg in a discernible rhythm. James stood and moved his chair to her side, pulling her close against him. She didn't want the comfort—she didn't want anyone to touch her—but she couldn't make herself pull away. The adrenaline that surged through her body like fire to the ends of her limbs left her feeling weak.

Her eyes burned, slowly filling with tears. She didn't want them to come, because she knew once they did, they would never stop. "Why?" she asked, feeling the vulnerability that must be written on her face. "Why did you . . . why did you . . ." She felt herself gasping for breath, choking on nothing but air.

Isabelle's shoulders slumped and she relied wholly on James's support to keep her upright. They had been so alone! Her family had been completely, utterly alone with hardly any money, and then her parents had died. She and Claire had lived on the streets . . .

"Phillip," Genevieve said, her voice having regained its usual authority and strength, "please retie William's hands and take him to my tent. Guard him with your gun and shoot him in the leg if he so much as flinches. Maude, will you please awaken Mr. Deveraux and ask him to stand watch with Phillip?"

Maude murmured her assent, and the three left the room after Phillip had tied William's hands together again behind his back. William hobbled from the room with his feet still tied together and wisely remained silent.

Genevieve pulled her chair close to Isabelle's and leaned forward but didn't attempt to hold or touch her.

Isabelle couldn't bring herself to look at the woman. "Were you ever going to tell me? Was I ever to know?" she asked, sounding very much like a child, even to her own ears.

"Isabelle," Genevieve said, her tone soft but firm. "I asked you about your family, more than once, if you'll recall. You told me that under no uncertain terms you wished to never have anything to do with your father's parents, that they had betrayed and hurt him for daring to marry your mother. You said that if you ever saw your grandparents, you would tell them you despised them and that if they tried to have any part in your life, you would summon the authorities."

"I was a young girl!"

"Yes, you were! And I was determined to have a part in your life, determined that you not live on the streets with your little sister! If the only way I could do it was by withholding the information that I was your grandmother, then so be it!" Genevieve took a deep breath and continued. "You made yourself very, very clear. More than once. And there was also Claire to consider. I wasn't about to allow her to disappear so that you could salvage your pride."

Isabelle felt her chest rise and fall, trying to calm herself but not knowing how. The worst of it was that Genevieve was right. She had left the woman no choice. It was clear that Genevieve had felt a fair amount of frustration, and Isabelle had to admit that she was entitled to it.

She lifted her head from James's chest and sat up a bit, glad that he kept his arm around her. Now she needed him close, afraid that if he let go she would collapse. "I wish," she said to her grandmother, "I wish . . ." The tears fell fresh. "I wish things had been different."

"Child, you have no idea how many times I have wished that myself. How often I berated myself for being so ridiculous about your father's choice of wife." Genevieve paused, her voice thick with emotion. "Your mother was a good girl and she adored my son. That should have been enough for me, but at the time, it wasn't. I will spend the rest of my life paying for that foolishness. My biggest regret is that it impacted you and Claire so profoundly."

Genevieve shook her head. "I looked high and low for you for years, well before I received news of your parents' deaths. I wanted to make amends, to bring them back home."

Isabelle shrugged, a small movement of one shoulder. "He was a proud man; they were a proud couple." She accepted the handkerchief James handed her and wiped her nose and eyes. "He would have died before going back home." She laughed, pained. "He did."

"He probably felt as though I'd left him no choice," Genevieve said. "If I were him, I would never have come back either." She paused for a moment and then leaned forward, reaching for Isabelle's hand. Genevieve gripped it with fingers that were ice cold. Without thinking, Isabelle wrapped both of her hands around Genevieve's hand, seeking to warm it.

"Isabelle, I am so sorry. No matter how many times I say it, it will never be enough, but I am so incredibly sorry. It is my sincere hope that sometime before you die, you might find it in your heart to forgive me."

Isabelle looked at the woman she'd known so long as her benefactress. How would she have reacted if Genevieve had told her of their connection all those years ago? She would never know, but one thing she did recognize in herself was her father's stubborn streak. Her pride was her biggest downfall.

"I forgive you. Of course I do," Isabelle said. "I am stunned, but in truth I cannot blame you. You were right—I left you no choice. Mine and Claire's lives were better from the moment you found us, and for that I will always be grateful. And if things had been different—I might never have taken the path I did. I don't regret that at all." She paused for a moment and briefly closed her eyes. "Absolution," she murmured.

Genevieve nodded once when Isabelle looked at her.

"That's what you gave me as the reason for being in Egypt."

"Yes," the older woman murmured. "It has been a long time in coming." Genevieve straightened in her chair. "We have much to discuss, but the rest can wait for later," she said. "As to why William has been behaving so horribly, I have no clue." Her face clouded. "Or perhaps I do. You'll excuse me, I'm sure. James, we are going to need the police again, and Isabelle, although I'm relatively certain William will not speak freely in front of you, perhaps you might sit outside the back of the tent and hear what he has to say. If you wish."

"Very well," Isabelle said and nodded. She rose on shaky legs and James stood with her, tucking her arm into his.

He held out his other elbow to Genevieve, and as they left the tent, he remarked, "A thorn between two roses."

Isabelle closed her eyes and rested her head for a moment against his arm. Turning her head, she placed a kiss on his bicep.

* * *

Thaddeus Sparks ran from the slumped form at the latrine, fighting the pain and black spots that danced in front of his eyes, threatening to pull him under. He held the knife that Montgomery had intended to kill him with; it was now bloodied and slippery in his grasp. Tempted to throw it to the ground, he instead tightened his grip on it, unwilling to leave it for someone else to find.

The guard who had followed him to the latrine in the aftermath of the chase and chaos that had awoken the entire camp would not be alerting them to Sparks's whereabouts anytime soon—Sparks had made certain the man was dead before he left the scene.

He made his way to his tent in the workers' compound, his fingers shaking as he wiped his hands as clean as possible against his trousers. He fumbled with the tent fastenings, trying to calm his breathing so as not to awaken anyone. Once inside, he hastily, if awkwardly, changed his clothing and stuffed the soiled things, including the knife, into a sack.

His head pounded unmercifully; he very nearly gave in to the urge to lie down, if only for a few minutes. He had to keep his wits about him, had to carefully plan his next move. His focus had now shifted and narrowed in on one thing; he had to find the jewel, and he had to leave Egypt.

* * *

Bits of dialogue slipped in and out of Isabelle's dreams. William's voice, the bitterness, the hatred. Genevieve's answering tones, her frustration and pain.

". . . why would you keep something like this from us, Mother? And then to assume we wouldn't know, wouldn't realize who she was?"

"She didn't want anything to do with her father's family, William, and—"

"Then you should have let her be! Stephen left the family, Mother, left all of us. His progeny with that nothing of a woman he married have no right to anything that is ours!"

A slap, then, harsh and crisp. Isabelle imagined William might bear his mother's handprint on his face for some time. She had sat outside the tent, as Genevieve had suggested, and listened for over an hour to William's harsh litany of objections to Isabelle having anything to do with their family.

One thing was clear—Eli and William were her uncles. It certainly explained the sense of familiarity she'd felt about Eli from the beginning. That she hadn't figured it out from the first was surprising. He strongly resembled Isabelle's father, both in appearance and gentleness of spirit.

Isabelle slept late the next morning, awakening only at the feel of a cool hand placed against her forehead. She opened her eyes to see Sally kneeling at her bedside, her face concerned. Isabelle took Sally's hand into her own and gave it a squeeze.

"What time is it?" she asked Sally.

"Half past nine."

Isabelle groaned and sat up. "You should have awoken me earlier," she said.

Sally looked at her with serious eyes. "Genevieve wouldn't let me. Are you well, Isabelle? She said I should ask you about what happened last night."

"Where is Genevieve now?"

"She's speaking with the police. They brought several reinforcements this time. I think they're afraid to leave the site—things keep happening here every time they go back to headquarters." Sally paused. "I heard Maude tell Phillip that the Egyptian authorities are holding William in a small jail in the village near the river until it can be clearly determined what kind of charges he will face and where. And here's something you'll not believe—Sparks escaped last night. Killed his guard. Belle, what is going on?"

Isabelle closed her eyes. "Let me dress, and meet me in the dining tent. I need to speak with James as well."

Sally left the tent and Isabelle quickly dressed and fixed her hair. She stepped out into the bright morning air, feeling much the same and yet somehow changed. She had a blood connection to someone other than her sister, and it had been a long time since she felt it. She hadn't realized she'd been missing it. It was foreign, though. An unfamiliar emotion—a joy that tangled itself with an irrational resentment for which she knew she couldn't hold Genevieve responsible.

"You're looking exceptionally lovely," James said as he strolled over to her tent, hands in his pockets and moving with the grace of someone very comfortable in his own skin.

She shook her head. "I look wretched and you well know it." She paused. "James, I . . . I . . ."

James placed his finger gently on her lips. "It doesn't matter."

"It does matter," she said when he moved his hand. "Please, I need to say this and I don't want to. I'm sorry for reacting so fiercely . . ."

"And I'm sorry for making you feel like you had to answer to me. That was not my intention."

She nodded. "I know."

James was quiet for a moment. "You're going to have to learn to trust me, you know."

"And you're going to have to learn to be patient with me."

He smiled and put one arm around her waist, pulling her close. "With pleasure. And as much as I hate to have to share you when I really would rather take you somewhere far, far away, Jackson Pearce has some things to tell us, and he's insisting that it be only you and me."

Isabelle looked beyond him to Sally, who stood waiting at the dining tent. "I need to talk to Sally for a moment first," she told James.

She walked over to Sally and took her hands. "The short of it is that Genevieve is my grandmother."

Sally's mouth dropped open, and Isabelle nodded. "As for the rest of it with William, will you be patient for a few moments while I speak with Mr. Pearce, or whoever he is?"

Sally nodded and shook her head as though clearing it. "Phillip is going to go with me to the cave, actually—we're going to see if we can do anything to help repair the damage in the burial chamber. Alice and Jean-Louis are already up there."

Isabelle nodded, thinking. "I suppose Alice is wearing her necklace . . ."

"Why should that signify?"

"I'll explain my theories on that later as well."

Sally pulled her forward into a quick embrace. "I can't decide now whether or not to like Genevieve."

Isabelle laughed. "She's fine. But I thank you for your loyalty, nonetheless. I have much to . . . think about." She watched with a sense of nostalgia as Sally ran to join Phillip, who took her hand in his arm much as James routinely did with Isabelle. "They seem to like each other," she said to James.

"Oh, he likes her more than just a little," James said as his eyes followed the pair disappearing down the path to the cave. "I think his intentions are growing quite serious. Come, my lady, we have some mysteries to unravel."

Once inside Pearce's tent, the doctor excused himself with strict instructions that his patient not move a muscle. He propped the man's head and shoulders up on some pillows and quietly left.

James slid a chair over for Isabelle and then sat on the vacant cot. Isabelle watched "Jackson Pearce," who regarded them with steady eyes.

"The things I tell you must remain between us, otherwise my life is forfeit," he said, wincing as he shifted.

"Fair enough," Isabelle said, "if you'll tell us your real name."

"My name really is Jackson Pearce. My last name is MacInnes. My friends know me as Jack MacInnes." He paused. "Jackson Pearce, the professor, was my maternal grandfather. I overheard the news of his passing when Genevieve told William."

James and Isabelle were silent, giving him the time he seemed to need to continue.

"I'm an agent with the British international police," he said quietly. Isabelle leaned forward to hear him better. "My task was to infiltrate an organization that calls itself the Federation. They are an international group of powerful men who are searching for three legendary stones referred to as the Greek Stones. One is the Jewel of Zeus, the next is the Jewel of Poseidon, and the third is the Jewel of Hades."

Isabelle glanced at James.

"I believe you may be in possession of the first. Or at least know of its whereabouts." Jackson looked at both of them and then shrugged slightly, eliciting another wince. "My assignment is to keep the Federation from taking control of any one of the stones, let alone all three."

"Why is that?"

Jackson sighed. "My government doesn't trust the Federation and fears what they will try to accomplish when in possession of the stones. They want me to find them first and bring them home. Truthfully, I have different plans for them. I want to destroy them."

28

"Why do you want the stones destroyed?" Isabelle asked.

Jackson MacInnes closed his eyes. "My grandfather was an avid student of the Greek Stones. He knew everything there was to know about the legend. I've always been skeptical, myself, but there does seem to be some sort of . . . fanaticism . . . that takes hold of people who actively search for it."

"Was your grandfather one of those?" James asked.

Jackson shook his head. "No, thankfully. He never did look, but he dug up every detail possible . . . one of those details told of the daughter of a pharaoh who bore the sign; she was a true heir to the stones and was spirited away by relatives who feared for her life. Her father was dangerous and wanted her for procurement of the jewels, nothing else. A false story concerning her reputation was circulated and she disappeared from sight. They brought her here, obviously."

He paused, again shifting on the cot.

"Would you like a drink?" Isabelle asked and motioned to the cup on the bedside table. He nodded, and she handed it to him. He sipped carefully and gave it back to her.

"So you found the expedition here and the Federation assigned you to become part of it?" James asked.

Jackson shook his head. "I was sent to trail Sparks, whom they had hired because they knew he had been looking in India with Phillip, who bears the mark. Ultimately, they want Phillip. What they don't know is that someone more valuable, in terms of the legend, is also here."

"Alice," Isabelle said.

Jackson nodded. "Supposedly the true heir to the stones must be female. Males may bear the mark and may find themselves led toward any one of the stones, but they are complete and . . ." he gave a little wave with his hand, "powerful only when owned by a female who bears the mark."

"How on earth did you know that Alice bears the mark?" Isabelle asked.

Jackson sighed. "Her mother. We had a man inside the Banbury Estate who acted as the family's butler. He saw and heard everything. Wasn't hard, from what I know about the lady."

Isabelle nodded. "She was loud. Uncouth."

"Our man was also the one who told us Lady Banbury had removed the jewel and was taking it to India. She said it was because her husband wanted it." He paused and closed his eyes. "Well, at any rate, this is my story. I'm telling the two of you because it's obvious you know I'm not who I claimed to be, and I want you to understand the power of these blasted stones. Or perceived power, at least. It makes people do foolish, crazy things."

James frowned. "I know. It took my brother across the world."

Jackson nodded. He had been speaking in low tones already but now dropped his voice to nearly a whisper. "I need your help. I don't know how long it will take me to heal, and I fear the Federation is losing confidence in me. They will kill me."

James leaned forward, resting his forearms on his knees. "How can we help you?"

"We must find the second stone—you do have the first one?" He paused and waited while they reluctantly nodded. "And then we find the third. My grandfather believed it to be in Greece. Alice is the key to destroying them."

Isabelle drew in a breath. "You know of no other females with the birthmark?"

"No," Jackson said. "I'm sure you can understand why that information is not easily obtained."

"We will need to discuss it with Alice—obviously this is something we can't do without her willing cooperation," James told him.

"You seem to be a rational sort," Isabelle said and Jackson inclined his head. "How crucial is it, truly, that Alice play a part in this thing? I would hate to needlessly place her in danger."

"Let me say this . . ." Jackson paused. "If it's all an elaborate story, and the stones are still destroyed, so much the better. If, however, there's some strange truth to the legend, then I'd rather be sure we do it correctly." He shook his head. "My grandfather heard some odd stories from time to time . . . things that convinced him there is an element of the supernatural to the stones. And he was a rational man himself. If the Federation, or Sparks, even, were to get hold of any of the stones, I fear our chances of destroying them would be complicated at best. And there is the fact that although Lord Banbury claimed to never be affected by the stone itself, we don't know what could happen should they fall into the wrong hands."

Isabelle considered his words. She wished she could dismiss the whole of it as utter nonsense. The fact of the matter was, though, that the jewel in James's trunk seemed to have some sort of supernatural power to it. And there was also the fact that Alice's and Phillip's birthmarks burned when in close proximity to the jewel.

"I believe we are close to finding the second jewel, and we haven't even been actively searching for it." Isabelle explained the reaction of Alice's birthmark in the cave, the cryptic outbursts from two native Egyptian women, and the necklace that seemed to act as a charm. She tapped her fingers on the chair's armrest. "There are three stones . . ." she murmured, "and we know that just one by itself reacts to proximity with people who bear the mark."

"And?" James asked when she paused.

"What if . . ." She wrinkled her brow. "Suppose there is something to this legend. What will happen when the three stones are joined?"

Jackson opened his mouth to reply then closed it. He finally gave a small shrug. "I don't know. I don't . . ." He shook his head. "I never could get any of the Federation members to tell me exactly what they hope to accomplish by possessing them."

"The stone actually vibrates near Alice and Phillip," Isabelle whispered. "It glows slightly and hums."

"Isabelle, what are you suggesting?" James asked her.

"I'm suddenly feeling very apprehensive. There's something clearly strange about these jewels. Suppose they fall into the wrong hands? I'm beginning to feel the possibility is a very real threat." She turned to Jack. "How far-reaching is the Federation, do you suppose?"

Jackson briefly closed his eyes. "Too far for comfort, I'm afraid. They have spies everywhere. They knew not only about Sparks but certainly about Phillip and the fact that all of you were looking for him. They knew of Sparks's intentions before he even left the States."

"How many countries are involved? How many have an active stake or voice in the Federation?" James asked him.

"At least nine that I know of. Likely more."

Isabelle drew in a breath and slowly let it out. "I wish Allan were here," she murmured.

"Allan?" Jackson asked her.

She nodded. "Pinkerton. We could use a network of our own."

"I suppose we'll just have to work with what we have," Jackson said and winced again as he shifted his position.

"Did Sparks say anything to you last night?" James asked. "Were you awake with him for any length of time?" James asked Jackson.

"I should say so. He unburdened himself completely as though all fault lay with Mr. Montgomery. William had been planning to have Sparks sneak into your tent the night you were buried in the cave and scare you somehow. When he saw you leaving, and then the girls following, Sparks reasoned you were going to the cave and he devised the plan as he went, paying two other workers to help him. That shot you fired grazed his skin, in fact. Sparks was also responsible for the whispering you heard outside your tent, Miss Webb."

Isabelle nodded. "William confessed nearly everything to his mother last night. He tried to scare me with the note and by whispering on the *dahabeeyah*. He also placed the snake in our tent himself, and Adelaide was outside at the time and saw him do it. She approached him that night and made some sort of blackmail threat. He later gave her the note that said to meet him at the cave at two o'clock."

Jackson nodded. "And Sparks was there, waiting for her."

"Yes. Supposedly, William told Sparks to scare her, nothing more.

Something must have gone wrong, though, because they fought and Sparks killed her," Isabelle said.

"I don't understand why William was trying to frighten you away," Jackson said.

"I am heir to part of Genevieve's fortune. For years William has been under the impression that my father's portion would go to him. He wanted me to leave before I could somehow discover that Genevieve is my grandmother." She shook her head. "As if I ever would. If I hadn't figured it out by now on my own . . . Well, at any rate, the business with him is finished. Incidentally, who is Catherine to you?"

"She works for the Federation," Jackson said. "Lives in Cairo with her uncle. I've successfully avoided her for nearly a year—I've passed myself off as Italian with the Federation, but she's from Britain and has relatives near my home in Scotland. I resemble the rest of my family; I knew once she met me that she would see through my disguise."

"Why do you think they sent her?" James asked.

"To check on me, most likely. There are those members who haven't trusted me from the beginning."

Isabelle stood and placed her chair back in the corner of the tent. "We have much to discuss with the girls, and if we are to find the stones, we need to move quickly. I'd like to see this business done."

"How soon will you be fit enough to travel?" James asked him.

"The doctor told me I shouldn't move for at least a week. I can't stay down that long, though," Jackson said. "The bullet passed through my side, and he stitched me in both the front and the back. I'm hopeful that if I am careful enough, I won't tear it open."

"What will you tell the Federation?" Isabelle asked.

"That you have given up on the idea of finding a jewel here and that you're moving on to Greece. I'll tell them I need to go with you to secure the jewel for them."

James had risen with Isabelle and he now placed his hand on the small of her back. "We'll speak with the girls and let you know what they say. We can protect your identity as a British agent, if you'd like."

Jackson nodded. "That would be best, I believe. Tell them I work for the Federation but have become disenchanted with their motives."

"Rest well," Isabelle said. She paused and turned to James. "Perhaps we should keep a guard posted outside the tent."

* * *

The night air was cool, as usual. James walked beside Isabelle as they made one final trek to the cave. Phillip, Sally, Alice, and Jean-Louis were also with them, and the mood was subdued.

Alice had insisted on telling Jean-Louis the details of the legend, and in the end they had acquiesced. There was a fondness between the young couple, and as the mystery seemed largely solved, she trusted the Frenchman. He had listened to the crazy story with an open mind, which James appreciated.

On approaching the cave, James greeted the two guards he had hired himself and told them he was relieving them for a time, that the others needed to examine some hieroglyphs in the burial chamber and wished to avoid the superstitions of the locals by taking the women in. The excuse was flimsy but held as the guards were content with the fact that they would still be paid for their brief break.

He took up his post at the base of the path, and the other five entered the cave without him. He saw them light the lanterns, and then the glow slowly disappeared. As he paced slowly back and forth, he looked up at the night sky and considered recent events. Never in his life would he have imagined he would someday be looking at the stars in Egypt. He was concerned about the path upon which they were embarking but was hopeful that maybe, for once, they could pass some time before being threatened, abducted, or shot.

These were his last thoughts as something smashed into his head from behind and the world went black.

* * *

Isabelle watched with interest as Alice and Phillip together examined the wall where Sparks had attacked it. Pieces of hieroglyphs had come off in chunks, both large and powder-fine. Jean-Louis had done his best to piece together much of what could be salvaged earlier in the day, and the Staffords had been nearly beside themselves at the destruction, not only of the wall but the mummy herself.

Isabelle crept to the sarcophagus and placed her hand on it. Ibis was due to be transferred to the artifacts tent in the morning. Harry and Henry were confident enough that they had done what they could to best preserve her condition while still in the cave. They feared that, once removed, she would deteriorate quickly if not properly treated.

The lids had been replaced for the day, and she once again rested in the dark. Isabelle had been in awe of the preservation of the body. To know that the young woman had once walked the earth, had a life filled with drama and intrigue, and had born a birthmark similar to those that Alice and Phillip both had was amazing. Perhaps the eeriest part of all was the edge of a talisman that had protruded from beneath her bandages during Sparks's onslaught, although he had apparently not seen it. The Staffords had discovered it later as it poked out from beneath the wrappings. It matched, to the last carving, the talisman Alice possessed.

As she traced her fingertips along the rim of the sarcophagus, Isabelle looked up at Phillip and Alice, who had narrowed in on one particular place on the wall, to the side of the majority of Sparks's destruction. Alice pointed to a spot and glanced over her shoulder at Jean-Louis.

"Look at this," she said to him, and he joined her, asking Phillip to move the lantern closer.

Jean-Louis looked, removed his glasses, polished them, and replaced them on his face. He nodded and looked over at Isabelle. "Here are the three symbols," he said. "Just as in the other places."

Alice had removed her necklace and was absently rubbing her spine. Every so often, Isabelle noticed Phillip doing the same thing.

"I hate to say this," Isabelle whispered, "but we may need to dig into the wall." She glanced at Jean-Louis, who winced. "Do you feel the same intensity if you're across the room?" she asked Alice and Phillip.

They shook their heads. They had started at the far end of the chamber and slowly worked their way around the perimeter twice. Both times had found them at the same spot.

Jean-Louis had brought a bag of tools from the artifacts tent, and he now went to it and withdrew a chisel and mallet. Drawing in a deep breath, he returned to the wall and said to Alice, "Where?"

Alice's brows drew together. "Are you certain you want to be the one to do this, then?"

Jean-Louis nodded. "Here?" He pointed to the symbol of the ibis.

"Yes," Phillip said as Alice nodded.

The Frenchman slowly began to cut into the wall, managing to chisel around the part that held the three symbols, removing it in one solid piece. He handed it to Alice, who held it reverently. Inch by inch, he dug into the wall, pausing to question Isabelle about the size of the stone. She showed him with her hands, and he continued.

Before long, the sound of the chisel against the stone changed in tone. He glanced over at Alice and carefully worked his way around the object he'd encountered. He hammered and chiseled, working the stone around the object into a fine powder that dislodged when he scraped it out and blew into the hole. After what seemed an interminable amount of time, he began to pull at something. It was stuck fast and took several more rounds with the chisel against the stone holding it in place before he was able to produce a metal box. He worked it to the edge of the opening and then turned to Alice and Phillip.

"Perhaps one of you would like to do the honors?" he asked, wiping a bead of sweat from his brow. His jacket had long since been shed.

Phillip held his hand out to Alice and she handed him the carved stone she still held. Biting her lower lip, she put her slender hands up to the box and reverently pulled it out of the wall. She carried it over to Sally and Isabelle, who stood back on the fringes of the activity. Isabelle motioned toward a light that hung on the wall, and the group moved in for a closer look.

The box was simple and crude, with no ornamentation whatsoever. Alice glanced up at Phillip. "Do you feel it?" she asked him.

He nodded.

The box was free of any kind of lock or clasp, and Alice ran her fingers along the edge before slipping the tip of her forefinger under the lid and lifting it up. As it moved, she then grasped it with her whole hand and pulled it off.

The stone was identical to the Jewel of Zeus in shape and size. But whereas Zeus was iridescent purple, the stone Alice held was orange. Isabelle breathed in and touched it gently with her fingers, finally grasping it and pulling it out of its resting place. It was the size of her palm, and oval in shape. As she held it to the light, the color changed to a mixture of orange and yellow.

"I'll take that." The voice that came from the doorway broke the awed silence, and Isabelle flinched as Alice nearly dropped the stone. She took it from the girl and faced Thaddeus Sparks, who looked exhausted but otherwise none the worse for the wear.

29

Sparks held a gun, and Isabelle wondered if she could get to hers before he noticed.

"Where is James?" she asked, her heart pounding.

"I want to see your hands," he said to them all. "Especially yours, Miss Webb. Hand me the stone very slowly."

Phillip's stance was aggressive—the very image of a wolf preparing to lunge. "I should have killed you when I had the chance," he gritted out.

"Undoubtedly," Sparks said, his odd green eyes visible in the dim light of the room. "Miss Webb, the stone."

She hesitated and he waved the weapon. "I will shoot them, one by one, until you give it to me," he said, his voice rising in anger.

Isabelle's jaw tightened. So close to her weapon! She didn't trust him not to follow through on his threat. He'd already killed a woman and several guards. What little conscience he may ever have possessed was long gone. When she thought of James's probable state outside, her knees nearly buckled. She slowly moved closer to Sparks.

"First, hand me your bag," he said and motioned with his gun.

Gritting her teeth, she removed it from her shoulder and handed it to him.

"And now the stone."

It was smooth against her fingers, and cool. She wanted to hurl it at his head but instead placed it in his outstretched hand. He slipped it into the shoulder bag, which he then placed over his head and across his body.

Sparks had several lengths of rope he'd dropped behind himself on the floor. He picked them up and tossed one to Phillip. "Tie up your gentleman friend," he said. He directed Phillip's movements, watching as Phillip tied the knots, his knuckles tightening on the gun when Phillip didn't pull the ends tightly enough for his taste. His roar of anger echoed off the walls, and Phillip, his own rage clearly visible on his face, tied Jean-Louis's hands and then ankles more securely.

Isabelle had slowly begun to inch her way closer to Sparks, but he caught her out of the corner of his eye and backhanded her across the cheek, sending her sprawling. "I will shoot them!" he screamed at her, cocking his weapon and aiming it at Sally.

The room spun and Isabelle squinted her eyes in an effort to steady herself. She tried to stand but fumbled.

"Stay down!" he yelled, backing up to better see the whole group. He instructed Phillip to tie up Sally and Isabelle, and then Sparks, himself, tied Phillip with a threat to put a bullet in the back of Phillip's head if anybody moved.

"Now, young lady," he said to Alice, "I've recently discovered there are not one, but three jewels. I'll be needing your assistance." He smiled, and with the slight widening of his eyes, Isabelle began to see the insanity Phillip said he had witnessed in the man while they were in India. "We are off to Greece."

"You'll not touch her!" Jean-Louis roared from his position on the floor.

"Come over here!" Sparks yelled at Alice. "Or I shoot them all!"

"Alice, don't move!" Sally yelled through her tears. "We'd all rather die!"

Isabelle's eyes widened at Sally's dramatic pronouncement, but she soon found herself wincing as Sparks swung his arm toward Sally and fired a shot. The girl dove to the left as he squeezed the trigger and the bullet exploded behind her and into the sarcophagus, missing her by inches.

Isabelle screamed out and lunged over, struggling to get to her knees. Sparks, now wild-eyed and panicked, pointed his gun at Isabelle, but before he could fire, he was tackled from behind.

Isabelle gaped as she saw James, who had taken Sparks to the floor but now seemed to struggle with his own sense of balance.

They grappled, but James had clearly been hurt and was no match for Sparks. James closed his fingers around the gun, which had clattered to the floor, and Sparks grabbed his wrist, wildly smacking James's arm down against the floor.

James bent his hand, and as Sparks smashed his arm downward, James flung the gun out into the corridor. When Sparks released James and ran to find the gun, James staggered to his feet and followed him into the dark corridor. Isabelle heard Sparks cursing and then grunting as James's foot connected with his ribs.

Sparks muttered a curse and then ran, James trying to follow. One set of footsteps echoed into the distance, and Isabelle heard James fall.

"James!" she screamed.

She saw him slowly appear from the dark, leaning against the corridor wall for support. "James," she breathed, tears gathering, the fear nearly choking her. "Have you been shot?"

"Walls closing in . . ." he murmured. He fell into the room and collapsed across her lap. Phillip, meanwhile, had made his way to Jean-Louis and was working at the knots that bound the Frenchman's hands. Isabelle twisted her hands and tried to untie her own knots, rubbing her wrists raw in the process. She bent her head down and listened for the sound of James's breathing. In her own agitation, she couldn't determine if he was still alive.

Alice worked to untie Sally's hands and feet, then helped Phillip and Jean-Louis. Sally ran to Isabelle's side with a lantern and examined James.

"He's breathing, Belle," she said. Sally ran her fingers carefully along James's head as Alice worked to untie Isabelle's hands. "There's a large lump on the back of his head, here, but I don't think it's bleeding much. Probably he was hit with a rock." She looked at Isabelle with a ghost of a smile. "I know how he feels."

Isabelle appreciated Sally's attempt to stabilize her spirits. She murmured her thanks to Alice as her hands came free from the ropes and wiped at her nose and her eyes. She gingerly touched James's head, feeling the large bump for herself. "It's a miracle he didn't shoot him," she said as Phillip and Jean-Louis made their way to her and Alice untied her feet.

"The sound would have carried for quite a bit outside," Phillip said. "With everyone alert to mayhem these days, he probably didn't want to take the chance." Phillip rubbed his forehead and bent down, assessing his brother.

"Perhaps the pharaoh's daughter was watching over him," Alice said.

"Her or God," Phillip answered, his tone grim. "Either way, I'm grateful."

* * *

Isabelle's rest was fitful, and she awoke to the feel of a hand over her mouth. She sucked in air through her nose and was preparing to make any noise she could when her nose was pinched shut and a voice whispered close to her ear, "Isabelle, it's Catherine. I need to speak with you outside. I'll remove my hands but you must be still."

Isabelle blinked and tried to clear the fog from her thoughts. She nodded and tried not to cough as Catherine released her. The woman stood and motioned for Isabelle to follow her under the tent fabric of the back wall. As she dusted herself off and straightened, Isabelle rolled her eyes at the inefficiency of the guard who was supposedly standing watch at the tent. She followed Catherine, dodging behind the other tents until they were some distance from the small street.

"What are you doing here?" Isabelle whispered. "And what time is it?"

"Half past four," Catherine whispered back. She crept farther from the camp and took shelter under a gathering of trees. "I haven't much time," she told Isabelle. "I need you to get a message to Jackson Pearce."

Isabelle glanced at Jack's tent, which was guarded by two men. Catherine followed her gaze and nodded. "I couldn't get in to him."

"What's the message?"

"The Federation has sent men to kill him. I got the message yesterday when I went ashore and met with my contact. They're on a steamer that will arrive later today by noon."

Isabelle inhaled and held it for a moment before releasing the breath. Would things never be simple again? She looked at Catherine, who was dressed in an Egyptian robe and headdress. Her face was uncovered for the moment. "How do I know you're not trying to lead him, or me, for that matter, into a trap."

Catherine shook her head. "You don't. I'm giving you the information to do with it what you will. In the next twenty-four hours, he will likely be dead. I would think they will wait until the cover of night, but I can't be sure."

"How did you return so quickly?" Isabelle asked.

"We weren't far down the river. We were traveling by *dahabeeyah*. When I heard the news, I told the Burnses that I had business back here and caught passage on a steamer headed back this way."

Isabelle considered the matter, rubbing her forehead. She was so incredibly tired. "What have they said of the rest of us?" Isabelle asked. "Anything?"

Catherine looked at her for a moment before responding. "According to my contact, they want Phillip, but now even more so, Alice. None of you are safe here."

"Why are you warning us?"

Catherine paused, apparently indecisive. "I . . . there are too many innocent people involved now. It was another matter entirely when I dealt with the corrupt."

"What will you do? If they get word that you helped us, it won't bode well for you."

Catherine nodded. "I will tell them I've had an offer of marriage back at home and try to gracefully extricate myself. There is someone . . . that much is real enough." She shrugged. "I don't know that they will ever let me go—I suppose that's a price I will pay for my greed."

"I wish you all the best," Isabelle said. She felt a kinship with the woman. Theirs was a murky business.

Catherine nodded once and pulled her facial veils into place. "God speed," she said. "The steamer I came in on is set to leave at half-past seven for Cairo. That gives you three hours." She turned and walked away quickly.

Isabelle watched her disappear into the distance. Weary to the bone, she then made her way to James's tent. Making her identity known to the guard, he raised an eyebrow but allowed her entrance. She hesitated, unsure of the best course of action. If she startled the men too much, they would make noise and awaken the entire camp.

She began with Phillip, whose bed was closest to the door. She gently tapped his shoulder and whispered his name. He awoke with a start and grabbed her wrist but released it when he realized who she was. She bent down close to his ear and told him everything Catherine had said.

He leaned up on one elbow and rubbed his eyes. Shaking his head, he sat up and swung his legs over the side of his cot. He scratched the back of his head and yawned, muttering something under his breath. "I will tell Jean-Louis," he whispered. "You awaken James."

James was groggy in the extreme, and when he realized Isabelle was kneeling at his bedside, he smiled crookedly and put an arm around her shoulders, attempting to draw her close.

"James," she said in his ear, "we must go."

"Go where?"

"Phillip and Alice are in danger. So is Jack—we have to leave now for the river and board a steamboat."

"Let's stay here," he said and rolled toward her, smashing her throat against his shoulder.

"James!" she hissed, choking. "Listen to me!"

In the pale moonlight that shone through the light fabric of the tent, she saw the moment his eyes opened fully and he registered his surroundings. He looked at her in shock and sat up, groaning at the movement. Placing a hand at the back of his head, he closed his eyes and scrunched his face in pain.

"Please, do not tell me I just heard you say we must leave," he murmured to her.

"Shh, yes. I need to tell Jackson and the girls. Are you well enough to get dressed?"

He looked at her with one eye still closed. "You are not going to awaken Jackson."

She shook her head. "Don't be ridiculous. You don't know what to tell him."

"Take Phillip with you, then," he whispered when he saw that Phillip and Jean-Louis were already dressed.

She nodded and stood, asking Jean-Louis to see about securing a donkey and cart as quietly as he could possibly manage. "We need to leave with as few people knowing as possible. I'll tell Genevieve, though," she added as she motioned for Phillip to follow her. She felt a twinge of sadness at leaving Genevieve with so many questions unanswered.

Phillip accompanied her to Jack's tent, where they dismissed his guards and entered. Phillip quietly woke him up and Isabelle delivered the message from Catherine. The man looked groggy and exhausted. "We're taking a cart," she said. "You will ride in it, along with the trunks. Can you manage with only one of yours?"

Jackson nodded. "I have only one."

"Phillip will retrieve it from your tent. When the cart is ready, we'll come and get you."

"Nonsense," he said and moved, trying to hide the pain. "I'll not be carried like an infant."

"I carried you once before," Phillip told him.

Jackson eyed him askance and shoved himself into a standing position. "Just bring me a fresh shirt from my tent, if you will. I do believe the doctor threw away the bloodied one."

Satisfied Jackson was in capable hands, Isabelle left, first to awaken the girls, and then to tell Genevieve they were leaving.

Genevieve received the news with a fair amount of shock. "Are you certain you can trust her?" she asked Isabelle.

"A few days ago I would have said no. Now, I'm relying on instinct. And even if it weren't true, we need to leave. Alice isn't safe as long as Sparks is close by. I worry about you as well."

"We will be fine," Genevieve whispered. "We have nothing he wants."

"Will you stay and finish the dig?"

Genevieve nodded. "One more month is all the time we have on it, at any rate. Where will you go?"

"Greece, most likely. Athens first, I suspect. I'll wire you when we arrive. And then home, assuming all goes well."

"Take this with you," Genevieve said and retrieved something from the bottom of her trunk.

The bag was heavy, and Isabelle knew it was filled with money. "No," she said firmly and handed it back to Genevieve.

"Stubborn girl, it's but a fraction of your inheritance. Now take it, and use it to care for those with you. Don't make them suffer because you have pride. The money *is* yours."

Isabelle stiffened. "I have money."

"You also have others in your company who may have exhausted their funds, or close to it."

Isabelle had her pride but was no fool. "Very well," she said. "Thank you." She stood looking at Genevieve for a moment, feeling as though there was much more to say.

Genevieve reached for her and Isabelle embraced her. She felt her grandmother smoothing her hair and rubbing the back of her knuckles gently across Isabelle's cheek. It still smarted from where Sparks had hit her earlier.

"You see, my girl? You weren't abandoned. I was there all along. I love you, Isabelle," Genevieve whispered in her ear. "I always have."

Isabelle's throat tightened. "I love you too." She closed her eyes and admitted the truth. "I always have."

* * *

In the end, the entourage needed two carts. They each took one trunk of belongings, leaving anything else behind for Genevieve to ship home. They also expanded their number by one—Jean-Louis wanted to join them, and Genevieve gave him her blessing. She said she would console the poor Stafford brothers, who were bound to be left reeling come morning when they found that more than half the expedition was gone. There were enough archaeologists at the neighboring sites who were anxious to get their hands on the cave, though, and she insisted the Britons would be placated.

Isabelle asked her to please bid her farewells to Eli, whom she hoped to visit when they were all home. William, she didn't care to ever see again.

Epilogue

December 25, 1865

WITH ALEXANDRIA FADING AWAY IN the distance, Isabelle stood at the stern of the ship and looked one last time upon Egypt. The trip down the Nile to Cairo had been uneventful, and both James and Jackson rested well.

Maneuvering through Cairo undetected by any of the Federation who might recognize them, and certainly Jack, took a bit of planning. Rather than staying at Shepheard's, they slept one night in a local establishment and then secured passage the next morning on a train bound for Alexandria.

The train ride had been excruciating. The rails were inconsistent, causing the train to sway violently from side to side, and the compartments were cramped in the extreme. Nobody in the party slept well, and it was a relief to finally reach Alexandria.

Two days in that port city had them staying inconspicuously out of sight. When they did venture out, the women wore veils and robes, the men robes and turbans. The men had also stopped shaving, hoping the facial hair would help them blend in with the general populace. Their sun-bronzed skin also aided in their disguises, except for Jean-Louis, who was more pink than brown.

A bit of discreet questioning and a certain amount of bribery proved that they were a couple of days behind Sparks. Traveling by himself, he had had the luxury of moving more quickly than the group, especially given that James and especially Jackson were still trying to recover from their wounds. Sparks had boarded a steamship bound for

Greece just ahead of them.

Isabelle breathed a sigh and left the stern for the bow. The blue of the Mediterranean spread out before the ship, and she was anxious but hopeful. Arms encircling her from behind had her smiling and she leaned back into James's solid frame. One arm came around her waist, and the other he positioned out front. In his hand was a small box.

"Merry Christmas," he whispered to her.

She smiled. They had had an informal Christmas Eve dinner the night before at a small restaurant with several other Coptic Egyptians who were celebrating the holiday. It was an odd Christmas that year, to be sure. It was one unlike any of them had experienced to date.

Isabelle reached for the box, her hand trembling. Closing her eyes, she opened the lid. She opened her eyes and looked at a beautiful solitaire diamond. Leaning her head back into his chest, she said, "When did you buy this?"

She heard the smile in his voice when he answered. "In Calcutta."

Gasping, Isabelle turned in his arms. "*Calcutta*? James! How could you have known I would accept it?"

He reached down and captured her mouth with his, lingering, savoring. He pulled back and ran his thumb along her cheekbone where the bruise from Sparks was finally beginning to fade.

"I knew in Bombay."

Isabelle closed her eyes again, a tear escaping and slipping down her face. "I love you so very much. I am afraid," she admitted, "but I know I would rather be with you than not."

He chuckled. "I love you too, Isabelle Webb. Please, for heaven's sake, will you marry me?"

"Yes. If you promise you don't have any other wives at home."

He laughed out loud and pulled her in for another kiss. "I promise."

About the Author

N.C. Allen is fascinated with the Egyptology craze of the late nineteenth and early twentieth centuries and has enjoyed placing Isabelle Webb in this setting. She plans to one day visit Egypt and see firsthand what her characters have already experienced. In her spare time, the author carpools endlessly, is a news junkie, and enjoys spending time laughing with her family and friends.